COMMEMORATIONS

COMMEMORATIONS

Hans Herlin

Translated by Eric Mosbacher

St. Martin's Press • New York

Madrid, October 7 1969

She led the way down the steep steps that led to the bank safe deposit. Her hair was curly, and the skin of the back of her neck was very dark, even for a Spaniard. I was aware of nothing but her neck and the thin gold necklace round it, and her legs, which were just as dark-skinned under her light stockings, two thin legs under a tight blue skirt. I looked at her legs and the back of her neck and tried not to think about the money, to avoid seeming too agitated.

She led me to a table at which a man in a bluish-grey uniform was sitting, and told him my name. He pushed a ledger towards me and pointed to a space between two lines where I should put my signature. I signed myself Hans Pikola and followed the legs down some more steps.

The Banco Español de Credito, though it is in the Paseo de la Castellana, one of the best-known business streets in Madrid, is not one of those modern marble palaces; it is an old and venerable institution, and to any ordinary mortal hiring a safe there is totally out of the question, because its safes, like the best seats in the bull-ring, are handed down from generation to generation. But nothing was ever impossible to Fritz Lehr; he had hired a safe there jointly in his name and mine. That did not prevent me from having a sudden feeling of total disbelief that the money would be there.

'Your key, señor.'

3

I had not realised we had reached the steel strong-room. It was narrow, with a high ceiling, and we were standing opposite a wall with a large number of locked compartments; the varnish round the keyholes was scratched. The woman had put her key in the lock of one compartment and was waiting for me to produce mine. Her blouse was open at the neck. I noticed the gold cross on her dark skin, and I remembered that Julia never wore jewellery.

'Your key, señor,' she repeated with a smile.

I had had it in my hand the whole time. It was warm and moist, and I was surprised that it fitted, and that it turned in the lock. She moved aside a small flap, pulled the dull-gleaming metal box half out, and smiled at me again. She pointed in the direction of some tables, and left. A perfume I did not recognise disappeared with her. I was alone, in a deep underground vault that suddenly smelt like a burial chamber.

I took my bag and the metal box over to the tables, which were separated by shoulder-high partition walls, like election booths. The only other person present was an old lady; she was sitting at a table with a lot of papers in front of her, cutting off coupons, which she arranged in a neat pile. I noticed she was using her own scissors, not the pair hanging on a string at the side of the table; the scissors were small and golden, like the Spanish woman's necklace. She wore a lot of rings and bracelets, which tinkled whenever she used the scissors.

I disappeared into my booth, put the empty bag I had brought with me at my feet and the metal box on the table in front of me. I was surprised at how small it was, and again had the feeling that the whole thing was a silly game, one of those children's games in which one is blindfolded and led around in a circle in the wrong direction. I was prepared to find the box empty when I opened it.

I unlocked it, lifted the lid, and rested it against the wood at the back of the booth. In the middle was something

4

wrapped in a soft yellow cloth; the money was all around it. I did not have to touch the thing inside the yellow cloth to realise what it was; when I discussed the enterprise with Fritz Lehr I had wondered where the weapon would come from. I could hardly take it with me in the aircraft, and I knew no-one in Madrid who could have got such a thing for me. I had simply not bothered my head about it, as if I had known all along that I would find it here.

I gazed at the bundles of bank notes. The strange thing was that, though the uncertainty was over and the money was there, I did not feel the pleasure I had expected. It was rather like when I worked out how much $250,000 was in D-marks. When Lehr mentioned the sum I had thought it must be a good round million. A million was a magic figure, much more than $250,000. Then, when I looked up the exchange rate and discovered that the dollar had fallen again and that I should get only DM 3.80, which meant it was not a million marks but only 950,000, I was disappointed. I felt cheated, as if I had been robbed of the missing 50,000 marks, as if I were entitled to a million exactly.

The money disturbed me. It was in new $100 notes, packed in neat, rectangular bundles, as neat and clean as if they were metal blocks; in the bright artificial light the paper looked grey and unreal. I stared at the money as if it were in a non-existent currency. I picked up one of the rectangular blocks, and it still did not feel like money. I pulled out a few notes; they were cold and smooth and lifeless. I began counting, one bundle after another, miscounted, gave it up, and tried putting the notes back in the bundles. They no longer fitted perfectly into the bank's narrow yellow wrapping, and for the first time I began to feel that this was real money. I started again, simply taking notes out of the bundles, quickly counting them and then putting them back in the bundles as best I could. Meanwhile the old lady had risen to her feet with her box under her arm, and as she passed she glanced at me over the partition and smiled, as

if we were partners in a conspiracy; it was her smile that finally convinced me that what I was counting was real money, twenty-five times $10,000, a million marks, or only just short of a million.

A million marks. It was time I got used to the idea that it could belong to me, though first there was a job for me to do, after which it would belong to me, Hans Pikola, photographer, who had always been a failure in money matters, had always been satisfied too easily. I had wondered whether my old bag would be big enough, but of course it was, there would be no need to leave any of my things behind in the hotel. No-one would notice me, no-one would pay any attention to the man who in a few hours' time would leave the Hotel Fénix with only a single bag, would cross to the side of the street that was sunny in the afternoon, would pass the shops without glancing at them, being no longer interested in the window displays, since everything in them was now within his reach; a man walking more quickly than usual to get to the taxi-rank, almost imperceptibly dragging his right foot, or at any rate dragging it rather less than if he had spent a long time taking photographs in the open air or working in the dark-room.

No more taking photographs for Hans Pikola. No more advertising photographs, which really got one's goat—wasting three rolls of film before you caught the foam overflowing the top of the glass of beer just at the right moment, only to find that it had not been quite cold enough, with the result that the droplets, which were intended to suggest coolness, had disappeared. No more children's fashions, with models who were more affected than the grown-up professional stars. In fact no more people, no more faces at all. Julia had filed all my photographs in big steel filing cabinets —15,000 of them, the harvest of thirty years; that made one and a half pictures for every single day and, heaven knows, that was enough. There was only one picture I should like to have had, one of myself, carrying my bag, before getting

6

into the taxi to take me to the airport. It would *not* show
some of the things that a man of fifty does better not to
reveal to a young woman of twenty-four: the artificial right
knee-cap; the three missing lower left ribs; the two-thirds
of the stomach removed by operation; the artificial lower
jaw with those splendid-looking false teeth, each of which
cost more than a camera; and, really quite incidentally, the
spectacles with lenses of 2.5 diopters. 'How old are you?'
Dr. Blum had asked when he examined me three days ago.
'Fifty? But that's perfectly normal at your time of life, particularly in your job. The deterioration of your eyesight is
a perfectly normal phenomenon of ageing, and in fact in
your case it has set in relatively late.' The photograph would
show only a tall, thin, fair man with a narrow face, the face
of a non-smoker and non-drinker, a man who spent a great
deal of time in the open air; a rather crude, ordinary face, a
type you might well see wearing mountaineering clothes in
a mail-order catalogue, in climbing boots and tough cord
trousers. He would need only to have his hair cut. It was
too long for a man of fifty, and stood out over the back of
my shirt, but Julia liked it that way; it was she who had
persuaded me not to have it cut for the past six months.

Julia. I was twenty-six years older than she; and Dr. Blum,
who had married a girl forty years younger than himself,
had told me that the whole secret was having plenty of
money. 'All you need is plenty of money and it's all right,'
he had said. Here was the money. All I would have to do
was to fetch it later, in an hour or two hours' time, when I
had done the job I came here to do.

I took the yellow cloth out of the box and unfolded it.
In contrast to the money, the weapon looked used and very
real indeed. It was an American army .45 automatic. I took
out the magazine. It was loaded. I put it back, and tried the
silencer, which was lying next to it; it fitted the barrel perfectly. It was a powerful weapon, much too powerful for
the purpose for which it was intended, a single shot at short

7

range, for the man now waiting for me in his room at a motel in the Avenida de Burgos. A man who had never seen me, though I knew him well. I weighed the weapon in my hand, feeling slightly sick.

I had to make up my mind. The weapon or the money. If I took him the money, I should get five thousand dollars. If I took the weapon and killed him, all the money would be mine. The decision was mine only, but I did not feel I had any choice. Fritz Lehr had not sought me out for nothing, he had summed me up correctly, counting on my hate to gain the upper hand.

I took the pistol and put it in my pocket. I put the bundles of notes in the box, locked it, and put it back in the only open compartment. I locked the compartment, and put the key back in my pocket. I picked up my bag and walked towards the narrow exit. The steel chamber was more like a burial vault than ever.

I had so often imagined the rest that I acted as if in a dream. Opposite the bank I went down into the Metro and took it to the Plaza de Castilla Then I took a bus to Chamartin, from where I took a taxi to the corner of the Avenida de Burgos and the Avenida de Manoteras. From there I walked, carrying my bag in my left hand, keeping my eyes open for the Renault works.

It was a depressing industrial neighbourhood, and out here the Avenida de Burgos, the Spanish National Road No. 1, was one of those wide, unfriendly traffic arteries that seem to have no beginning or end and look the same everywhere, with their filling stations and rubbish dumps and cheap refreshment shacks. There were few houses, so there was an unrestricted view across the plain all the way to the Guadarrama mountains, which were covered in a light grey haze, though I thought I could see snow on the peaks. In the bank, particularly in the steel vault, I had felt like a stranger, but here, remarkably enough, I felt completely at home, as if the whole scene were familiar and had nothing new, un-

8

expected, or surprising to offer. The gas-holder rusting away on the right, the scrap-yard in which old, unserviceable buses were dumped, the car cemeteries, the single-storey supermarket with a lot of little flags on top—I felt as if I had come this way a hundred times, that I had known every inch of it for years; and when the motel appeared on the left, just after the Renault works, as Lehr had said, I knew I had reached my goal.

The motel lay about twenty yards back from the road. It was a low, flat building, as depressing as the neighbourhood itself. Red paint was flaking from the exterior. Steps led up to the entrance, the reception desk and a restaurant. The bedrooms lay along a corridor over the garages. Behind some timber wainscotting you could see the narrow, brown-painted doors with the room numbers. On either side of the entrance there was a rather pitiful patch of green, otherwise there was nothing but a dirty grey concrete surface, with oil stains outside the garages. A red neon light over the entrance, an arrow that kept flashing though it was broad daylight, failed to relieve the shabbiness of the place. But it was a perfect bolt-hole for the man whom I was going to see. No-one could approach it without being seen; there were no trees or buildings, nothing whatever to restrict the view.

There were only three cars outside the garages, all old models. At the edge of the road there was a filling station which I had to pass. A man in a stained overall was using a hand-pump to refuel a car. Otherwise there was no-one in sight. In spite of the neon sign, the place looked empty and desolate. Nothing altered as I approached; on the contrary, the doors now looked as if they led nowhere, as if the whole thing were nothing but a façade, like a film set with nothing behind it, so that if you opened the doors you would see nothing but sky.

Room 16 was the last room on the right at the end of the corridor. There was a car outside the garage that belonged

to it—*outside* the garage, not in it. No doubt the key was in the ignition and the tank was full. I noticed that there was another small flight of steps at the end of the garage next to room 16, so that he could reach the car in a flash. It really was an ideal spot from his point of view; it was precisely what a man used to hiding himself would choose. He had done nothing else for twenty-one years. That made no difference to me. I could not think beyond the moment when I would knock at his door. It was impossible. It was impossible to imagine that I would go in and see a face that I had seen only once in my life before, and that only on a photograph that showed a man twenty-five years younger than he was now. I could not imagine killing him, but I also could not imagine not killing him.

First I went to the car under room 16. It was an old Dodge. I opened the door on the driver's side and, sure enough, the key was in the ignition. I leaned over, half turned the key and watched the arrow on the petrol gauge. As I expected, it slowly moved until it came to a stop at 'full,' which gave me a sense of satisfaction. I put my bag on the driver's seat, took out the pistol and put it under my belt. A practiced eye would detect it at once, but that did not matter, because if he were sensible that was what he would expect. He could never feel secure; not for one moment in the past twenty-five years had he been able to feel secure; his alertness might have increased or it might have abated; both were equally possible.

I went back to the entrance. I wanted to make absolutely sure; he might have grown suspicious and changed rooms. During all these years he must not only have felt fear but have developed a sixth sense for danger. After successfully living in hiding for twenty-one years it must have become practically second nature. There were no curtains on the restaurant windows. I could see no customers inside, but only a man behind a bar with a transistor set in front of him. I walked into the entrance hall. There was a desk

there, and a rack on the wall with sixteen cubby-holes. The key of No. 16 was not there. There was also a placard showing the departure times of trains and another showing forthcoming cinema atttractions. I could hear the radio, but no-one took any notice of me.

I went behind the table and found the big black book in which guests' names were entered. I leafed through the pages until I found his name; he had arrived four weeks previously. He called himself Clemente Stoeber, but that was not his real name.

The signature bore no resemblance to that which I had so often found in the files and had scrutinized over and over again. Then his name had been Karl Boettcher, and his signature had been illegible, as doctors' signatures generally are. This one was legible in the way that a child's signature is legible. Looking at it, at the strange name, I wondered why I had taken all this trouble, travelled all this way, to kill a man who signed his name like a child. . . .

I

I know now how and when it all began, but at the time, of course, when the silvery-grey Mercedes drew up under the chestnut trees beside the old town moat and Christina Lehr got out, I had not the slightest suspicion. It was the second week of September 1969, and posters were going up everywhere for the elections on the 28th of that month, even in the Augsburg suburb of Lech. I lived and had my studio in one of the dilapidated houses there.

It was a fine, hot day, but the houses looked dilapidated even in the sunshine; the paint and the stucco ornaments were flaking away, the windows were unpainted, the balcony railings rusty. The water level in the moat below the remains of the old town wall had sunk, the water was stagnant, and when there was an east wind it was better to keep the windows shut. There was a path along the moat, and that was where the car drew up, in the shadow of the chestnut trees. I noticed it only when someone called out my name.

I stopped, surprised that the voice should have changed so little in fifteen years, for it was fifteen years since I had last seen her. I had of course followed her career, from Christl Stempa to Mrs. Christina Weinberger, then to just Christina, the famous model, and finally, for the past few years, to Frau Christina Lehr, wife of the well-known building contractor.

First to emerge from the car were her legs, her long,

slender legs; the fact that she wore stockings was not perceptible at first glance. Then came her equally long and
slender body, which seemed not so much to be covered by
a dress as to have had something green—green paint perhaps
—applied directly to the skin; and last to appear was her
face; the first thing you noticed when she smiled was that
her two front teeth were too far apart.

With her there emerged the smell of the leather upholstery
of the new car and a whiff of perfume, but all I noticed were
the teeth and the gap between them. This was never to be
seen in her photographs; in the old days when I photographed her she simply wore a false tooth that closed the
gap. I had forgotten this, but now remembered it again.

'Hallo,' I said. 'Hallo, Funny Face,' which had also been
one of her names.

She came nearer, and I could not help thinking that all
great photographic models are exceptions to the rule. Whoever said that, it applied to Christina, still applied, though
she had long since abandoned that profession. She must
now be thirty-nine or forty. She was too flat-chested, too
thin, too tall—she was just over 5 ft. 10, if I remember
correctly—and an endless amount had been written about
her size in shoes, which was seven or seven and a half,
I think. The effect she produced had nothing to do with
ordinary standards of beauty, but everything to do with
that special radiation that is peculiar to the great models;
they are just *there*, fully and completely, all the time, they
create a special mood, they animate . . . and as we walked
off together I felt this still applied to her.

She had locked the car, dropped the key in her bag, and
put her arm in mine. 'I wasn't really sure that all this still
existed,' she said. From the way she spoke and the construction of her sentences you could tell she had lived in America
for a long time.

'Nothing changes here,' I said. 'Not a great deal, at any
rate, and it never will change much. This is not a town that

likes change.' In fact a great deal had changed, of course, but I did not want to talk about the past. 'What brings you here?'

'I come here every so often. I've got an astrologer whom I go and see every now and then; he certainly wouldn't like hearing himself described as that, but that is more or less what he is.'

We had reached the house; its dilapidated condition could no more be denied than could that of its neighbours. She looked it over as if she were comparing it with her memories. 'You hated it even then,' she said, 'and all you wanted was to get away from here.'

'Yes, but I'm still here, as you see.'

'The sign isn't there any longer. Aren't you still a photographer?'

'Yes, what else could I be?' I looked at her. 'But no more models.'

Inside the house was actually worse, with the marble floor that had once been white and the remains of the Art Nouveau windows. There was a lift, a monstrosity of latticed metal; the brasswork gleamed, but it had been condemned by the town surveyor's department and had been out of action for years. She smiled, as if anything else would have been a disappointment to her. 'Really, very little has changed here.'

There was no need to show her the way. She knew which door to use, the studio-flat was still in the same place, the two big inter-connecting rooms were unchanged, except that they were more over-crowded than ever; there was too much furniture, too many pictures, too many things I had accumulated, both valuable and otherwise. She moved about in the chaos as if she could have found her way in the dark. She picked things up and put them down again, stopped in front of the glass case with the collection of clocks, looked at the backs of the books on the shelves, inspected three enlargements I had made and hung up to dry. I too realised

14

how little had changed here, apart from the row of gleaming metal filing cabinets in the neighbouring room in which my prints and negatives were filed.

I wanted to free a chair for her, but she sat on the edge of the low divan, on the big fox-fur cover.

'Are you still married to her?' she asked.

'Yes, still.' I had to work it out. 'We've been married for twenty-seven years. Will you have a drink?'

'No, thanks. And how are things going between you?'

She asked the question so simply and naturally that I answered as naturally as I could.

'They're not,' I said.

'I always said you weren't made for married life.'

'And I didn't think you were either.'

'How wrong can one be. On the contrary, the exact opposite is the case. I'm ideally fitted for marriage. It's still the easiest way for a woman to lay her hands on money. Even when I was a little girl I wanted to be rich. I never wanted any presents but money, I didn't want dolls or toys, what I always wanted more than anything else was money. It's my natural disposition, it's constitutional with me, and it was also the lesson that I learnt from life. You can buy practically everything for money, and I don't like people who won't admit it. I always knew I wanted money. It makes you feel more secure. That's what it does.'

'You must have earned a great deal of money when you were a model.'

'A model earns a great deal, but she spends it too. You can't keep money if you're a model, you have to fulfil expectations. I don't know one of us who got rich by it. And then you know where the money comes from, you know how you had to sweat for it, I don't call that being rich. You're not rich until you stop asking where the money comes from, and if you're a woman you can get that only from marriage.'

'And what's being married to Fritz Lehr like?'

15

'O.K., I think. He gives me what I want, and I try to give him everything that matters to him. And we have two children. Don't ask me for photographs, because I haven't got any, but I'm a good mother. They're three and five, a boy and a girl. Does that surprise you?'

'I read the newspapers, including the newspapers that print that sort of thing. I read about your children and your parties, and when you open art exhibitions, and I see photographs of you surrounded by long-haired young artists, and I wonder . . .'

'That's what everyone wonders.' She laughed, showing the gap between her teeth. 'Everyone would like to know whether I sleep with them . . . no, my marriage is O.K., within limits, but life is like that. But if you knew I was back, why didn't you get in touch? After all, you and Fritz used to be friends.'

'We lost sight of each other.'

'Haven't you ever seen him again?'

I had seen him, but what was the point of talking about it? What was really an event was seeing Christina sitting on the edge of the divan in her green, sleeveless dress, with her legs tucked underneath her. She was still sitting in the same position, and had not moved. It was this ability of hers to remain absolutely motionless that had made her so easy to work with. She could, if necessary, sit for hours like that, wearing heavy make-up, in the hot glare of the lights, until her muscles sometimes began visibly to twitch from cramp and tears came into her eyes and had to be blown away with a hair-dryer. Her pictures showed no trace of these physical ordeals.

'Did you ever see him again?'

'Once.'

'And?'

'It was a bit awkward.'

'If you don't want to talk about it. . . .'

16

'Why not? It was simply rather difficult after so many years. We hadn't seen each other since 1945. It was in a restaurant in Munich, and he was playing the big shot. It was one of those smart places where the waiters look down their noses at you, but they were all dancing attendance on him. It wasn't the right occasion for a reunion. At first he didn't know what to say to me, but then he showed me photographs of his children and the American wife he had at the time. At all events, I finished up knowing all about his new house and the estate at Steingaden and his latest turnover figures. But I can't really claim we had anything to say to each other, and since then neither of us has made any effort to see the other.'

'When was that?'

'Eleven or twelve years after the war. It was before you came back. It must have been in 1958, yes, it was soon after my accident.'

'You had an accident? You used to be a good driver, rather on the cautious side.'

The accident had happened two years after I took over the postcard publishing business. I needed the car because of the large amount of equipment necessary for the different open air and indoor pictures. Once before I had had valuable equipment stolen, so I bought a dog that I left with the car—it was so fierce that I could leave it unlocked without worrying. That day I went off to take pictures of a loop of the Lech, it was a pretty inaccessible spot, and when I came back the car was empty and the dog was dead—it had been poisoned. I felt so sick and angry that I must have driven like a blind man, and probably too fast into the bargain. It was an autumn day with a strong, gripping wind, and it caught the light car when I came out of a stretch of wood.

'I was lucky,' I said. 'The car was a write-off, but I only had to have three ribs removed, and my lower jaw was

broken, nothing that couldn't be rectified by a good oral surgeon. Look, I've never had such beautiful teeth in my life before.' I thought again about Fritz Lehr. 'Things were simply a bit difficult between us. Perhaps there were things we simply didn't want to talk about.'

'I think you'd get on all right now. I hope to see more of you from now on. You know our house on the lake, between Utting and Holzhausen, just beyond the Augsburg sailing club grounds? We're practically always there now. Of course the place isn't quite the same as in the old days, I've made some changes, but the park is exactly the same, we haven't cut down a single tree. But it's dreadful, I keep on talking only about myself. How are things with you?'

'They're as you can see.'

'Do you still paint?'

'I've never painted.'

I did not like this subject of conversation. I did not want to talk about the past. It was a closed chapter, and that was how I wanted it to remain.

'And you swore never to come back to this town if you ever got away from it,' I reminded her.

'Oh Pikola, the things we swear when we're young. You're quite right, we should never be reminded of them. I shan't talk about your painting, and you won't remind me of the things I swore. Besides, I've really forgotten all that. Just now, when you called me Funny Face, I really had to rack my brains to remember who first called me that, and when. I'm not afraid of the past any more, I never dream about it as I used to. The only thing a woman of my age has to be afraid of is the future.'

I looked at her, shook my head, and said: 'You look better than ever. You've never looked better in your life.'

'I shall be forty in three weeks' time. Forty. You know what that means to a woman?'

I could have told her that I only needed to think about

18

Thea, but I said: 'You don't look as if you were twenty, but you don't try to. Perhaps that's why you look as if you were thirty.'

'Now you're talking like my doctor. *Youth is wasted on the young*, isn't it? Real life begins at forty. My doctor says it's the age when the biggest jump in a woman's value takes place—she's better in every respect. She looks better and feels better than ever. She's more attractive, more experienced, more sensuous. Above all, she's more sensuous. It's now that she gets the right men. They just fall into her lap. Everything falls into her lap, because she's sure of herself. My doctor tells me that once a fortnight and, to cap words with deeds, he gives me those marvellous Vitamin E injections and pumps me full of those even more marvellous oestrogens.' She laughed. 'That's what you see in me. The right oestrogens tone up your skin, put gleam in your hair, firm up your breasts, provided you have any . . . Well, they spruce up your vagina too, not to forget your clitoris. Well, you know how outspoken these doctors can be.' She moved for the first time. She rose, came over to me, and rested her hands on the side of the chair in which I was sitting. Her face, her green body, were over me. 'Might your wife suddenly walk in?'

'No. She's at work, and in any case she never comes into this room. Sometimes I think she believes terrible things take place here. Actually she hates this room.'

She resumed walking up and down the room. Over in the corner where I developed my films there were two red lights. She switched them on, and looked at me, smiling.

'Tell me, she said, 'are you as good as you used to be?'

She had always asked such direct questions. She was the only woman I knew who could ask such questions, and the only one whom I answered in the same way. So, suppressing a year, I said: 'I'm forty-nine.'

'But Pikola, that's something you don't forget.'

I was not sure she was really talking about me.

'Do you have problems with him?' I asked, feeling I was talking like a doctor.

'Not exactly problems,' she said in a completely matter-of-fact voice.

'Girls?'

'What makes you think that?'

'It could be. He's a year older than I, and they say. . . .'

'No, not girls. I'm not afraid of the girls of the present day. They're prettier and cleverer than we were, and I have plenty of opportunities in our house of watching them when they're on the trail. Perhaps I know the wrong girls, but those I watch making up to our managers at the week-end are all as cold as ice—they've got all the tricks at their finger-tips, but they take not the slightest pleasure in it, they're in deadly earnest the whole time. I've done all that myself in my time, but I wasn't so cold. I was always prepared to give something in return. No. Fritz sees through them. In that he's a man of wealth, I mean a man of inherited wealth. He can tell at once when someone is after his money, *only* after his money.'

I could not help thinking of Julia, who was a girl too, but not like the girls she was talking about, and not like Christina either, but I had no intention of talking about her to anyone.

'No, it's not a question of girls, unless perhaps one turned up who was quite different. . . . But sometimes, after a meeting or when he comes back from abroad and he thinks no-one will suspect anything, he goes to one of those massage parlours in Munich, *massage and swimming pool, also for non-swimmers.* He always goes to the same one, Micklich, 51 Arcisstrasse, ring twice.'

'And you know all about it?'

'I think it's better that I should.'

'You've always been so very direct.'

'Yes, I know, it's not very feminine.' She had moved over to the window, where there were roller blinds, so that I

could darken the room in the daytime while I was developing. She let them down. In the light of the two red lamps that were still alight the green of her dress disappeared. 'Since I left you I've tried to work everything out,' she went on. 'That's not the worst thing I could have done, or is it? I think my dreams are in order. I wanted security, and I've got it. But of course I'm no longer the woman I was. What was I like then?' She did not wait for an answer, but bent over me. 'I want you to sleep with me,' she said.

I tried to remember the colour of her dress, but could not. In the reddish light it was the same colour as her skin. I did not notice how she undressed, where she put her clothes, whether she was wearing anything but the dress.

When I was in bed by her side she said: 'The first time you slept with me I was just over sixteen, and you were my first man. I'm your creation, don't forget that.' Suddenly she was quiet, her hands moved, and then she laughed beside me, very gently, as if it were possible to laugh in a whisper, and just as gently she said: 'You feel like old times . . . very much so.'

The roller blinds did not completely exclude the light. I looked at the two strips of light and said to myself it was high time I bought new ones. There was much that restrained me, too much. Why did I not tell her? The past cannot be brought back, though she seemed to think it could, and who was I to refute her?

II

Afterwards she was as natural as before. She dressed without my really being aware of it. She did not have to look for anything, and she left nothing lying about. She seemed to need only a few quick movements to tidy the bed. And when I pulled up the blinds and saw that her dress was green, she was again squatting in her original position on the edge of the divan. She opened her bag, glanced at herself in a mirror, decided that she needed no powder or lipstick, and adjusted her hair without a comb, with her hands only. She took a watch from her bag, glanced at it, and said:

'Tell me, have you kept the old pictures of me? Can I see them?'

This gave me time—time to go into the next room and look at the grey metal filing cabinets. First I looked under C, C for Christina, but there there was nothing but press cuttings, a whole series of front pages from *Vogue* with pictures of her, pictures from the early sixties not taken by me. I opened the S drawer and found a packed file with a cross reference: Christl Stempa, see also Christina, Weinberger, Lehr. Whatever Julia did, she did impeccably. I opened the file; most of the contents were photographs taken for press advertisements: Christina as a 4711 Sparta girl, or saying to another girl, 'Ten minutes ago you gave me a Spalt tablet, and now my headache's gone'; also there

were many pictures of her modelling hats by Velois, beach-
wear by Hödesmann, poplin coats by Jobis, ski suits by
Bogner. They all dated from 1948 to 1950, and to me they
all seemed a hundred years old. I went on searching until
I found one particular picture, a 2½ × 3½, a bad print on bad
paper. I took it and went back and handed Christina the
file.

She spread the pictures round her on the big bed. I sat
in my chair and looked at the small, bad, amateur snapshot
of an American military jeep, with an American lieutenant
in the passenger seat and a boy behind the steering wheel
wearing a uniform that was an exact replica of the lieutenant's, down to the little ship and the rainbow-coloured divisional sign. The windscreen had been lowered, and you
could see the boy's face plainly. He had both hands on the
steering wheel, and was smiling broadly. His two front teeth
were too far apart.

The snapshot was of her, Christina, Funny Face, taken
at the time when I first met her in July 1945. In the background you could see the American barracks. I looked at
the snapshot, which was now twenty-four years old, and I
was not sure whether Christina wanted to see it; I was not
even sure that I wanted to be reminded of it myself.

I was told her story by Lieutenant Duncan, the American
officer in the photograph, and she told me some things herself; and I gathered a great deal from the dreams she had
after she came to live with me. What was the point of resur-
recting all that now? I remembered the roller skates, of
course; Dresden in wartime, and a young girl scouring the
streets on roller skates to find out where it might be possible
to earn a little money, watching cars in the Old Market for
20 pfennigs an hour or selling worms to men fishing in the
Elbe—she told me a great deal about that. But she spoke
very little about her home, her two brothers who had been
killed in the war, her father, who was a blacksmith unable
to follow his trade because he had lost a hand in the First

World War and had never got over it, and her mother, who had to go out to work and tried to persuade her daughter to work too. *Why are you always sitting around polishing those roller skates? I can't see what's left to polish on them.* And off the girl went again on her roller skates, which were expensive ones, firmly attached to her white boots, wearing a thick shawl and mittens, for it was cold in February 1945, and next day, the 14th, was her mother's birthday. She had a shopping bag over her shoulder, though there was nothing to buy in the shops; it was her last year at school, and in the afternoon, when lessons were over, off she went. She was a resourceful girl, and knew where she could steal some flowers.

They caught her at it and locked her up. She had no identity card, and *one night* would not do her any harm; there would be time in the morning to check the name she gave, Christl Stempa, and her address and the story about her mother's birthday; in February 1945 there were so many refugees in the town and so many thieving children, it would all be cleared up in due course. But during the night the big air raid on Dresden took place. The girl, still wearing her roller skates, was in a big communal cell, and they left her there during the raid. Part of the building was hit, and in the confusion next morning she managed to run away.

That morning even the streets were blazing, because the asphalt caught fire; that was the one thing that she told me over and over again and that kept recurring in her dreams. The hot asphalt stuck to the wheels of her roller skates and brought her to a standstill; she struggled out, but they got stuck again, stuck solid, and she could not move. *I'm stuck* she cried out in her dreams, and then woke up and turned over towards me, and said, 'Have I been dreaming?'

In the Kaulbachstrasse her parents' house no longer existed; in fact no houses were there at all, and there was no point in digging for bodies. Someone helped her to unscrew the roller skates from her boots, a boy who would have been

able to talk to her about his dead parents, but no more did so than she did.

There were many such boys, and she joined up with them. She had no relatives in the town. The school was still standing, but the boys laughed at her. Who would think of going to school now? She did not like the boys laughing at her. So she cut her hair short and stayed with them. They roamed about and stole—without ration cards you had to steal—and moved on ahead of the approaching front. She accompanied the gang to near Prague, and then to Vienna and Salzburg. By now she had been wearing boy's clothes for a long time and called herself Christian. She was in Bad Reichenhall when the war ended, and there she saw her first Americans. Still wearing her white boots, she watched them helping themselves to German prisoners' watches, rings and other valuables. A young lieutenant, looking around for something to snap with his newly-acquired Leica, called out to the boy: 'Hey, you, yes you with that funny face, come here, what's your name? What's your name, funny face?' I looked at the old photograph, and saw a face, a smooth, unlined face; there was nothing to remind one of the girl with the worn white boots, not even the teeth.

'What picture is that?' I think she had asked that several times already. I was not sure whether I ought to show it to her, but I rose and went over to her.

'It's of you and Lieutenant Duncan. Do you remember him?'

She looked at the print for a long time without anything changing in her face. Then she said:

'Of course I remember Duncan. He gave me the first piece of advice that was of any practical use to me in my life.' Then she fell silent, and looked at the snapshot just as I had. I did not want to tell her of what memories the snapshot stirred in me.

It was not unusual at that time for American units to

adopt as a mascot one of the innumerable boys who were roaming the streets. They kept such boys for luck, a talisman, as others kept a company dog. Duncan's company kept Funny Face. She accompanied them to Augsburg in a uniform specially made to measure for her, complete with the rainbow that was the divisional sign. She lived with them, ate in their messes, watched their films. She had the key to Duncan's ration box and his jeep. But, almost overnight, the end came; the combat troops were withdrawn, and Christina's life as a mascot was over. It was then that she came to live with me. Thea was in Transylvania, and I did not even know whether she was still alive.

Christina had put the photograph down. 'Do you still remember that we ended by going with him all the way to Bremerhaven? And do you know the last thing he said to me just before he went on board? *Smile and advance*. That day I was dressed as a girl for the first time for a long time, and he bent down and kissed me on the cheek and said: "Never look back, Funny Face, just smile and advance." It was good advice, and I've always tried to follow it.' She made a movement with her hand. 'I didn't know you had kept all this.'

'You're right, one shouldn't. But a photographer is always worried at the idea of somebody turning up some time and asking for a particular picture or negative that he once took. He can never throw anything away, he has to keep everything.'

'Those weren't bad times, were they?' she said. 'I mean, we were badly off, but all the same it was a good time, I mean with all those good intentions we had. Do you ever remember the ice hockey? Do you remember that game at Garmisch? Incidentally, how's that knee of yours? That happened in the game at Garmisch, didn't it?'

I still had the knee, but all the rest was far away and long ago, a past that no longer existed. Jacques Fath had seen pictures of her and wanted her to model for him, and

in 1950 she had gone to Paris alone. Three years later I met her again. By that time she was Mrs. Christina Weinberger, recently married to an American army officer, and her ship, the *America*, was sailing to New York from Le Havre next day. *Smile and advance*. She really had followed Lieutenant Duncan's advice.

'Why didn't you come across with me at the time? You could have, as you know. We should both have gone a long way, and perhaps you might still have been the first man in my life.'

'Perhaps we might have gone a long way,' I said. 'But I certainly shouldn't have remained the only man in your life.' There were also other things. There was Thea, who in 1950 was at last able to come to Germany, and the child Julia, whom I did not want to talk about. But Christina seemed to read my thoughts.

'You haven't told me anything about Julia,' she said. 'She must be grown up by now, a young lady. How old is she now?'

'Twenty-four.'

She rose and looked round the room. 'I can't see a picture of her anywhere. Haven't you got one?'

'No.'

Perhaps it was stupid to say that. But I did not want to show her any photographs of Julia. I showed photographs of Julia to no-one.

'No photographs? Is she pretty?'

'I don't know.'

'Is she like you?'

'They say so.'

'You must bring her with you. She won't remember me, but I still remember her. She was always terribly serious when we went to see her at that convent and then said good-bye and left her there alone. Promise me you'll bring her. I'm giving a garden party on my birthday. You're invited, and you must bring Julia. After all, it's my fortieth

27

birthday. You'll still remember the date, September 28th, born under the sign of Libra, ruling planet the sun. It's a Sunday, and I'm giving a garden party. Zgodda, my astrologer, has promised me it's going to be a fine weekend, and so far his predictions have always come true; he's absolutely dependable so far as the weather is concerned.'

She had suddenly been totally transformed into Christina Lehr, the cool, elegant, industrialist's wife who surrounded herself with left-wing intellectuals, and I was someone who had been allotted a role in the plans for her garden party.

'Oh, but you haven't got a car, I'll send one for you.'

'Julia will bring me,' I said.

'Very well, I shall count on you then. You'll be getting the invitation. I must go now, but I hope we shall be seeing much more of each other in future?'

This was the moment, standing by the door, when she first mentioned the idea of my writing and illustrating the centenary volume. I must say that at the time I did not take very seriously either that or the invitation to the garden party for which the weather was *unquestionably* going to be perfect. The feeling I had at the time was that, as I had done something for her, she felt she must reciprocate, but that it had struck her at the last moment that the invitation to the garden party was not sufficient recompense for my *services*. Perhaps I was unfair to her, perhaps it was simply her way of distributing little favours to men, left-wing authors and progressive artists and photographers whom she had once known. *Little favours are the things you're remembered by.* Was that perhaps something that Mr. Weinberger had taught her?

At all events, it appeared that the firm of Friedrich Lehr was celebrating its centenary on November 1 1969, and the idea was to publish an illustrated commemorative volume in honour of the occasion.

'You can do it easily, Pikola, you have an eye, and you have the right flair. If you agree, Fritz will get in touch

with you, or his brother Gottfried. So that's settled then, isn't it? As I said, I hope we'll be seeing more of each other in future.'

I was in a strange mood when she left, and did not take what she said about the centenary volume seriously, and so it was a complete surprise when Gottfried Lehr telephoned two days later. But none of that was in my mind when Christina said good-bye and I stood at the window and watched her walk away. She got into the car body first, and then she drew her long legs behind her, and I watched her putting on a pair of long white gloves. She turned the car, and as she drove past she waved with her left hand; the gesture was not aimed at any window in particular.

The pictures were still scattered all over the bed, and I gathered them together. I was glad when they were back in their files in the metal cabinets. I stood there, gazing at them. It suddenly struck me that they were like a row of grey tombstones; it was a good thing to see them firmly anchored there, burying the past. What was the use of re-membering? There was no connection between the girl on the bad 2½ × 3½ photograph and the woman whom I had just seen again. Was not Christina a striking proof that it was always at all times and in all circumstances possible to make the best of the painful business that is called life? Or was Thea right when she said that if I were able to start my life over again I should again fail to get what I wanted and should repeat all the mistakes I had made?

I also said to myself that one should really not venture into the proximity of the wealthy if one was not one of them; and today I should add that one should not venture into the proximity of the happy if one is not one of them.

III

Thea changed the places where she kept her drink, but a good place to begin looking for it was in the side drawers of the dressing-table in the window niche. I had not been to her bedroom for a long time, and the sight of it was a shock. In the morning she was always in a tremendous hurry; after an evening with the bottle it must have been hard to pull herself together to face another day, to get up, let in the light, dress, have breakfast, and give instructions to her mother's nurse with the taxi waiting outside. The whole room suggested a hurried departure—the half-open wardrobe door, the clothes on the bed she had taken out but not put on, the open chest of drawers, the pair of stockings in which she had discovered a run at the last moment. Her violet silk dressing gown lay at the foot of the bed—violet of all colours. The empty glass was on the bedside table, the heavy ruby glass she always filled in the living room last thing every evening before going to bed; it was the last glass of many, but the most important, to help her to go to sleep.

The dressing-table was the last surviving relic of a former bedroom suite, and the glass top was almost invisible beneath an array of half-empty tubes, powder boxes, bottles of nail polish, half of them presumably dried up, too many bottles of perfume and samples that did not mix; and scat-

tered about in the midst of all this, like small, exotic animals, were combs and eyelashes—these last in particular looking like an angler's artificial flies; and all this in broad daylight, for the dressing-table was right under the window. What a struggle must take place at it every morning. Yet none of this was perceptible when Thea left the house and went to the waiting taxi; from my window, from which I often watched her, all that met the eye was a good-looking, middle-aged, not unsuccessful career woman.

The doors at the sides of the dressing-table were locked and the keys were not there, but I knew where to find them. We had played this game of hide-and-seek for years, particularly at the beginning, when it worried me much more. I have known many drinkers—there are plenty in the photography business, which often involves long periods of waiting about—but no man is as good at that game as a woman is. Not that she was a drinker in the sense that she struck people as such; she was, I think, what the doctors call a functioning alcoholic. In the company of others she behaved quite normally, and she was always ready to deny that she drank; she merely needed a pick-me-up after a tiring day.

I found the key in the pocket of her dressing gown. The right hand compartment of the dressing table contained wigs. Most of them were arranged on plastic foam heads, but one was hung over a still unopened brown glass bottle with a white label and gold lettering, *distilled and bottled in Scotland.* I took it, and opened the window before leaving the room. What I was doing suddenly struck me as pointless, but now I had to see it through.

The flat on the same floor opposite my studio was quiet; the whole house, occupied by quiet, elderly people, was quiet; but now I could hear a different sound, thirds, fifths and quarters, a pause and then it started all over again, this time triads and the whole octave; Thea's mother was having her piano tuned. It was in the sitting room, a white Blüth-

31

ner. No one had played on it for the past ten years, but Thea's mother had the tuner in every three months.

When I entered the room the piano tuner had finished and he was putting his things away. He told me what a wonderful instrument it was; nowadays they couldn't make them like that any more. The old lady smiled at him from her chair by the window, and said that also there were no more *voices* like those in the old days, female voices in particular. According to her story, and the faded newspaper cuttings that she kept in three leather albums, in the years after the turn of the century Olga Valmy (she insisted on using her maiden name) had been the soprano star of the Bucharest Opera, and the first Salome who not only sang the part but danced it. She talked everlastingly about those good old days, and about her voice, though the principal theme of the press cuttings was her escapades with Russian nobles. Sitting there in her chair by the window with a table with a lot of medicine bottles beside her, she was still a beauty. Her hair was silvery white—Clairol's Silk and Silver—and was held in place by a thin net. She used a great deal of make-up, but with her dark skin and dark eyes it was not very noticeable.

As soon as I was alone with her I began looking for the bottle of Kirsch. She kept her eyes shut, as if taking no notice of what I was doing, but she had very thin eyelids, which gave you the feeling that she was watching you all the same, and suddenly she said: 'You'll have trouble with Thea.'

I had found what I was looking for; a litre bottle of 60 per cent pure Kirsch.

'Don't you want to go on looking?' she said. 'Are you sure *I* haven't hidden another bottle somewhere? Here, in my chair, for instance? But you wouldn't dare to come too close to *me*. It would be a pretty kettle of fish if I suddenly collapsed and died in my chair. How would you explain *that* to Thea?'

In spite of this death threat, which was her favourite

32

weapon, I have never known anyone with such a strong will to live. If only Thea had had one-tenth of her strength.

'Why don't you help her?' I said. 'She'd certainly listen to you. You're always with her, you could stop her drinking, but instead you actually encourage her.'

'What makes you think she drinks? What reason have you to suppose she has touched a single drop lately?'

I pointed to the half-empty bottle of Kirsch. 'All I know is that yesterday it was full,' I said.

'And Thea drank it, of course, and not that person who calls herself a nurse and can hardly speak a word of German. But all I'm worth in your eyes, of course, is a Turkish woman who pokes her nose into everything, steals my records and helps herself to the drinks.'

The nurse came every morning before Thea left for work. She cleaned up, looked after the old lady, and made sure she took her medicine. She was a very quiet, shy person, the wife of a doctor at the West Hospital. It was quite certain that all my mother-in-law's accusations against her were false.

'That was your idea, of course, foisting a Turkish woman on me,' she went on. 'All these Turks are thieves. They are a nation of thieves, born thieves, all of them.'

'And Rumanians are born drinkers, aren't they?' She always managed to make me say things I did not want to say.

'I'm not a Rumanian,' she said.

'Your father was.'

'My father. My father. What a father he was. A lousy Rumanian, like they all are. You're all the same, you men, but I've finished with you, and Thea will finish with you too.'

She was a charming old lady, sitting there with her hands folded on the crocheted rug over her knees. In the early years I had always assumed her to be an ally of Thea's, and this had certainly been a mistake. I was nearly at the door when she suddenly said:

'I saw her. Not that you believe I didn't see her. So you

now let them into the house when Thea is out? The older you men are, the more shameless you get. You drive your shamelessness to the limit, as if I didn't know.'

She said this without a trace of feeling, and that strong old heart of hers certainly did not beat faster. I went out before she could say any more, taking the bottles with me. They were to make possible a conversation with Thea, pointless though it seemed, because I knew how such conversations ended. Generally they did not even happen, because when Thea came home she disappeared at once. I decided to go to the station to meet her.

I went back to my studio and put the bottles on the shelf next to the bed and looked at them. I felt I could do with a strong drink myself. But you don't drink if you have had two-thirds of your stomach cut away. Suddenly I had to laugh when I remembered that I had met her only because, literally on my last day in Africa, an over-zealous Englishman in the 11th Hussars had fired three rounds of his submachine gun into my body. And it struck me that for years I had not thought so much about the past as I had today.

IV

Election posters were going up all over the station square, and I watched men pasting them up while I waited. One man was adding the second half of Kiesinger's face. It was the right side of the face, the one with the eye with the drooping eyelid, which made him look tired and resigned. The trouble was undoubtedly ptosis, either congenital or a symptom of old age, and it could easily have been removed. Why had he not been advised to have the operation? But it was a thoroughly bad picture. Why did they insist on photographing him with his mouth open? A politician can be allowed to smile on an election poster, but if so he must have his mouth shut; showing his teeth gives a man an expression of excessive personal ambition, of unscrupulousness. Adenauer knew this, and showed how it ought to be done. On his election posters he always had his lips closed or actually pressed together, a reticent man looking down almost contemptuously at the chaos of our times.

But that was no affair of mine. I was no longer concerned with public relations, I took no more photographs of people. After thirty years I had had enough of photography, the most objective of the arts, though it can lie so brilliantly. Photographers are generally held to be very sensitive people, but the truth is rather the opposite. We are dull, stale people—only the film we use has to be sensitive. To us things are cut-outs. We see something, cut it out, shut off every-

thing else and no longer see it. That is what we have to have a gift for, for cutting out; and later in the dark room we have to decide whether to make another cut-out out of the cut-out.

Once upon a time Thea had believed me to be an especially gifted photographer, better than the rest; what she meant by that was only that I was better at faking. That is really what she told me when we first met in Athens twenty-seven years ago, when I took my first photograph of her. She was the most touchingly unsuccessful singer who ever appeared on a stage to entertain German troops. I photographed her and gave her the enlargement, and she looked at it in astonishment and said: 'Is that me? It's extremely flattering. Do I really look like that?' That was the whole point. She told me only what became clearer and clearer to me in the course of time, that is, how much one can fake and lie in photographing people, so much so that in the end I gave it up. I did it for twenty years, using my Rodenstock, the right film, the right paper and the right cut-out to bring out a person's best, most attractive features. It earned me a reputation.

Those who wanted to be flattered in this way patronised the photographer Pikola, who could be depended on to destroy every disadvantageous picture immediately, including the negative. He would never let you see an eye half-shut or too wide open because of the flash-light, or a hand that shook and was distorted as a result. I showed people at their best, even in the most difficult circumstances, even in times when you had to work really hard to find it and had to cover off a great deal.

On my photograph of Max Schmeling—I had begun with sporting pictures—it was the only one I took of him when he was not fighting, but posing in the studio with his fists raised and all the light behind him—he looked as if he had never received a blow in his life—may he forgive me, because I know he could take them as well as give them—and

36

because of the lighting even the broken nose he already had at that time was not displeasing and created an impression of strength. So it was not surprising that during the war I became a photographer in a propaganda company, and in that capacity was assigned to Rommel, the desert fox himself. If you still remember the pictures of Rommel, I always made sure he had his goggles over the peak of his cap and that his field glasses were hanging round his shoulders; and on every single one of my photographs of him you will always find a map, which was my trademark, so to speak, whether he was in a tank or in the cockpit of a Fieseler-Storch or outside his tent; the map was always spread out in front of him, suggesting space, wide horizons, vast enveloping moves, strategic superiority. In my pictures of Rommel in Africa throughout the years from 1941 to 1943 he always looked like an undefeated general, and in fact he was never really beaten, was he?

But the day came when I had had enough of it and stopped photographing people. In 1956 I took over the postcard publishing firm, whole cupboards full of prints and negatives, and only photographed views—bends in rivers, churches, sailing boats on a lake and gravestones, which were a particular favourite of mine, little ones lying neglected by the roadside, recording calamities such as the coach and horses that collapsed, killing two people, gravestones in small country cemeteries and others in town cemeteries with curious inscriptions, like 'Mummy, please come soon too.' To Thea all this travelling about taking ridiculous views for postcards seemed a deplorable waste of talent—never having a picture in *Life* or in any of the big exhibitions, with nothing to my credit but a single book of photographs which was really good. This referred to a volume called *Faces*, which was a collection of unsold portraits. Otherwise there were only those mindless albums *Perfect Close-ups, How to Make Cut-Outs* and *Models in Photography*, ninety-six pages, paper boards, DM 4.80—and post-

cards, postcards and calendars. She felt ashamed every time she passed the sign outside—Hans Pikola, Publisher of **Cal-endars** and Postcards—so much so that I ended by removing it. I, the most talented and least successful of them all. . . .

She was not on the first train, but another was due a few minutes later; both left Munich between 4.30 and 5.00. She worked in Munich, and commuted every day. She never failed to catch one of those two trains, both of which had a restaurant-car with bar. During the day she did not touch drink, but had her first in the train on the way home. When I went to Munich once a week on Julia's free day I used to meet Thea at the station in the evening. She always automatically made for the carriage next to the restaurant-car, and she was always particularly irritable and nervous on these occasions. I eventually realised why it did not suit her to have me travelling with her. It meant that she had to control herself, because my presence spoilt the moment for which she had been waiting all day, the first drink, the first step towards the other bank, to the land without thickets and thorns, where marriages were happy and children got top marks, the land of which she wanted to go on dreaming. For what they gave her was not just alcohol, but an elixir that nourished her dreams. All the waiters on the trains knew her, she had no need to tell them what she wanted, and her first glass was empty and the first flush appeared on her cheeks before the train pulled out. She drank the first glass very quickly, in a single draught, and waited impatiently for the second which, however, she was in no hurry to drink; it was sufficient to have it in front of her and to hold it, and it lasted her for the rest of the journey.

She could not have expected me to be waiting for her, for I had not done so for a long time, so she walked up the broad stairway and passed without seeing me. She looked very well groomed in her brown suit with her brown crocodile bag under her arm; her legs were a little too thin for

her body; she always had a struggle to keep her weight down. She looked exactly what she was, one of those independent women who do a job and are successful at it. But I always saw something else in her. She had her father's face, the big cheek bones, the bright eyes, the fair complexion. Basically it was a very simple face, classic in its simplicity, rather like a piece of furniture in which all the lines and shapes are right. But she spoilt it by the wrong make-up, too red lips, too dark eyebrows, and the dark wigs she nearly always wore. As her job was beauty culture, one wondered why she did everything wrong for herself. The impression it made on me, now as always, was that it was an act of self-destruction—as if to say others must not love what she no longer loved herself.

I had let her pass me, and I followed her; for a while I actually walked by her side. When she walked more quickly, I did the same. She looked at me for a moment, neither surprised nor angry. She actually smiled.

'I thought I'd fetch you,' I said.

'Nice of you,' she replied, as anyone else would have.

'Have you had a tiring day?'

'Not too bad, it has become just routine. And what about you?'

'Nothing out of the way.'

She went towards a taxi, next to which a young man in a leather jacket was waiting. He was young, with long, curly hair. I saw him raise his hand in greeting from some distance away, but he dropped it when he saw she was not alone. I had forgotten that she had the same taxi to take her to the station in the morning and fetch her in the evening every day.

'Let us walk for a bit,' I said. 'It's such a fine day.' When she failed to respond, I added: 'I can pay him for the fare he's missing.'

'There's no need to,' she said. 'I pay him for the whole month.'

39

She walked on towards the taxi, and the young man opened the door. She got in and sat down, and he closed the door behind her. He seemed not to expect me to get in too; at all events, he made no move to open the door for me but went to his seat. For a moment I was tempted to let her drive off alone, but then I went round and got in on the other side and sat beside her. She said nothing, and lowered the arm-rest between us. This made her golden bracelets and chains with coins on them tinkle, and I felt she was wearing too many of them for her small wrists and her hands, from which you could still tell she had once played the piano.

The young man drove off; I could see his eyes in the front mirror as he looked at Thea and said with a smile: "Well, how many of those rich ladies did you deal with today? Facials? Do you really do that?'

Obviously Thea used to talk to him about her work on their daily trips. She had now been doing this job for several years; she worked in a beauty parlour. It was run by a Hungarian woman and was called the Ilona Institute, Medical Centre for Total Beauty Treatment, and it was a very exclusive and snobbish establishment for rich women.

I had once been there to fetch Thea; there were soft, near-white carpets, white leather armchairs, transparent plexiglass desks, soft music from invisible loudspeakers, and of course *les machines*, the glittering chrome instruments by which Ilona swore; she never referred to them except as *les machines*, insisting on the French, though nearly all of them were developed and manufactured in Germany and exported all over the world. There were vaporizers, blowers, toners, special rollers and brushes that removed dead cells with ultrasonic speed. But Ilona's holy of holies was an instrument that by means of galvanic currents sprayed under the pores of the skin a serum specially prepared for her from amniotic fluid. The thought of those instruments, and the men who drove Ilona's silver-painted station-wagon to farms three times a week to fetch the amniotic fluid, which

was taken from unborn calves, sometimes followed me into my dreams. A quite special odour, rather like a mixture of incense and that given off by an ultra-violet ray lamp, was exuded by all these instruments, which were attended to chiefly by Thea. Suddenly I thought I detected it in her as she sat at my side. Because of my presence the driver had fallen silent. I had spoilt his daily chat.

I remembered that Thea had once tried to run away with a young man. That had been five years ago; he was a young and promising painter, ten years younger than she. He had won a prize and a residential bursary to the Villa Massimo in Rome. She had pretended she was going to Rome to attend an Avon conference, but both of us were very well aware that she had no intention of ever coming back. But six weeks later she came back, in a worse state than ever. She never heard from the young man again, and I never heard of him either—I mean, I never heard of his being successful; he was never more than promising, which was certainly why things went wrong between him and Thea; for Thea's problem was her craving for perfection.

It had taken me a long time to realise it, but the source of her unhappiness was that she wanted too much perfection, in herself and others, and she was continually disappointed when people turned out to be less than perfect. The problem in our marriage was that she saw something in me that I could not fulfill. She had loved me, and she had loved Julia, too, and those whom she loved had to be specially perfect, must have no weaknesses and make no mistakes. Others she might perhaps have forgiven, but us she could not forgive.

The driver was still disgruntled when at last he pulled up outside the house. He got out and opened the door.

'The same time to-morrow morning?' he asked.

'Yes, the same as usual.'

That was all they said, but it sounded like a code, a secret language they used in the presence of a stranger. When we

were inside I took her arm and tried to lead her towards my studio.

'What's the meaning of this?' she said. 'Leave me alone, please.'

'I want to talk to you.'

'Why? What is there so important to talk about? I'm tired. At least let me get home and relax. I've been in these clothes all day long.'

She was nervous and restless, and glanced at the door which was the only thing that separated her from her bottle.

'I want to talk to you.'

But she did not give up yet. 'Very well, I'll just go up to the flat and tell mother I'm back.'

'She knows you're back. She's sitting at the window and saw us arrive.'

I had unlocked the studio door, and she followed me over the threshold, cautious and tense, and she stopped stiffly near the door.

'Won't you sit down?'

'Tell me what you've got to say. I've had a tiring day. I. . . .'

She spotted the bottles on the shelf. For a moment I thought she was going to fly into a rage, but instead she seemed to relax. She flung her handbag on the bed, and in doing so she drew nearer the shelf with the bottles, as if unintentionally. She tried not to look in that direction, but it cost her a tremendous effort of self-control, and suddenly I noticed the lines round her mouth and her rather too full face.

'This daily travel takes too much out of you. You always say . . .'

I realised she was not listening. No matter what I said, the thought of how to get to the bottle would be stronger. I was afraid she might *ask* for it, and so I fetched a glass. I filled it half full and put it down near the bottle. I turned

away and began tidying up some books and papers that were lying about, standing with my back to her, to give her a chance to drink unobserved. I heard her move, pick up the glass and drink, and waited a little longer. Then when I turned again I noticed the empty glass next to the bottle. She smiled. It was not a very happy smile, but it was better than her remoteness in the taxi.

'You seem to be on very good terms with the taxi driver.'

'Was that what you wanted to talk to me about? Yes, I am on good terms with him. Taxi drivers and dining-car attendants are marvellous to talk to. They listen, don't you see. It's part of their job. Of course it's still better to talk to a total stranger you know you will never see again in your life, then you can really let yourself go.' She had got over her inhibitions, or whatever they were, and helped herself from the bottle without replacing the cork. Her bracelets tinkled as she drank, and this time she kept the glass in her hand.

'Well, what is it? What have you got to say to me? I've really had a tiring day.'

'Why must you always wear those wigs?'

I was furious because I'd had an urgent feeling that we must talk, and now I was unable to think of anything to say. But that was the trouble, it was all so trivial, but our life consisted exclusively of these trivialities about which we battled, like two perverted warriors who had long since forgotten what they were fighting about but could not stop slashing at each other.

She suddenly put her hand in her dark hair and pulled it off. She flung the wig towards the bed where her bag was, but missed, and it fell to the floor.

There were grey streaks in her fair hair. I liked her much better like this, particularly when she pushed the hair back from her brow with one of those helpless gestures of hers. She stood there as if turned to stone; only the muscles in

her face twitched, as if she realised too late what she had done; it was as if she had done something indecent in my presence.

'Don't look at me like that. I know what I look like.'

Her voice betrayed the first signs of hysteria, as if it were the first thing about her to be affected by alcohol. 'But what I look like is nothing in comparison to what I feel. If you could only see that.'

'Don't worry, it's written on your face. At all events, I can see it.'

'You can't see anything. And you're not even interested. I ought to swallow one of those little cameras they photograph people's insides with and have the picture enlarged and framed. A nice little camera in my heart, what a picture it would take.'

'Perhaps you ought just to try and give up drinking. You'd probably feel much better.'

'Better? Do you think it makes any difference what I wake up with in the morning? A hangover from drink or from crying my heart out?'

Normally this was something we never discussed; we had given up mentioning the fact that she drank. The glass in her hand was empty, and she was struggling to pluck up courage to fill it again in my presence. I had not remembered things were as bad as this. Sometimes they were better, sometimes worse, and sometimes there actually seemed to be reason for hope. It occurred to me that she had been dealing all day long with women like Christina and that she had had to flatter them in the most real sense of the word.

Christina was an example of how it was possible to survive misfortune and turn it to one's advantage, but it was not that that occurred to me now; all that was in my mind was how unfairly life had treated Thea.

As always in my life, I could not find the right things to say. What Thea lacked, after all, was balance; she was

44

desperately searching for a little balance, even in the glass she still had in her hand. I tried to make amends for everything, and said: 'Why don't you change, and then we could go out somewhere? We could go have dinner somewhere or, if you don't want to see people, we could get the bicycles out of the basement and go out to the Sieben-Tisch woods.' I tried to take her arm, but she withdrew it. There was an expression of mistrust on her face; perhaps this harmless suggestion of mine merely reminded her of the tennis courts in the Sieben-Tisch woods where I used to practice with Julia. 'You say what you prefer to do.'

'It will be better if I don't.'

'Please, let us talk. You've always complained that I don't talk to you enough.'

'It's too late now.'

'Perhaps it's this house. Perhaps we ought to move. I could do my job anywhere. Perhaps . . .'

"Don't use that word, I hate it. *Perhaps* I should never have got married. *Perhaps* I should never have been born . . . What's the good of it? Who was she?'

'Who was who?'

'The girl.'

'What are you talking about?'

'The girl who was here.'

She pointed to the bed.

'You think that just because I drink I can't see and smell and taste. No, don't tell me who she was. Was she a model? And she wouldn't? You were too old for her? Is that it, you're too old for them already? They can never be young enough for you, can they?'

One of her fixed ideas was that I used my job to *get girls*, and that was why she hated these rooms, where she no doubt imagined that things *happened*. By this time I was ready to give in; I give in easily after so many vain attempts.

'Very well, let's stop talking,' I said. 'It was only an at-

tempt. There's no need for us to go on talking. Don't keep your mother waiting any longer.'

She picked up her wig from the floor and took her bag.

'What's the point of this? Why make such a fuss? What is there so unusual about us?' she said. 'Look round and you see nothing but broken marriages. So take it easy. Marriages either break up or are broken up, I don't know why or whose fault it is, but that's simply how it is.'

She had drunk more than I had thought. She must have filled her glass again without my noticing it, or perhaps I had not wanted to notice it. She could not stand still, the floor might have been gently heaving beneath her feet. A false tone crept into her voice as she went on: 'I'm glad I'm getting old, I'm glad I *am* old. What you see is just the last quiverings, but don't worry, they'll stop too, soon you'll have two old women in the house.' She laughed hysterically. 'And then you'll be able to sleep with anyone you like. I'm only surprised you haven't plucked up courage yet to try with Julia . . .'

'Stop.' I had been expecting this. At this stage I always expected it, for this was what she always ended up with. 'Don't mention that subject again, because if you do I shall leave immediately, and I shan't come back. You know that that is the agreement between us. It will be better if you go now. Don't worry about the bottles, I'll bring them over.'

That is exactly what I did. Then I left the house, hurried through the streets, telephoned to Julia from the main post office and told her I was coming to Munich the next day. In what remained of today I would go to see my father at his printing works to discuss calendars.

The firm still called itself Pikola Brothers, Printers and Publishers, but that was a very grandiloquent name for it. A glance at the showcases next to the entrance gave an accurate picture of its present state. The glass was encrusted with dust and dirt, so that it was hard to make out what

was inside. The contents had certainly not been renewed
for more than ten years, and were faded and stained with
damp; they consisted of specimens of print and letter head-
ings and marriage and death announcements, an aristo-
cratic lady's blue visiting card, and in the middle the only
relatively new product, a brief newspaper cutting now
more than four years old in which the words 'formerly
Ludwig Pikola, book printers and lithographers by appointment to the royal court' were underlined by hand.

The cutting had appeared on the occasion of the firm's
centenary; it referred to the centenary without mentioning
the firm's decline. Thus it was four years older than Lehrs,
the building contractors, and if I mention it it is not because
my father plays any important part in this story, but simply
because it underlines the contrast between a family firm
that rose to riches in the course of a century and another,
once prosperous, firm that equally steadily declined.

The greater part of the former printing works had been
given up; part served as a beer store and the rest was used
by a dealer in devotional articles. All that remained was the
composing room and a room with a few superannuated
presses. Thick dust lay everywhere; it covered the rolls of
paper and the steel shelves on which the blocks for the postcards were kept, and the typecases seemed filled solely with
dust. Old posters announcing church meetings hung on the
walls, and a list of Gothic types.

Apart from printing my postcards, calendars and 35mm.
booklets, which was not done here, my father had handed
over the business ten years previously to a rather dubious
individual, a former headmaster, who published a small-
sized fortnightly printed on cheap paper with articles such
as 'Can spanking with the flat of the hand really do any
harm?' or 'Caning in English public schools,' together with
a larger number of small advertisements with wordings like
'Domina, passionate disciplinarian, offers imaginative and
pleasurable training.' The man made a good living out of

this and lived in a villa in a suburb of Westheim, and was in all other respects a very worthy-looking man in his fifties, with a wife and four children. The fact that the old machine on which the diocesan newspapers had once been printed was in this profitable use failed to register with my father. He had bought himself a place in an old people's home and parted with the works on the sole condition that he might spend the day there and might sometimes do some printing there himself. He had a corner separated from the main area by low partition walls, and this he had turned into a small, over-crowded office, where he sat at a desk covered with papers and drawings; the neon light had to be kept on even in the day-time. The shelves all round him contained the files in which he kept his correspondence with church officials, civil servants, anthropological museums and private scholars, as well as the books he needed for his real interest in life, for he was an amateur archaeologist, continually on the trail of ancient Roman burial places in the Lech area.

Thea could never stop making derogatory remarks about the cranky, hopelessly unbusinesslike old gentleman, hinting that I might well end up like him myself, for in her eyes he was merely a crackpot and a total failure. That is certainly what many people took him to be, for, as I have indicated, the firm was once a famous one in the printing world. It had been in existence since 1865, and the great breakthrough came with a contract from the General Staff for the reproduction of all the maps for the official history of the 1870-71 campaign. This, as well as contracts from the British Ornithological Society, remained the firm's speciality, and during the First World War a large proportion of the necessary war maps were printed by Ludwig Pikola.

But the end of the War led to a ban on the printing of maps and the dismantling of machinery, and inflation did the rest, particularly after my grandfather's death in 1919. Of his three sons, of whom my father, then aged twenty-

three, was the eldest, only the youngest would have been capable of carrying on the business; only he had the technical knowledge and the interest, but in 1931 or 1932 he was stabbed to death at Harburg, outside Hamburg, where he had gone to fetch a Swedish printing machine. He got mixed up in a street fight between Communists and the SA; at all events, he died of stab wounds.

At the time I was twelve or thirteen, and the reason I remember it so well is that it was so often talked about at home. My father took me to the funeral of the victims—of whom there were a number—at the Ohlsdorf cemetery. Before 1933 they always said it was the Nazis, the SA rowdies, who had my uncle on their conscience, but after 1933 the story changed and everyone said he had been knifed by the treacherous Communists. When I asked my father about it later on, he merely said that either version could be correct; the affair had never been cleared up.

The second of my father's brothers was killed at the Jablunka Pass in the first few days of the Second World War.

Religion, the Catholic Church, was one of the pillars of my father's life. He was certainly a German nationalist; he welcomed the 'wiping out of the shame of Versailles' and the elimination of 'excessive foreign influence' in economic and cultural life, and above all he was pleased at the restoration of order and the removal of the unemployed from the streets. But the banning of the Catholic Young Men's Association alarmed him, and the campaign against monasteries and convents that began in 1936 and 1937 roused his indignation. In 1939 he was arrested and sent to Dachau for reprinting and distributing a statement published by the Bishop of Münster, the later Cardinal Galen; it was a protest against the highly secret euthanasia programme, the killing off of incurables and the insane.

He was released from Dachau after six months, and never wasted another word on that period. In the meantime he had lost most of his printing contracts, and few dared offer

49

him new ones. The paper shortage allegedly caused the diocesan newspapers to cease publication, and the business he did with letters of indulgence fell away. Just then, thanks to the intervention of Gottfried Lehr, he secured the contract for those well-known reproductions in colour—in postcard size and made from signed photographs—of all the winners of the Knight's Cross of the Iron Cross; so huge was the demand for them that it engaged practically the full capacity of the works for the rest of the war.

But at bottom my father was totally uninterested in the printing business. He had never got over the fact that his father's death had forced him to drop the study of archaeology that he had just begun. His hero was Schliemann and his dream was Peru and the Incas, but in 1919, when he had to go back to the printing works, he had to content himself with the Romans and began investigating the morainic topography of the Lech. In fact he acquired something of a reputation, if only in scholarly circles. His 'Plans, Profiles, and Descriptions of Burial Mounds in the so-called Lech Area' are familiar to historians and anthropologists. He discovered burial mounds of the Hallstatt C period, and the villa of a dealer in purple dye named Clephas; altogether he discovered 242 burial grounds, twenty-nine of which had been 'unfortunately ruined by over-zealous excavation by unqualified hands.'

Another discovery for which he was responsible was that of the plague burial ground at Kaufering dating from 1630, together with 'the cart with felt-covered wheels in which during the plague bodies were taken noiselessly by night to the burial place in order not to alarm the living beyond due measure'.

Money was another thing that had never interested him, and did not interest him now. He put all the firm's profits into his excavations, and into strange patents for 'tools for improved excavation techniques'. So it was not surprising that Thea should always be holding him up to me as an ex-

ample of a talented individual who had frittered away his
talents. Thea said: 'The pair of you are just the same. You
could have done so much with your lives, and you've done
so little. Doesn't that place depress you, that dusty glass box
in which he sits all day long? His whole life has been nothing
but idle dreams and wasted opportunities.' Nevertheless, his
Excursions into the Past, a popular version of the accounts
of his archaeological finds, was now in its thirty-sixth edition.

True, all this, in contrast to the history of the firm of
Lehr, was hardly suitable material for a commemorative
volume. But I cannot say that I found it depressing; on the
contrary, I spent a great deal of time with my father in his
glass box, listening to the latest account of some burial
mound that he had discovered; and after my talk with Thea
I went to see him again. We discussed the reprinting of a
series of postcards and the printing of a calendar that had
to be delivered by the end of the month. He listened reluc-
tantly, and then went on talking about his burial mounds
and grumbling at the forestry administration, which had
used one of his burial chambers for keeping logs in and had
ended up by ruining it completely.

There he sat, his deep-set eyes unnaturally enlarged by
strong spectacles, with his white hair that was always freshly
washed, wearing a black suit of thick material and a black
tie, the image of his father, whose photograph, together with
that of Schliemann, was on the wall. As so often, I wondered
what happened when a man's life ran out, when what had
once been a broad riverbed could no longer be filled with
water. Would it not be better to die when the right time
came? But what was the right time?

At all events, the answer was not be had from him. He
might be expected to be embittered, to complain about the
many blows he had had in his lifetime. He did nothing of
the sort. A great many things had happened, of course, two
world wars and two inflations, that was quite enough for
him. But, in his view, there was nothing special about the

way things had gone for him. *My life has really been a perfectly normal one, you know.* The one thing in his life that he regretted was that he had not had more time for his excavations, that he had never gone to Peru and the Incas, but had had to content himself with the Romans.

As he stared silently at an outdated calendar on the wall, my mind's eye shifted, and I saw exactly what was going on in Thea's flat.

Thea, in her violet dressing gown, with her coffee and the bottle in front of her and the telephone on her lap, dialling number after number and having interminable trivial conversations with friends or fleeting acquaintances, in a kind of desperate craving to communicate; it was her communion service, so to speak, her confirmation that the life of others also consisted of trivialties. And then the last drink, the ceremonial act of filling the ruby glass, her real communion cup, the blood that brought her sleep and oblivion—until next morning the alarm clock rang, her hand moved out of the bed to switch it off, and she slowly sat up and looked about her and hoped that nothing remained over from the day before, because if it did, how could she begin a new one?

V

The hotel in which Gottfried Lehr had lived since 1945 was
a tall, narrow building called The Green House, a residential hotel, and I was very surprised when he told me on the
telephone that he still lived there. Ever since my school
days—I went to the same boarding school as the two brothers
—I had associated the Lehrs with wealth and elegance, and
this place suggested neither.

The district of Munich in which it lay was full of antique
dealers, and one shop was next door to the hotel. It special-
ised in clocks, and in the old days, when I still collected
them, I had bought quite a lot there, and I had listened
again and again to the owner's story of his escape to the
west in 1945 with all his clocks loaded on a horse-drawn
cart. In the window there was a piece of which I should
have liked to ask the price; it was a pocket sun-dial in an
ivory case. Most sun-dials of that kind were made by Augsburg masters, and I had a good collection of them, but the
shop was shut.

The entrance to the hotel was in a passage on the right.
The door was shut, but I remembered there was an automatic opener. Most of the guests were permanent residents
like Gottfried Lehr, and so knew about it.

Gottfried Lehr had the whole top floor to himself. A
wrought-iron grating separated the fifth floor from the

fourth; the white-painted door to the flat was shut but not locked; there was no bell and no name-plate.

I heard voices when I went in. For a moment I hesitated in the passage, which was lined with indirectly lit glass cases full of the silver cups and badges that Gottfried Lehr had won at tennis, but one of the doors opened and a young man came out. When he saw me he started. He was very thin, very fair and had curly hair; in fact he was the type that Gottfried Lehr had always liked. The colour of his hair was too light to be real. He wore high-heeled shoes, close-fitting brown trousers, a brown silk shirt open at the neck, and a belt the buckle of which was almost the size and shape of a small monstrance.

He looked at me haughtily. 'How did you get in here?' he said. 'Is he expecting you?'

I took no trouble to answer, but walked towards the door through which he had come.

Gottfried Lehr was standing by the window that filled the whole of one side of the room. Perhaps seven years had passed since I had last seen him, but standing there in white trousers, white pullover and a white shirt open at the neck, with his dark hair carefully parted, he was exactly as I remembered him in the old days. This was exactly how Gottfried Lehr, the great tennis player, used to wait by the umpire's chair during the breaks in the game, with a towel round his neck and a glass of lemonade in his hand, calm and relaxed, while his opponent wiped off the sweat; then he would return relaxedly to his place at the base line—he was always the first to do so. All that was necessary to complete the picture was the sound of tennis balls and the umpire's voice ringing out over the court: 'Advantage Lehr'; in my memory the advantage in all games always lay with Gottfried Lehr.

He put something down on a shelf and came towards me, showing me the left side of his face; his right ear had been struck by a tennis ball in a game with one of those smash-

54

hitters whom he despised, though he would no doubt merely have referred to him as one of those players who continually charged at the net with as much style as a bull in a china shop. The ball had torn off a part of the ear and affected his hearing on one side, but that was not the real reason why he turned the other side towards me; he would never voluntarily impose anything unaesthetic on anyone. Not till we had shaken hands did he take any notice of the boy with the fair curly hair, who had followed me.

'You'll be wanting to go now, won't you?' he said to him.

'Why are we quarrelling?' the boy exclaimed. 'Why won't you let me talk to you? The amount they want is chicken feed to you. I thought you'd jump for joy when you heard the place was obtainable. It's a unique site, quite close to the Bayerischer Hof, I'd get a first-class clientèle there. If you want to get anywhere in the fashion trade nowadays, you've got to invest. And you talk about the high rent and the installation costs. When I think of what you spend on a ridiculous toy. . . .'

'I don't want to discuss the matter any further.' There was no trace of sharpness in Gottfried Lehr's voice.

'I've got to say yes today.'

'You mean you've got to say no.'

'I could find someone else. Or do you think that's out of the question?'

Gottfried Lehr smiled. 'Not out of the question, but rather difficult.'

'You'll regret it. I'll pack my bags and go, and . . .'

'That's where we got before. It's a pity you've learned so little. It's just like tennis, you haven't grasped the basic principles. The most important is that games are not won by the player who wins the most points, but by the player who loses the fewest. That's what tennis is all about—keeping the ball in play. That's the whole secret of the game, it even makes it possible to beat a player who is better than yourself. Pikola, tell him I'm right.'

But the boy gave me no chance to say anything.

'What rubbish you're talking now,' he said. 'I can't stand old gentlemen who kid themselves that they're young just because they can return a ball over the net.'

He was now nothing but a wretched little queer, and I was surprised at Lehr's remaining so calm. His only reply was the changed expression on his face, a mocking smile, a silent signal to the young man not to go too far and to clear out while the going was good.

'To conclude the matter,' he said finally, 'the answer is no. I'm not investing any more money. I don't take it amiss that you asked me, but you know that I don't allow myself to be coerced into anything. If you accept that, well and good, we can forget the whole thing. That's all, and now please leave us alone.'

The boy seemed to want to say something else, but then he remembered my presence. He turned and strode from the room.

I felt uncomfortable for a moment, but Gottfried Lehr behaved as if nothing had happened. He poured me out a glass of tonic water, remembering that I took it without ice and not out of the refrigerator, and said, 'Nice of you to come. I've got all the centenary material, but look, I want to show you this first. You're not pressed for time, are you?'

He took from a shelf a small wooden box that opened to form a flight of steps. Then he produced from a small compartment two carved wooden figures, each the size of a matchstick. They were painted, and represented two acrobats, one of whom sat with outstretched legs on the shoulders of the other. 'Now watch,' he said. He stood them in a hollow on the top step and withdrew his hand. At first nothing happened, but then the top figure began slowly moving forward until it was standing on the step below, at the same time lifting the other figure upwards until it was sitting on its shoulders; and so it went on until both reached the bottom step.

56

Gottfried Lehr watched it with the fascination of a child.

'It's called the Vienna circus acrobats,' he said. 'It's an extremely rare eighteenth-century toy. If you do manage to lay your hands on one, the mechanism is sure to have been damaged. The whole secret is a thread that runs through the two figures' shoulder joints. It took me a whole year to find someone able to repair it.' He put the figures away, shut the box and put it back on the shelf, which was filled with other old toys, still with the same expression on his face, the childish and at the same time slightly self-mocking smile of a man who had suffered no disasters in his life.

'Are you surprised at me?' he said.

'Not really. Before coming up here I was considering whether or not to buy a pocket sun-dial. That's not much more useful.'

'Useful? What's the use of useful? The world is full of useful people. I've always been a completely useless person At any rate, that's what Fritz would say of me, and my father most of all. If you ask me what I've really done during this past year, I should have to reply that I've devoted it exclusively to getting those Vienna staircase acrobats into working order again.'

He looked towards the door, where the fair young man had reappeared, this time carrying a suitcase. He said nothing, but stood there in a dramatic posture. When Gottfried Lehr did nothing to detain him, he disappeared.

'I'm sorry,' he said to me. 'Generally my family rows don't take place in the presence of third parties.' Then he added: 'He'll come back, you know.' It almost sounded as if he regretted it. 'I challenge them to leave me, but they never do. After a day or two they come back again, back to the manger. He has been living with me for a year, and after a year they're hooked. All those expensive shirts and shoes, and a belt that cost more than he earned in a month a year ago; and all the other things, of course, the silk dressing-

gown in the bedroom, and the champagne and, don't forget, no more worrying about the neighbours or the police. Does all that sound very disillusioned?'

'I should say cynical.'

'Really?'

The expression on his face changed, or perhaps it was just the colour of his skin, which grew lighter, as if his blood had thinned.

'You remember the inscription over the entrance to the centre court at Wimbledon?' he went on. 'If you can meet with triumph and disaster and treat those two impostors just the same . . . I only try to accept my successes and failures with equanimity, as a good tennis player should. Do you ever think about the old days?'

Gottfried Lehr was five years older than I. Nowadays the difference was of no importance, of course, but at school it had been enormous. At that school the junior boys had to fag for their seniors, performing services ranging from shoe-cleaning to cleaning and tidying rooms. It was part of the system of suppression powerfully supported by the school authorities, and it made me hate the place even more than I should have done in any case. Gottfried Lehr was one of the few senior boys who did not take advantage of the system, and on top of that it was thanks to him that I took up photography. He and his brother Fritz took me to the Winter Olympics at Garmisch-Partenkirchen in February 1936. It was the ice hockey that interested us most, and it was with his camera that I got that shot of the only goal scored by the German team against England. England were the favourites, and in fact were the ultimate winners, but that goal made the result 1-1. The German goal came so suddenly and unexpectedly that my picture was the only usable one, and Gottfried Lehr sent it for me to the *Berliner Illustrierte Zeitung*. Not only was I paid 150 Reichsmarks for it, but my name appeared in print for the first time in the special Winter Olympics edition of the *Berliner Illustri-*

erte. That was the first time I profited from the Lehrs, but not the last.

The boarding school the three of us went to was at Schondorf-am-Ammersee. I hated the years I spent there, and if the Lehrs had not been there, I'm not sure whether I could have stuck it out. My friendship with them gave me a special position, for both Gottfried and Fritz were already great tennis players—Gottfried won the German youth championship three times. That meant release from the weekly ten hours of instruction in Nazi ideology, from service twice weekly with the Hitler Youth, and from three hours a day written work, because all that time was needed for practice; it also automatically raised their average marks in all other subjects—and mine too. For, even though I always remained a tyro in relation to them, they insisted they needed me for training—I think because I was able to keep the ball in play for them when they practised and did not mind spending a whole hour playing the same ball to the back hand.

I went on benefiting from their friendship; Gottfried Lehr put work my way that enabled me to accompany him as a press photographer to the Davis Cup matches in which he played; and at the beginning of 1939 I went with him to Zagreb and Prague, Milan and Warsaw, as well as to the last tournament before the war at the end of August 1939 at Bad Pyrmont. By that time Gottfried Lehr had been banned, but Fritz played in it. The tournament was for the Pyrmont Jubilee Cup, but it could not be played out properly to the end, because on that Saturday and Sunday games were continually being broken off by the arrival of call-up telegrams for the players.

In those pre-war years Gottfried Lehr was certainly one of the best baseline players in the game. His play was never very adventurous or exciting, but he had steadiness and endurance; you only had to watch him on the morning before an important match spending a whole hour on the court practising lobs until he could place the ball within

half an inch of his opponent's baseline. His game seemed slow, he never seemed to be in a hurry; the only rule he kept to he had picked up from the American Bill Tilden, who was his model in many ways: 'Never change your game when you're winning. Always change it when you're losing.' Gottfried Lehr in his day was capable of beating any of the players that counted at that time, and he had to his credit wins over Ritchie, Manuel Alonso, Fred Perry and even Donald Budge.

Strangely enough, the one person whom he could never beat was his brother. Fritz Lehr was a player who was always on the point of getting to the very top but never got there. He would win the most difficult games and then lose the easiest. He played entirely without style, but the secret of his successes lay in his ability to extricate himself from the most awkward situations and, above all, his determination to fight to the point of exhaustion. His matches were dramatic battles, and as a result he was always a favourite with the crowd, even when he lost. It was a way of playing with which Gottfried had no sympathy, and after losing to him a number of times he subsequently kept out of his way. But from 1939 onwards that was no longer necessary, for Gottfried Lehr was quietly banned; his taste for fair ball boys had become known, he did not play in any of the wartime championships, and even getting married did not help him. In 1945 he promptly secured a divorce and began playing again, but he refused to take part in tournaments or championships, though at thirty-two he might once more have got into the top flight. The last tournament in which I saw him play was a private one arranged by an American colonel in Munich in 1947. There were weeds on the court, the nets were patched and had a musty smell, many of the players wore street-shoes from which they had removed the heels.

'Do you still play at all?' I asked.

'If you mean play, no, I don't. I just practise a bit, to test

my reactions. I go and hit balls across the net early in the morning when I have the court to myself. I sometimes think it's a bit absurd to have all those cups on display outside like that. One should let the past be the past. You know from my father what happens if one doesn't do that.'

His father had also been a tennis player before the First World War, and had won everything that was to be won at that time, including the Kaiser's Prize. He beat the famous R. F. Doherty to win the Grand Master Prize at Baden Baden, and in 1914 he was in the German Davis Cup team that met Australia at Pittsburg. It was rather like the Pyrmont tournament in 1939, because the club management withheld the news that war had broken out between Germany and Russia until after the last singles had been played. Friedrich Lehr took an Italian ship to Genoa, but the British took him off at Gibraltar and interned him. A year later he was exchanged and went back to his home near Memel on the Baltic Sea, and it was there that he discovered what had happened to his collection of cups, for which he had built a special room at his country house at Friedrichsruh. The Russians had overrun the area, set fire to the buildings, and the cups had been either stolen or destroyed.

Gottfried Lehr looked at me as if to assure himself that I still remembered all this. 'Fifty silver cups,' he said, 'twenty gold cigarette cases, and one with the Crown Prince's coat-of-arms and signature. Everything he had ever won. In fact he never got over it, and his whole ambition in life was to win them all back after the war. That's my earliest memory of my father, practising on the hard court behind our house in Memel early in the morning before he went to business and late at night by artificial light. After the war he wanted to get back again, but of course he never did. When the war was over there were other things to think about.' I watched him as he seemed almost to recite some of this, as though this apparently meandering reminiscence were quite purposeful. As, in the event, it all proved to be.

61

'You remember whom my father blamed for the loss of all those cups? Not the Russians, but Dressler. That's what the old man is like. He blamed the young major in command of the Germans on that sector of the front for not preventing the Russians from occupying the estate; in his view, the whole of the German Eighth Army should have concentrated on the defense of his cups. What's the matter? Shouldn't I have reminded you of all that?'

That young Major Dressler—the subsequent General Dressler—was the father of Julia's mother, and I really did not want to be reminded of these things.

'How is your father' I asked.

'Very well indeed. He's nearly eighty-five, and he's as litigious as ever; with him going to court is a sign of good health. I hardly ever see him. I've always been the parasite of the family, which suits me excellently.'

I looked at Gottfried Lehr, sitting with one leg over another in his immaculate white trousers, with his long, slender, carefully manicured hands over his knees. I knew it was a senseless question to ask, but I asked it because I was interested.

'Did you ever think of trying to make money?'

'Once,' He laughed. 'I was seventeen or eighteen at the time. I went to see a so-called tar works, in connection with which the old man had a lot of patents, it was a monumental affair. I inspected the whole outfit, made them show me everything, watched the men at work, and decided that making money was too dirty and tiring, especially in the building industry. All I can say is that I knew it was not for me, it satisfied none of my senses, if you like.' Again he laughed in that self-mocking manner of his. 'Fritz is really the one who's best fitted for the business. He's most like the old man, he's a chip off the old block, and it's a pretty tough block. In our business what's needed is cannon-ball tennis, you don't get anywhere with gentle lobs.'

He had taken me into the library. He cleared the table

and spread a lot of papers on it, including a brochure in a faded violet cover, another one in blue, and a set of yellow, faded galley proofs.

He picked up one of the brochures, the violet one. It was a slender production, and I could see the title: *Twenty-fifth Anniversary of the Firm of J. W. Lehr, Builders and Timber Merchants, Memel, 1869-1894.* That must have been in the grandfather's time.

'That was the only commemorative brochure that appeared in normal times, so to speak,' he went on. 'Otherwise we always had more or less bad luck with them, they always fell due at the most unfavorable times. The fiftieth anniversary was in 1919, immediately after the last war. The seventy-fifth anniversary was in 1944, and it didn't appear at all.' He pointed to the galley-proofs. 'Do you remember that the type was set at your father's works? He insisted on a very tasteful Roman type, but it couldn't be printed because of the paper shortage.'

He picked up the 1919 volume, the blue one, with an Art Nouveau ornament on the cover, an elaborate 'L' in the shape of a plant. He leafed through it, and I noticed he had underlined a number of passages.

'You can feel my father's hand,' he said. 'Listen to this: *The times through which we are passing are not suited for celebrations. Germany's misfortune permits no glad, festive mood.*' He looked at me over the top of the brochure. 'Don't take that too literally. The firm was not doing at all badly; the war had led to huge expansion. The old gentleman was always brilliant at adapting himself to changed circumstances, and spreading pessimism was one of his gimmicks Listen to this: *Bad times lie ahead. Immeasurable difficulties face us, particularly in the building sector; immeasurable consequences will inevitable flow from the impoverishment of our fatherland and the resulting taxation, which deprives the employer of most of his capital and profits.* These must be his own words, though Fritz could still come up with the

same grumbles about difficulties in the building sector and unfair taxation.

'This one's even worse,' Gottfried Lehr went on, picking up the proof of the 1944 volume. 'Nowadays it's simply unreadable. To a large extent it's totally unintelligible. Were we really like that? Did we really express ourselves like that? Was that the way we talked? We didn't just build, we constructed edifices, we didn't just make concrete but *worked ceaselessly at the focal point of the mightiest defence wall of all times.* Construction jobs were still further elevated by being turned into *works of honour.* Nothing is ordinary. The firm was then working on two Autobahns, one from Elbing to Königsberg and the other from Breslau to Forst. There's a whole chapter about it. The chapter heading—"The Reich Autobahn as Cultural Memorial"—just about sums it up. It says that building those roads is not a technical job, but *a cultural task which the firm tackles with a sense of dedicated responsibility, a building task which it carries out with a sense of mission, an opportunity to show character.* It keeps talking about how our building must match the greatness of our times. You'd better forget all that stuff.'

'You mean we should simply ignore the whole period?'

'No, not ignore. That's not possible. And not necessary. The upsurge in building in those days was not due just to the Nazis; it was part of the whole economic development. I'm not sure it's necessary to go into the Autobahn building we did, and the work we did for the party. And who cares nowadays that we had 5,000 men working on the Atlantic Wall? There are plenty of other things to illustrate the work we were doing then. Bridge construction. And in particular the sports centres which were always one of the firm's specialties, beginning with the first hard courts for the Berlin Sportsground Society, the famous Sport Palace; that was in 1910. The covered courts at Bremen were the first of their kind in Europe. And don't forget the Post Office workers' housing estate at Leipzig, which was really a model of

that kind of co-operative development. Those were jobs that were and remain impressive, both technically and from the aesthetic point of view.' He evidently thought he had gone a little too far in what he had just said, so he qualified it. 'Not that I want to suggest that the old man cared very much about the aesthetic aspect. He has been at daggers drawn with architects all his life, he thinks them an unnecessary waste of money. I once asked him what a successful construction job was in his opinion. "A successful construction job," he said, "is one that yields a handsome profit at the end of the day." '

'He won't want that as a motto for the commemorative volume?'

'No, he wouldn't go as far as that.'

'Do you think I should have a talk with him?'

'I think you should go and see him. I don't know whether he'll have anything to say about the volume. Very likely all he'll tell you is that he owes his health and fitness purely to his refusal for many years past to eat any food contaminated by chemicals, and that all the crops on his estates are produced with natural manure only. That's his hobby-horse now; he supplies the whole family with his produce. You certainly must go and see him to have his photograph taken for the volume; he has refused to be photographed since 1945.'

'He lives on the Steingaden estate?'

'Yes, since my mother's death he has lived there with my sister. And of course you must talk to Fritz. I know Fritz has pretty definite ideas about the contents, and he wants to discuss them with you before you begin. That's why I don't want to say any more on the subject, I propose to confine myself to the externals. I think a centenary justifies something impressive.'

He put the brochures and proofs aside and spread a number of old photographs on the table. He said he had started collecting them, and that he visualised the volume as con-

sisting chiefly of illustrations—as many pictures and as little text as possible. So the format must be large, with text in three languages, German, French and English. He had also been considering what paper to use; he had in mind either an MD Brilliant or a Zanders Special. There could be 500 copies of the ordinary paper-bound edition, and a special edition of fifty numbered copies, bound by hand in a fine Morocco or raw silk, samples of which he had already ordered.

'Do we agree, then? There need be very little text; what needs to be said about the firm's history can all be said in the captions. Its growth can be shown statistically; turnover figures, numbers employed, etc., can be shown graphically or in tabular form. Above all, the illustrations must show *people*. You would have to take the necessary photographs: a crane operator in his clean blue overall and yellow helmet, workers with their attaché cases and thermos flasks during a rest period; a driver in the cab of one of those huge cement lorries. All people connected with the firm, who work for it, and are proud to be associated with it. . . . Do I sound like the old man?'

At all events he sounded like a member of the family, and I could not help thinking how close to each other the members of this family were.

'The greetings at the front of the volume, they raise a rather delicate problem,' he remarked. The elections are just coming up, so we shall have to write to both Kiesinger and Brandt. But they'll do that at the office. They'll give you all the necessary information.'

'It all sounds as if there won't be much left for me to do.'

'But don't let that mislead you into asking Fritz for too small a fee. My father was a rich man of the old school. He kept the money together, saved and economised, particularly in relation to his family, his wife and children. But Fritz has to be surrounded by people who cost him money— that's why Christina is just the right wife for him. She satis-

fies his vanity, not least by the sovereign manner in which she spends money. I mean that quite seriously. If Fritz is asked for too little money, he feels suspicious. He believes only in what has to be paid for. In that he's like an American, and it was certainly no accident that his first wife was American. He believes in money. So don't ask for too little.'

'What shall I ask for?'

'I suggest 10,000 marks, 5,000 down and the rest on completion.'

'Isn't that a great deal?'

'Yes, it is. But if you insist on it it will put his mind at rest, he'll feel you're going to do a proper job.'

The money reminded me again of what the Lehrs had done for me, particularly Gottfried. He had put me into photography, and put work my way. It had been his idea that I should join an army propaganda company. He had put me in touch with the Hamburg Cigarette Service, whose picture albums, for which there was plenty of paper even in wartime, appeared in editions of millions, and they paid well for their pictures. And finally, in 1943, after I was wounded, he organised my transfer to Reichsleiter Rosenberg's special staff, to which he had belonged since 1940.

This organisation had the job of confiscating so-called 'ownerless' works of art, which were assembled throughout Europe and at last transferred to Germany, chiefly in the central depôt at Neuschwanstein Castle. I arrived there in September 1943, and my job was to make a complete photographic record of every single art object. Hard though it may be to believe, this kept me busy until the end of the war. Apart from a few rooms kept open for ceremonial purposes, the whole castle, as well as some other smaller retreats in the neighbourhood, was crammed full of works of art. Everything was arranged on endless wooden shelves—oil paintings, engravings, drawings, miniatures, Gobelin tapestries, porcelain, faience, sculptures, bronzes, vases, silver, jewellery,

coins, books and manuscripts. There were more than 21,000 objects from private collections, including the famous collections of Maurice de Rothschild, Samuel Kahn, Jacques Seligman and David Weil. I made more than 800 negatives of them and the same number of glossy prints, which were bound in thirty-nine leather volumes.

These were all things I had long forgotten and wanted to forget, and I again wondered why Gottfried Lehr was reminding me of them. Why was he stirring all this up, what feelings was he thinking of rousing in me?

'Don't have any scruples in the matter,' he said. 'Just take the money.'

'It's not the money.'

'What is it, then?'

'Old memories.'

'I'm sorry if I've touched on a sensitive chord. I didn't mean to.'

'But you did.'

'But my dear Pikola, all that was a quarter of a century ago.' He looked at me. 'You took the death of Julia Dressler very hard, didn't you?'

Whether he did it deliberately or not, this only plunged me deeper into the past. I said nothing.

'You still feel, how shall I put it, guilty of her death?'

This took me completely aback, so much so that against my will I said: 'I have never felt guilty of her death. I hated those who were guilty of her death, that's all. I hated them from the bottom of my heart, and sometimes I do so still.'

'Those guilty of her death? You mean Boettcher?'

This was the first time for a long time that anyone had mentioned his name. Boettcher was the man at whom all my hate was directed. To my surprise, I realised that it, or the remains of it, was still alive; there was still a glow under the layer of ashes that could be fanned into flame again.

'But Boettcher is dead,' he said. 'You know he's dead. If

68

he were still alive, I could understand you. If he were still alive. . . .'

The sentence hung in the air between us; it was meaningful only to us, perhaps only to me. No more was said on the subject then. I have tried to write down only what was said and nothing else. Later it acquired a different meaning, particularly that last sentence, but now he dropped the subject.

A change had taken place in him; it had been noticeable for some time, chiefly in his face. All the Lehrs have bright blue eyes, which produce a strange effect against their dark hair, but now his eyes were grey, almost colourless. There were wrinkles in his smooth, light skin, as if it had loosened, particularly round the eyes. He had several times got up and gone to the living room, dialled a telephone number and asked for a Dr. Jacob, and he began looking at his watch more and more impatiently and at ever shorter intervals and listening for someone coming up to the flat. Suddenly he apologised and left me alone. I heard voices in the hall. The doctor's name was mentioned, and then they withdrew and all was quiet. I waited for a quarter of an hour. When Gottfried Lehr came back into the library, alone, the first thing I noticed was that the bright blue had returned to his eyes. He had taken off his pullover, and he was holding his left arm rather stiffly, as one cannot help doing after an injection. The effect it had, and the impatience with which he had waited for the doctor, meant that it could only have been some kind of amphetamine, but I was not interested in hearing about it, whatever it was. I pointed to the brochures and galley proofs.

'May I take them?' I said.

'Do you want to go already?' he replied, but did not seem displeased at the prospect.

'I think we've discussed everything, at any rate for the moment.'

'When will you go and see the old gentleman?'

I thought for a moment. I had promised to go to Garmisch with Julia for a club tournament. Most of the games would be uninteresting, and there would be long and boring waiting periods in between, but it was an excellent opportunity of being with Julia.

'Do you think I could go on Sunday afternoon? I could get a lift there.'

'I'll telephone him and tell him to expect you. Why not go and see Fritz straight away on Monday? He's always at Landsberg on Mondays. The head office is here in Munich, but that's where his planning office is, his royal household, as I call it.'

I still felt worried about what I had seen. In another man, dependence on someone like Dr. Jacob would mean a vulnerability, the chance of being put at a disadvantage. But then I realised that such a thing would never happen. I remembered the voice ringing out over the court. *Advantage Lehr*. The Lehrs always had the advantage.

VI

The voices came floating in through the open window from the court behind the house and were audible even in the hall-like dining room. Julia's voice was deep, while the old man's was surprisingly high and shrill. Every now and then she laughed, and said things such as: 'Say when it's getting too much for you,' or 'Would you rather I played to your forehand?' What he said was short and sharp. 'That's enough of those soft returns,' he said once, and then I heard him say: 'All right, now I'm warmed up. We'll play a set—and forget my age. And no more soft balls. I won't have them.'

I was not the only person interested. Two men in a dark livery were laying the table for dinner, making less noise than the two tennis players outside and, in spite of their solemn and serious expressions, you could tell they were not totally concentrating on what they were doing, but badly wanted to go to the window and watch; they were all ears for what was going on outside, the voices and the sounds made by the racquets striking the ball.

From where I was standing by the window I could see half the court. It was surrounded by high wire netting, parts of which were rusting away, and it was obvious from the state it was in that it had not been played on for a long time. The net sagged in the middle, and there were grey-green patches on the red surface where rain-water had stood. In some places the white lines had sunk in so deep that they

had ceased to be visible. Outside the court one of the watch-
men who had checked us on arrival was standing, this time
without an alsatian. Even from a distance his whole attitude
indicated that he, like the servants, was upset by what was
going on, by the total departure from normal routine. The
old man's three grandaughters, all wearing the same beige
riding breeches, brown boots and white blouses, were sitting on a bench that had been placed by the sideline.

The game was interrupted soon after it began, and Friedrich Lehr walked over to the sideline and said something to
one of the girls, who rose, laid her riding crop on the bench
and came running into the house. I turned when she came
into the dining room; the servants had disappeared, but a
woman, whose old-fashioned hair-do and three-quarter-
length skirt struck one immediately, was standing at the
table and inspecting their handiwork.

'He wants woollen socks,' the girl said to her mother. 'Two
pairs, and as thick as possible.' As she spoke she looked at
me, not unfriendly, but surprised at the presence of a
stranger. 'Why don't you stop him? He's overdoing it.'

My presence obviously prevented her from saying more,
and the woman seemed long to have given up questioning
her father's wishes.

'At least he's sensible enough to want socks', she said.
'Otherwise heaven knows what he might do to himself on
that hard court. You'll find them in the wardrobe in his
room, where the shirts are.'

The girl disappeared up a big wide staircase, and the
woman's attention reverted to the table. She moved some
glasses without taking any more notice of me.

On our arrival early that afternoon we had been received
like two interlopers. Friedrich Lehr's property near Steingaden—it used to be a castle or a monastery—lay in grounds
of about two hundred acres. The approach road led through
a valley, at the narrowest point of which it was blocked by
a gate with a hut beside it. I hooted, thus incurring the

watchman's wrath. He emerged from the hut with an alsatian on a lead. He was a man in his fifties, but even the belly that protruded slightly over his belt did not suggest he would be prepared to admit physical inferiority to anyone. He moved lightly for a man of his age and weight, and later we met more of these men on the way to the big house, all in the same uniform, blue trousers, blue shirt and tie, dark-coloured hats and with short-cut hair.

The one at the entrance told me off severely: 'What's the meaning of this hooting?' he said. 'I saw you long ago. What are you doing here? This is a private road. You can read, can't you? So turn around and disappear quick.'

If Julia, who was at the wheel, had had her way, we should have immediately turned round and done as he said. But I did not want to have come all this way for nothing, so I told him who we were and watched him go back to the hut and telephone from an instrument on the wall. Afterwards he was not much friendlier, but he let us through. We drove on, down a long, winding lane with fields on either side. Then came stables, outbuildings and greenhouses, and we rounded a bend and the house appeared, a long, low building with a green copper roof. I had been here only once before, with Gottfried Lehr, for art objects that I had had to photograph had been stored here too. Friedrich Lehr had bought the property in 1937 from a Jewish dealer in photographic goods in Munich who had emigrated to Cuba in that year.

The old gentleman received me without going out of his way to seem polite. He gave me no chance to open my mouth, and made it clear that he had not the slightest intention of contributing anything to the commemorative volume. He had never in his life attached any importance to personal publicity, he said, and at his time of life he was not likely to change. He abominated journalists and press photographers, and had never given an interview; the single picture that some swine of a photographer had taken of him in the dock

at Nuremberg was quite enough for him. Did I not know
that he had been stamped as a so-called war criminal and
sentenced to five years' imprisonment? Perhaps his sons
would like to put *that* in the commemorative volume. So far
as he was concerned, he would be only too pleased, he was
proud of it, and in any case they went their own way without
bothering to consult him; first the Americans had deprived
him of his rights, and now his own sons had done the
same. . . . It was a veritable tirade that he unleashed at me,
and it was hard to say how much of it was real and how much
was play-acting, because I had the feeling that he had himself completely under control the whole time. At all events,
the reception was very different from what I had expected.
But, just when I was preparing to go, Julia, who had been
carried off to the stables by the granddaughters to be shown
their horses, came in. I cannot remember what they said to
each other, but she and this self-centered, intolerant old
tyrant took an immediate liking to each other, and he suddenly insisted on our staying.

Outside the game had started again. I had watched the
old man preparing for it by putting on two pairs of thick
socks to protect his feet and save him from the shaking
caused by running about on the hard court; actually, there
was nothing out of the way about it, for many first-class
players did the same when practising. From where I was
standing I could not see Julia, but only this tall, gaunt,
white-haired old gentleman in a pullover that was far too
big for him. He hardly moved from the base line, but he kept
the ball in play, and once or twice I heard Julia exclaim in
astonishment when she obviously failed to deal with an easy-
seeming return. I saw her only when she came to the net,
sometimes making a gesture of appreciation when the old
man managed a deft passing shot.

I have a great many contradictory memories of the meal
that followed, perhaps because I was really watching only
Julia all the time, wondering what impression the evening

74

was making on her. What I chiefly remember was the room in which eight of us sat down to dine, the details, even including the decoration of the porcelain; those were things I was used to noticing. The room was obviously the former refectory; I found it cool and uncomfortable, and depressing in particular because of the pictures that covered practically every inch of the walls. Most of them were 'old masters' of a quite special type—Grützner, Waldmüller, Moritz von Schwind, the school of serene contemplation one might call it. They were valuable pictures, but all of them were in a bad state, as must have been evident to Julia in particular; they were dark and dirty, and in many places the paint had cracked. Between them were other paintings by artists unknown to me, a harvesting scene, a peasant family round a table, an Amazon with huge breasts and, over a carved stone fireplace immediately in front of me, so that I could not avoid seeing it whenever I raised my head, a painting of monumental proportions of a tar works, painted so realistically that the faces of the workmen were recognisable even from a distance.

I cannot remember what we ate, except that there were many courses; the two servants were kept continually busy. My neighbour, the old man's daughter, kept looking anxiously at the head of the table. Hadn't the game been too much for him? Wasn't he eating too much? There he was having yet another glass of wine. Her glances, and the way she kept dropping her head, betrayed her silent anxiety. She hardly touched her food and took no part in the conversation of her three daughters, which was mostly about horses, show-jumpers, though it took me some time to realise this, as they had names such as Elgar, Verdi, Gaetano and Cristoforo and the girls attributed to them qualities that were more human than equine. When one was close to them the three girls looked older, and they all had the broad faces and blue eyes characteristic of the Lehr family.

The eighth person at the table was an elderly gentleman

75

who had turned up at the last moment and was also the first silently to disappear after bending over his plate and consuming enormous quantities of food. He was a slightly built little man, and corresponded exactly to one's picture of a poor relation graciously received into a rich man's household. His name was Müller-Heydekrug, and Friedrich Lehr used him as a kind of librarian or keeper of the records; he bought for the old man all the literature in print about the Baltic, old files of the *Memeler Dampfboot,* and engravings. He had been a teacher at the German-language school at Heydekrug, was the author of poems about the Memel territory, and had edited an anthology about Germany's lost eastern territories. He had been sentenced by the Lithuanians in Kaunas to two-and-a-half years' imprisonment, which he had served at Ukmerge, and in 1938 he had become a member of the Landtag on the Memel German list. He had told me all this during the afternoon when—after the old man's surprising change of mood—I talked to him and got him to give me material for the early history of the firm for the commemorative volume.

Those were the things I noticed, but what I was really trying to do was to see the dinner through Julia's eyes. I had hardly had a chance to speak to her, because the old man monopolised her, and she sat next to him at dinner too. The pair of them conducted a conversation of their own in a low voice, which cut them off completely from the rest of the table. This was an unprecedented situation, as was evident from the expression on everybody's face, but there was a surprise for me too, and that was Julia's laughter. You didn't often hear her laugh, and she struck most people as a very serious girl. Those who met her for the first time often thought her proud; this had something to do with her face, her eyes, the green round her pupils. But she was obviously enjoying the old man's company and was completely at ease, which was unusual with her; she did not easily give herself to strangers.

This room, and particularly the pictures, should really have displeased her. Neither were to her taste, and she *despised* people who neglected pictures. But she seemed not to notice them. The two drank to each other's health, she laughed at the things he told her, she smiled across at me, and I thought I discerned what it was that was giving her so much pleasure, the big, festively laid table, the many different glasses, the table decorations, the silver dishes, the many persons and the buzz of conversation. I remembered what our meals together had been like for many years. When I went to see her in Munich we generally went out and had a quick snack somewhere, which did not really count. When I went with her to tennis tournaments, we ate in the rather depressing restaurants of the hotels we stayed at. She rarely came to Augsburg, and even her visits at Christmas and other holidays seemed to have stopped, not as a matter of principle on her part, but just because something always seemed to turn up at the last moment to prevent her. Sometimes we ate in her flat in Munich, the two of us alone; she took a great deal of trouble over it, but the kitchenette was separated from the living room only by a curtain, and the so-called divan-table was too low for one to be able to eat at it in comfort.

After dinner we moved to an adjoining room, which was smaller, being a covered veranda; the variety of furniture of the most different periods suggested an auctioneer's showroom. In places several carpets were laid on top of one another. There were cane chairs, and the table was covered with a green cloth, like a billiard table. There were pictures here too, and every gap was filled with framed photographs of girls with horses; in the earliest of them the girls still wore plaits and had barrettes in their hair.

They went off to the stables again immediately after dinner, and Julia and the old gentleman stayed on the veranda for only a short time. He had changed for dinner, into a dark suit, but I noticed that he still had on his tennis shoes

and woollen socks. The backs of his hands were covered with big liver marks, but the impression he created was not of old age—above all, age had spared his face. His blue eyes were sharp and clear, and the wrinkles round them gave him a lively, mischievous look. Except for a wisp in the middle, that looked like a cock's comb, his hair was cut short.

He asked me whether I had enjoyed the meal and why I had not touched the wine, a 1929 claret which was reserved exclusively for him. How could I expect to live to a ripe old age if I didn't drink wine? There were three things, in his opinion, that made growing old easier: a bottle of wine and twelve hours sleep a day and—the mischievous look in his eyes intensified—a few people around whom one could torment.

'Old age is a very strange thing, my dear fellow,' he said. 'Externally you shrink into a hideous old beast, but you still have the feelings of a boy of twenty-one. It was an excellent idea to bring your daughter here, and I very much appreciate it. I'm surrounded by the old, you see, and I include my granddaughters among them. I had actually forgotten that such a thing as a young woman whom it was possible to talk to existed. In this house the only subject of conversation is horses, and I have always regarded horses as totally unprofitable animals, the most unprofitable animals that exist —too much volume for too little performance. Do you know what my daughter spends on each of those horses? What with feeling it, grooming it, and the cost of insurance, transport and entry fees, it comes to between 15,000 and 20,000 marks a year, and only because she hopes one of the girls may get into the Olympic team. And what I prefer not to talk about is what riding does to a woman's figure. Have you looked at my granddaughters, I mean below the waist? Well, I shan't go deeper into the matter. You must excuse us. Your daughter would like to see my mineral collection. You'll be staying the night, won't you? I insist. My daughter

78

will get two rooms ready for you, won't you, Ehrengard? You'll see to it.'

His daughter made no reply, but indicated with a nod that she had taken cognizance of his instructions; their relations seemed to consist exclusively of his giving orders and her silent obedience. When Julia and the old man left I felt I must apologise.

'No, why?' she said. 'I'm used to it from him. He needs someone around him whom he can torment, and since my mother's death that's me. Of course he's irritated by the money I spend on the horses. It's my own money, but he thinks it's really his, of course. But more important than the money is being able to torment us. If you knew how he treated my mother. She counted for nothing in his eyes, and do you know why? For one reason and one reason only, all the sons she bore him were shorter than he. He used to be six foot three—since then he has shrunk a bit—and for a lifetime he held it against her that they failed to grow as tall as he.'

I was now sitting alone with her outside on the cool veranda. We sipped our coffee in silence, and I found her presence oppressive, for the feeling she gave me was of a woman who had been disappointed too often in life; in spite of the children she had borne, her body created the impression of growing old *unused*. And, of course, I knew to whom she had been married. As for her outward appearance, she did everything possible to emphasise the impression of ageing. Her presumably expensive brown tweed dress, obviously made to measure, for it would have been impossible to buy such a thing off the hook, served merely to drape her form; and on top of this, she wore brown woollen stockings, strong flat shoes, and no make-up; in fact she seemed to be trying deliberately to set herself off at a disadvantage. The only really normal thing about her was her eyes and her skin; she had the healthy colouring of a person who spends a great

deal of time in the open air, works in the garden and goes for long walks.

'I really didn't want to cause you any trouble,' I repeated. 'I hope the game of tennis didn't worry you.'

'And what difference would it make if it did? He takes no notice of what the doctor says, or of what I say. The only thing that surprises me is that he managed to see the ball. Normally he can hardly see anything at all. If he went out alone, I think he'd walk straight into the first car. He ought to have an operation, but he won't. He ought to wear glasses, but he won't. Not that he reads very much, I've never seen him looking at a book, he reads nothing but company reports, balance sheets and contracts. Look at this, he had it specially made so that he could do his jigsaw puzzles.' She pointed to one of the tables, at the end of which there was an oversize magnifying glass on a flexible metal arm. I noticed that the shelf on the wall was full of games, most of them jigsaw puzzles of all kinds, but especially of landscapes and maps. The flat boxes piled on top of one another all looked very new, not like games used by children. She took one and put it beside her.

'You don't mind if I do a jigsaw?' she said. 'We can go on talking. I can do them in my sleep.'

She began laying out pieces on the green felt, beginning with the corners. Before she began she glanced at her wristwatch, an old-fashioned round one with Arabic figures.

'Jigsaw puzzles are what we spend the evening doing,' she went on. 'My father and I either take the same subject, or at any rate the same number of pieces, and we begin at the same time. He insists on playing for money, otherwise he would be bored, he says; fifty pfennigs for each piece that either of us has left when the other has finished. Sometimes it comes to quite a tidy sum, because he prefers the puzzles with 3,000 pieces, and sometimes he finishes a hundred or even two hundred pieces ahead of me. He insists on payment on the dot and, as he never touches cash—he says he hates

money that has passed through anyone else's hands—he makes me write out a cheque.' She looked searchingly at me across the table, as if her thoughts were moving in quite a different direction. 'I generally lose,' she went on, 'and that's the end of our day—I sitting here and writing out a cheque and he standing over me making sure it's for the right amount. Tell me, what does your daughter do?'

We had not mentioned her, but she had talked about her daughters. They were all born between 1942 and 1945, and there were five of them, including twins, and they had names like Edeltraud, Sieglinde or Uta. They all bore the name of Lehr, for after her husband's death in 1947 she had reverted to her maiden name. All the girls were married, three of them to doctors, and one was in practice as a doctor herself. Three had equestrian ambitions—two in show-jumping and one in dressage—and they spent all their free time on the estate.

'She works at the Doerner Institute in Munich,' I said. As she looked at me enquiringly, I explained it was a state-run organisation for research into the preservation of works of art, especially pictures.

'Does she paint?'

'She would deny it vigorously and say that her job consists essentially of not painting. She won't have anything to do with the over-painting that is so often done. They preserve works of art, that's all. The whole thing has more to do with science than art. You have to know a good deal of chemistry and mineralogy and about protection against the effects of light.'

'But surely she went to the university?'

'No. What they need is expert craftsmen. They prefer a qualified cabinet-maker or organ-builder to someone with a doctorate in the history of art. Julia is a qualified goldsmith; her speciality is the cleaning of burnish gilding, the exposure of underlying layers of carvings and paintings.'

'My daughters went to the university,' she said in a resent-

ful tone. 'All that expense, and then when they had finished they couldn't get married quickly enough. If they didn't come here because of the horses, I should have nobody left. But I think it must be even worse for a father when he loses his daughter. She's the age, isn't she? How old is she?'

'Twenty-four.'

'Then it might happen practically any day. It was really hard for me. But they say that for a man it's even worse; after all, he gives his daughter away to another man, it's natural jealousy.'

'I don't know whether I'm a typical father in that respect.'

The jigsaw obviously occupied her mind very little. She fitted the pieces together with uncanny speed, and now that only a few gaps were left her hands moved even faster. As soon as she had filled the last of them she looked at her watch.

'Twenty minutes for 150 pieces. That's not bad, but not good enough; he would have been quicker,' she said, breaking up the puzzle and putting the pieces back in the box. Then she helped herself to a new one. 'It's a nice name, Julia. It reminds me of the last summer before the war. Julia and I were just about to take our last pre-clinical exam. You remember? I was jealous of her at the time for having someone to help her. *Gamma-picolinic acid is used as the parent substance for the production of Neoteben (isonicotinic acid hydrazide acid), which is successfully used in the initial stages of tuberculosis.* I always had a great deal of trouble with organic chemistry, and I had no-one to help me. Do you remember?'

'It's a long time ago.'

'But you must remember. Julia Dressler. It was the last summer before the war, and the first we spent back in Memel again. It was Fritz who brought you. You must remember, you were friends, I think he had you in mind for me, but there was no getting you away from Julia, so they said.'

82

It was beginning to get dark. Outside it was lighter than on the veranda, and I was glad, because she looked at me, and for the first time there was something like curiosity in her eyes.

'But that's extraordinary,' she said. 'You give your daughter the same name and say you don't remember.'

'I said it was a long time ago.'

If she had been a fellow-student of Julia's mother, she must have been about the same age, which meant that she could not be more than fifty-three.

The curiosity faded from her eyes, and her thoughts went back to her own past; she was carried along by a single current she was never able to fight.

'You never met my husband, did you?'

This was the question I was afraid of, the question I had seen coming.

What had I let myself in for? I had as good as buried the past, but they were digging up one layer after the other.

'No, I never met him,' I said.

'He was a doctor, a good doctor. We met in Königsberg soon after we qualified. He got his first job there, in charge of an SS X-ray team that was examining the whole population for signs of TB. In one year we compiled X-ray records of 400,000 people in East Prussia, that is, one person in every three in the whole area. You know what they accused him of later? Just because he was an SS doctor? None of them knew him. He was a man with a heart of gold, a good father and a gifted musician. During the depression he paid his way as a student by playing the piano. He loved music, Schumann, Strauss. . . . You know, of course, what they accused him of? Those disgraceful photographs of him that were published after the war. They couldn't leave him alone, even after his death they had to drag his name through the mud.'

Boettcher—I could no longer suppress the name, and the fact that she had been married to him. *He was a man with a*

heart of gold, strict, but with a heart of gold. I knew differently, but why remind her of it after twenty-five years, when I myself had forgotten.

It was quite dark by now on the veranda, but her hands still moved tirelessly; she had already put enough pieces together for the picture to be recognisable. I tried to see only her hands, and to think of her as just one of the many women who had lost their husbands at an early age, who were left alone after the war, and during that difficult time had to struggle through with their children as best they could.

She looked round to make sure we were still alone, and went on:

'They forced me to give up his name, my father and Fritz did, it was those two most of all. I had to identify his body, and I had to assume my maiden name again. They forced me to. I was forbidden ever to mention his name again, and the children were never told it, they still don't know it to this day. There's not a single picture of him here in the house, and I'm not allowed to put one up.'

She rose and switched on some of the lights. They shed a feeble, yellowish light that barely lit the corners of the room. Outside it was still lighter than in the house, as if it were floodlit. She went back to her chair. A simple black handbag was by her side. She opened it, moved aside a cheque book, and then produced a photograph, size 3½ x 4½.

'When the newspapers published that distorted picture of him I sent them this photo with a letter, but nobody published it. See for yourself, does he look like a criminal? What they attributed to him is nothing but a pack of lies. All those dead. Produce the evidence, I told them, produce a single witness to show that he ever killed anyone. But that's a subject that must not be mentioned in this house. Not one of them ever knew him, not one of them. And you didn't know him either, did you?'

She held the picture out to me, and if I had not taken it

84

from her she would not have noticed, for she was too carried away by her own memories, her own pain—one might have imagined that twenty-five years would be enough to offer protection against the past. My taking the photograph was a test to which I subjected myself.

Nothing happened; it was almost exactly like the moment when Gottfried Lehr mentioned the name; there seemed no longer any connection. It was an old print, much handled. Standing with one hand on his hip, he was looking straight at the camera. There was nothing striking about him except, perhaps, for the lips, which were narrow and pressed together; otherwise he had what one would have called an honest, open face. She was certainly right when she said he looked like a man with a heart of gold, strict, but with a heart of gold.

I had never seen him, and yet he had changed my life. I knew his signature; while searching through the files I had come across it again and again, written in the illegible fashion of most doctors' signatures; and I had built up my picture of him from that signature and notes in his hand written in the margin of other documents—the man whom I hated, who followed me into my dreams, existed more powerfully in my imagination than in reality. I handed her back the photograph. I said nothing, she did not seem to expect me to say anything. She put it back in her bag and finished the puzzle.

'Thirty-five minutes. That's good for two hundred pieces.'

She seemed to revert to the present without any transition. The light flickered, and kept alternating between bright and dim.

'It's because we have our own installation,' she explained. 'He had it put in a few years ago because they refused to grant him a special tariff. I believe it's totally uneconomic, our current costs us a vast sum of money, but that doesn't perturb him in the least. He loves quarrelling. Even when he doesn't allow anyone else into the house, the lawyers can

come and see him at any time of the day or night. For the past five years he has been fighting a case about a footpath through the estate. The local authorities claim it's a public right of way and are trying to force him to open it again. Not that it's a nuisance to us in any way, it runs through a wood a long way away from the house, but he blocked it with a fence. The case is now before the chief administrative court.'

'And who's going to win it?'

'He will, of course. At first it looked as if the local authorities could produce witnesses who remembered there had been undisputed public use of the path since their childhood, but after he talked to them they suddenly no longer remembered anything. The local authorities are now basing their case on old maps, but they'll disappear just as suddenly, I'm sure. The Lehrs are always on the winning side, that's something you ought to appreciate.'

She said this as if she were not one of them. She rose, as if sensing that her father and Julia were about to appear on the veranda.

'I'll go and see about your rooms,' she said. 'I'll send someone to fetch your things from the car.'

Friedrich Lehr looked after her as she left the room.

'Has she been trying to turn you against me?' he said. 'Don't believe everything she tells you. She always looks like a poor old woman who can't look after herself but, believe me, she's very well able to. She. . . .'

But what he said left me utterly indifferent; I did not care how they spent their days and evenings, or what lawsuits they fought and won. I looked at Julia; Thea had always been afraid that the tennis she had started playing at the age of eleven might spoil her figure. Many people associate women tennis players with short skirts, fat legs and powerful thighs, but when Julia went on to the court with three racquets under her arm she always looked like a too thin eighteen-year-old. The only result of all her tennis

was the strongly developed area of the left shoulder, for she was a left-hander. But, unless one knew about it, as I did, it was imperceptible under the black blouse she was wearing with black trousers and no jewellery.

'Look what I've been given,' she said, showing me a stone in her left hand; the nails were cut very short, otherwise they would have impeded her work. 'It's a beryl grown in mica-schist.' It was the size of a walnut. The deposits were the size and shape of bits of candy sugar, except that they were green. 'You must go and look at the collection,' she said, 'it's the biggest and best I've ever seen.'

'But she was not at all satisfied with the labelling of the pieces,' Friedrich Lehr said. 'And I must say she was quite right. Those labels are always getting lost. She gave me a very sensible idea, to put a small spot of paint on each specimen and write a serial number on it in Indian ink.' He looked at Julia. 'How would it be if I gave you a job? You could arrange the whole collection, and prepare a catalogue with all the points that matter—the names of the minerals, the accompanying substances, their composition, the place where they were found, the date of acquisition. The more carefully that is done, the greater is the value of a collection like that, so I'm not making you a present. Also you could buy items missing from the collection. It would certainly take you a year. How about it? I'll take you on for a year and pay you. . . .'

She interrupted him with her laugh.

'And my Holbein?' she said. 'What about my Holbein?'

So she had been talking to him about her work, the picture she was then engaged on.

'Your Holbein has been waiting for four hundred and fifty years, so it can wait a little longer. I haven't got much longer to live. And we could have the tennis court renovated and play an hour every day.'

'I'll think about it,' she said. 'What do you think?' she added, turning to me.

At that moment the old man's daughter returned to the veranda, so I did not have to answer. Our rooms were ready. I should have preferred to have left that evening, but Julia had had a long day; she had played two matches at Garmisch before driving me here.

The old man's daughter said that one of the servants would show us to our rooms, and that we should tell him what time we wanted to be called in the morning. Then she turned to her father and, without her saying anything, he nodded and sat down at the table with the magnifying glass. Later, when we walked through the hall again, I saw the two of them sitting at the green baize table with jigsaw puzzles in front of them.

VII

We were given neighbouring rooms in one of the wings. You could tell from the thickness of the outside walls that it was a very old part of the building. The rooms had been newly decorated; they had wood-panelled ceilings and green carpets, and each had its own bathroom. A door led into an inter-connecting balcony. There was a brightly painted double bed in peasant style, to which a piece had been added on either side to make it bigger; Friedrich Lehr was certainly a man who would think of something like that.

It was almost as if I could see through the walls to where he and his daughter were sitting at the table on the veranda, concentrating on winning the race to complete their jigsaw puzzle for money as if they had regressed to childhood. I was not tired. All I had wanted was to get away from them, but my thoughts had gone straight back to them again.

I picked up the papers and documents that Müller-Heydekrug had searched out for me and began looking through them, sometimes only picking out individual sentences here and there. I knew a great deal of it already, and needed only an occasional hint to refresh my memory. This casual and cursory way of reading actually made clear to me the main reason for the Lehrs' success; they took money-making seriously and, just as important, they always managed to be on good terms with the powers-that-be at any particular mo-

ment, and also they had a sixth sense for when the times were going to change.

In the first commemorative volume, published on the occasion of the firm's twenty-fifth anniversary, I found a favourite saying of a Lehr of the time that was as simple as it was revealing. It was *money-making is not to be trifled with*. This was Johann Wilhelm Lehr, the father of the man now busy with his jigsaw puzzle downstairs, who had laid the foundations of the family's wealth. He was a third generation member of a Lübeck family that had moved to Memel, and at the age of fifty he was still the master of a ship that took cargoes of timber from Memel to England; this was the kind known as Memel timber, which had enjoyed a world-wide reputation since the eighteenth century and had enriched the big timber dealers and saw-mill proprietors while Johann Wilhelm Lehr had not even managed to acquire a ship of his own. This was new to me. Then he had bought a ship on mortgage and secured a ten-year contract with the German South Sea Plantation Company.

In the 1870s the company had established large coconut palm plantations in Samoa for the production of vegetable fat and copra, but had difficulties in securing labor. The work was hard, and for every labourer landed at Apia, the capital of Samoa, the company paid £22 sterling. Johann Wilhelm Lehr spent ten years in the Melanesian and Polynesian islands; he established depôts where he assembled the labourers before shipping them to the plantations. He returned to Memel with the title of honorary consul of Samoa and enough money to buy extensive woodlands and six saw-mills and build himself a house in the suburb of Schmelz am Holzhafen. He became a member of the Memel Freemasons' lodge, and with that the family's future course was set; there was always a Lehr who took money-making seriously and was on good terms with the powerful. The story was so different from my father's.

During the Wilhelmine period the Lehrs were of course loyal to the imperial régime, which did not, however, prevent them from getting out of the war loans to which they had dutifully subscribed in good time and at a good price and investing the proceeds in commodities that would not lose their value, such as timber, iron, steel and even rubble, and moving their headquarters to Berlin. Under the Weimar Republic the firm supported the democratic parties, and actually secured a contract for 50,000 dwelling units a year from a Social Democratic Prime Minister; but they also had the foresight to replenish the coffers of the 'new, up-and-coming national party' when the right time came. For this they were suitably rewarded, but again they read the signs of the times correctly, and in 1944 they sold off their government securities, recovered all the money owed to them by the government, and employed lawyers to lodge war damage claims for losses suffered in the east. This time they moved their headquarters to Bavaria and strained every nerve to transfer as much as possible of their building machinery and stocks of raw materials to the same area, a task in which they were powerfully assisted by one last big contract for the construction of underground factories in the Landsberg area. Müller-Heydekrug described to me how in the last few weeks of the war all the documents relating to contributions to the Nazi party had been destroyed here in this house, while an accurate list was drawn up of all the contributions paid to the bourgeois parties during the Weimar period. Farsighted as ever, Friedrich Lehr had made contact by way of Switzerland with the Jewish dealer in photographic goods from Munich from whom he had bought the estate in 1937, undertaking when the time came voluntarily to pay him a substantial sum to compensate him for the low price he had paid for it at the time.

Looked at from this point of view, it was understandable that to Friedrich Lehr the twelve years of the Third Reich

should seem a mere episode, which had cost him a great deal with very little to show for it. Hence the noncomprehension with which he greeted his arrest after the end of the war. Müller-Heydekrug showed me the press photograph of him taken in the dock at Nuremberg; his face expressed nothing but contempt for his judges, as well as confidence that the 'mistake' would soon be rectified.

What did all this add up to? Simply to the fact that there had always and at all times been privileged people who were cleverer than others, luckier than others, who always came out on top while others went under. This was hardly a suitable theme for a commemorative volume—or perhaps at bottom it was. For, if one ignored certain details, it was the story of a family, of a man who in spite of all obstacles had forced fortune to remain on his side. If only it had not been true. It was also a fact that the unfortunate took a tremendous interest in stories about the fortunate and successful.

And on top of it all Julia had been charmed by the old gentleman. She was quite right to see him in this light. I did not want to tell her other things of which the Lehrs reminded me. I had never done so, and that was how I wanted it to remain. Julia's memories began with nuns in a convent, cold rooms, getting up at unearthly hours, endless prayers, and punishments for reading forbidden books such as Wilhelm Busch's *Pious Helen*, and that was enough; they began with reports in which she was praised for tidiness and cleanliness and blamed for disobedience and vanity; with photographs of a slender girl in a grey cotton dress; with a father who came to see her only at weekends and a missing mother whose place was taken by long, imaginative stories about a woman who had never existed.

I sat and listened for sounds from her room, but there were none. How often had we slept in adjoining rooms like this when I went with her to tournaments and club championships, and how often had I listened as I was listening

92

now; sometimes I also lay awake in the morning, waiting for the sound that told me that she too was awake—that of a skipping rope striking the floor, for she began every day with skipping.

The balcony ran along the whole length of the house. I did not know how much time had passed, because my watch had stopped; a bright white patch surrounded the building; floodlights fitted under the eaves at the corners were apparently left on all night.

The door to her room was half open, and she was sitting on the edge of her bed, wearing yellow towelling pyjamas. She had her back to me and was immersed in a book. Her left shoulder-blade moved under the cloth of the pyjamas when she turned a page. The skipping rope with red handles lay on a chair.

I knocked on the window-pane, once, twice, before she turned her head. Only then did she seem to realise where she was; she laid the book aside and asked me to come in. She always called me by my Christian name, as she did with Thea too. I drew a chair up to the bed. She had been reading a small grey pamphlet, the title of which I could not see.

'What have you been reading?' I said.

She smiled at me. She had washed, and her face was free of make-up, but with her reddish-brown hair, green eyes and very red lips there seemed to be more colour in it than before.

'What would I have been reading?' she said. 'Something serious, of course. It's a sin to waste a minute—that was drummed into me at such an early age that I shall never get rid of it. I found it over there.' She pointed to a narrow, built-in shelf that was full of books. 'I now know a great deal about the functioning of the heart. Do you know how long a heart-beat lasts?'

'Between 0.8 and 0.9 seconds.'

She looked at me in surprise, but dropped the subject and picked up the stone that was lying next to the book and held it in her hand, sitting upright in bed.

'Tell me about the old gentleman,' she said. 'I really thought him very agreeable, very different from your description of him. Agreeable isn't really the right word—I mean he's agreeably old-fashioned. He reminds me of something you once told me . . . Strange, he said he was a war criminal. He said it sarcastically. What's the truth behind it?'

'You like him, that's all that matters, isn't it?'

'That's why I asked, because I like him. Because both can't be right; either my feeling about him is wrong, or what you said about him is wrong. Tell me about him.'

I had really not gone to her room to talk about him, so I said nothing.

'Was he arrested after the war?' she went on. 'Was he sent to prison?'

'Yes, he was sentenced to five years' imprisonment, and they sent him to the fortress at Landsberg. I don't know what he told you, probably that he spent the whole time peeling potatoes. Actually his lawyers were able to go and see him and they appealed against his conviction. He employed American lawyers, he had no confidence in the Germans. After three years they got him out. By that time everything had changed, the blockade of Berlin had begun, the cold war was in full swing, and the Americans had realised that these trials of German industrialists were very foolish, because they were needed again. The whole thing had been a "demonstrable misunderstanding", as the Americans themselves said at the time. So content yourself with that.'

'What was he charged with?'

'There were a number of counts in the indictment.'

'Tell me one of them. Tell me something definite he was charged with.'

'The first count of the indictment was of having employed

thousands of foreign workers against their will and of having exploited them.'

'But that's happening again today, isn't it? Nowadays they're called guest workers, but they don't come here as guests, but because employers earn solid profits by employing them. You can express moral disapproval of that, you can blame the system if you like, but is there anything illegal about it?'

Another thing about her was that she could think clearly and objectively, like a man.

'At that time it was rather different,' I said.

'Different in what way?'

'In the first place, they were forced to do the work. Secondly, they were not only workers but also prisoners of war and concentration camp inmates. And thirdly, there were the conditions in which they were transported to the camps in the Landsberg area and the conditions in the camps themselves.'

'What sort of conditions? I don't see why you can't talk about it openly. Why is the subject so painful to you?'

'I could talk about it, but what would be the use? What is the point of telling you that many of them died before getting to the camps? Will it mean anything to you if I say that the food consisted of one litre of soup, five grammes of fat and 200 grammes of bread for a working day of from twelve to fourteen hours, and that the building sites of the firm of Lehr were particularly feared? Perhaps it will mean something to you if I tell you that in one of the camps in the last few days of the war three hundred and sixty persons were shot on the order of a certain doctor in charge because he was afraid to allow them to fall into the hands of the Americans in the state they were in.'

'Did that happen? What was the old man's defence?'

'That he knew nothing whatever about those things. That the whole story was nothing but slander and distortion. That nobody could prove that he knew anything about them.

That he wasn't the real target of the prosecution at all, but that the object was to denounce all German industrialists to the world as exploiters of slave labour, and that that was an exercise that would yield bitter fruit. He turned the tables on his accusers and accused them. We really ought not to go on talking about it.'

'But did he know? Of all those dead that you talk of, was there a single one who died because of him? Tell me, was there?'

I had said more than I had wanted to. I had always done everything to keep her away from these things.

'It's all such a long time ago now. We are made to forget. Forgetting is a very important human capacity. You can't live without forgetting.'

She had put the stone back beside the book. I remembered something she had said at the beginning of the conversation.

'What did you mean,' I asked her, 'when you said that his old-fashioned manner reminded you of something I had once told you?'

'It had something to do with mother.'

'I don't see what you mean.'

This was another area in which I had to walk warily. Not that I was unprepared for such questions. What I had told her about her mother had been as close to the truth as was possible. I had told her that I met Julia Dressler in the summer of 1939 on her father's estate on the Dange, eight miles from Memel, and that I had seen her again in 1944, when she came to see me at Neuschwanstein, and that she had borne a child, Julia, in December 1944. Soon after that she had gone to Berlin, because she had had no news of her parents for a long time and wanted to try to get them out of Memel. I told her that her train had been attacked by low-flying American fighter-bombers, that there had been so many deaths that it had been impossible to identify the bodies, and that her mother's grave had never been found.

By the time she was old enough to be told the truth this story had become so firmly established that it had acquired an autonomy of its own, had been filled in and adorned with so many supplementary details that it sounded like nothing but the truth, even to me.

'What exactly do you mean?'

'The story of how you met mother. The first time on the estate. Someone was having a birthday party, someone belonging to the family, an aunt, wasn't it, and you turned up when the party was in full swing, and there was that girl in a long pink dress, so you told me, and she curtsied to the aunt and kissed her hand, though she wasn't a little girl, but almost my age; she bent over the old lady's hand and kissed it, or, at any rate, that's what you said.'

'That's exactly what happened. I turned up right in the middle of the party and saw a young girl in a pink dress; at all events, I thought she was a young girl, and only when she turned and looked at me did I realise she was grown up.'

'She had my eyes?'

'Yes, you have her eyes, and a great deal more of her as well. When I took her for a young girl she was actually working hard for one of her medical exams.'

'And you fell in love with her at first sight?'

'Yes, the very first moment, when I saw her kissing her aunt's hand. It was old-fashioned, of course, but it didn't make me want to smile. She was rather like someone from another world, and that was how she always remained.'

'It's a long time since you talked to me about her. I always liked it when you talked to me about her.'

'There's not a great deal to tell you, you know.'

'Yes, I know, but I like it all the same. That story about kissing her aunt's hand, I could listen to it over and over again; you can tell from the way you tell it that you were in love with her. I wish we were still living in such times . . . Did you hear what I said?'

97

'Yes. In what sort of times?'

'When girls wore long pink dresses and could kiss an aunt's hand even at my age. Instead we wear jeans and . . .'

'I've never seen you in jeans.'

'That shows I'm old-fashioned too. Perhaps it's because of my job, the old pictures I'm always working on. I like old-fashioned things and old-fashioned men too.' She stretched out her hand and motioned to me to sit beside her on the edge of the bed. 'I'm hopelessly old-fashioned in everything,' she said, and looked at me enquiringly. 'It's very old-fash-ioned nowadays to be still a virgin, or practically a virgin, at the age of twenty-four.'

She said this quite naturally, simply stating a fact.

'Does it worry you?' I said.

She shook her head.

'No, it doesn't worry me. I hope it doesn't worry you.'

'No. In these matters fathers are very strange creatures, so they say. They're jealous of every man who approaches their daughter. They don't show it, but it comes out at last when things get as far as that.'

'Sometimes I think I *ought* to be worried. If only you could listen to other girls of my age. And when one sees the films and reads the newspapers one seems to be completely ab-normal to have left it so late.'

'You'll have your reasons.'

'Yes. One of them is you.'

'Me?'

'I don't mean you only. I mean you and Thea, your mar-riage, seeing how two people can torment each other year in and year out. It's really enough to put one off. You're not a very encouraging example. And everything you've always said, your warnings, which weren't directed only against you, but against all men. That's one thing. And besides, there are the young men themselves, I mean the young men of the present day.'

'What's wrong with them?'

98

'Nothing, except that nothing whatever is left in them that is in any way old-fashioned. You can do anything with them. You can play tennis with them, or go to the theatre, or argue with them, or dance with them. You sit with them at a discotheque in the evening talking about university reform, "the revolt against crusty and fusty authority", the reform of Clauses 218 and 175, reaching an understanding with East Germany, supporting the independence movement of young national states, and eliminating the relics of racialism, and in the same breath they look at you, quite surprised to discover that it's *you,* and they raise their glass and say: "Tell me, will you sleep with me tonight?" And then, when you say no, they nod, and say: "O.K., I only asked," and go on with what they were saying before. Do you see what I mean? They're not angry or offended, they just asked a question and you just answered it, that's all, it's perfectly in order, and quite likely the question will crop up again another time if the occasion arises. They all want to uproot all existing institutions by force and change the world, and admittedly it needs changing, but has everything got to be changed for that reason? I just look at things differently, as they were with you in the old days. . . .'

That was something she would be well advised not to do, but I did not say so. It was as quiet in the house as if it were empty apart from ourselves. There was something unreal about the light outside. I was sitting so close to her that I could hear her breathing; I could tell without looking how her breast was rising and falling beneath the yellow material. With only a slight, imperceptible movement I could have held her hand. I badly wanted to do so, but I did not. I thought to myself that sometimes in life some things repeated themselves and gave one a second chance, but I did not have the courage to believe it.

'At dinner this evening I had an idea,' I said. 'Suppose we took a flat together in Munich, with a studio for each of us.'

'What about my work at the institute?'

'Before we went to Garmisch I had a talk with your boss. He thinks you ought to set up for yourself. They have only six places on the establishment, and they won't get any more. So there's practically no chance of your getting any further. But if you set up for yourself they would certainly pass work on to you. You know very well that they have to turn down nearly all private work. Apart from the restoration work, you could give expert opinions and make valuations, for which there's a big demand, and the institute is not allowed to provide them. You'd do the same work and earn twice as much. It's only an idea, but I thought I'd put it to you.'

'I've thought of it myself. I've got to make up my mind between work and tennis, I can't go on doing both. At tennis I'm slowly becoming a veteran. I shan't get much further, and also I'm losing the ambition, and if I go on losing games like that one at Garmisch this morning, it would be better to stop . . . But what about Thea?'

'I'll talk to her. There's no hope of any real change between her and me. Will you think about my idea?'

'Yes. Though I can tell you straight away that there's not very much to think about.' She was no longer sitting on the bed, but lying on it, with the blanket drawn up over her breasts. 'It really would be abnormal,' she went on. 'Other girls of my age leave their parents.' She looked at me. I could not make out the meaning of the expression on her face. There was something dream-like about it, but I did not imagine for a moment that it could be in any way connected with me.

Two lights were on in the room. I switched off one of them, leaving the bedside lamp alight. I was on the way to the door when she said: 'Don't go yet, stay for a minute.' I turned, and saw her eyes, one of which was blueish and the other yellowish, which made them look green; her mother's had been just the same.

'It's to do with mother,' she said, 'or rather it's to do with this book.'

It was on the bedside table. I picked it up. It was a typed production for the use of students of the University of Königsberg, called *The Basic Facts of Human Physiology.* A strange feeling came over me while I held it in my hand.

'I wasn't really reading it,' she said.

'Oh? You seemed to be very deep in it.'

'Deep in it is just the right phrase. I don't know why I picked on it, I just wanted to read something and took it from the shelf, but then I just sat there holding it. I was really only sitting there holding it, and. . . . You'll laugh at me. I've never told anyone about this before. It's hard to explain, perhaps it's easiest to describe in connection with the pictures. Sometimes exactly the same thing happens to me with the pictures I work on. Now it's the Holbein, for instance. It's a painting by Holbein the elder, which was later over-painted.'

I had watched her working on the picture when I fetched her three days before. It was painted in 1504, and showed a family named Schwarz, in everyday clothing. Later on a member of the family must have disgraced himself in some way, for the minister of the church into whose possession it had come had had it over-painted. The men were given long white gowns, the women black capes and nuns' coifs, and wreaths of roses were put in the children's hands. These over-paintings were not in the least unusual, and one of the institute's tasks was to restore the pictures to their original condition. Julia explained the method to me; for the Holbein she used a paste called Panzol, which she applied successively to small areas of the picture; it softened up the over-painting until it was possible to remove it with a spatula or modeling stick.

'You've seen the process for yourself,' she went on, 'When you have applied the paste, there's nothing to do but wait.

101

Sometimes it takes twenty minutes for the oil paint to soften, and then you often have only a few seconds in which to remove it. You sit there with the smell of the paste and the paint in your nostrils for ten or twenty minutes, and during that time . . . you'll think me crazy, but suddenly my imagination ran away with me. I saw the church, the place where the picture hung, I saw the minister talking to the painter, I heard their voices and every word they said; it was as if I were actually there. This is not the first time it has happened, it has happened with other pictures too. I've never dared talk to you about it. Crazy, isn't it?'

'Exactly the same happened to me with the book,' she went on. 'I was sitting there, holding it in my hands without reading it, and suddenly I had the feeling that it had something to do with you and mother.'

'Me and mother?'

I had been holding the book in my hand the whole time, but now I had to put it down.

'I saw you and I heard you. It was summer. There was a white bench and, strangely enough, a lot of birds. I heard them chirping and I heard your voices. You were asking her questions and she was answering them.'

'I told you about that,' I said. 'It was the summer when she was working for her exam. I was hearing her. I've told you all about that.'

'Of course, but I saw her. You've never shown me a picture of her, but I saw her, I saw her quite distinctly, I could describe her to you.'

She was right, I had never shown her a photograph of her mother; there was only one still in existence, and that one I did not want her to see.

'And I heard your voices. It's only natural that I should recognise yours, but I also heard her voice answering you.'

I tried treating all this lightly.

'And what questions did I ask?'

'They were about breath noises, listening to the sounds

102

that come from the lungs and the diagnoses that could be made on the strength of them.'

'And what did she answer?'

She closed her eyes as if to help her to concentrate. When she replied, slowly and hesitantly, there was a different tone in her voice. 'Vesicular breathing . . . sounds like wind in the leaves . . . bronchial breathing . . . sounds like a sharp German *ch* sound . . . amphoric breathing . . . sounds like the noise made by blowing over the top of an empty jug or bottle.'

For a moment I was speechless. Then I said: 'You must have read that in the book.'

'Is that what it says?'

I opened it, found the passage, and showed it to her. She was now sitting up. Suddenly she seemed to be freezing without the warmth of the blanket. She put her hand through her hair. She was pale and shaken by all this. Then she tried to smile, but suddenly there were tears in her eyes.

'I'm simply tired and overwrought,' she said. 'And I haven't got over losing that match this morning. What was the matter with me? How could I lose against *her?* She got me down with those mindless lobs of hers. It was a bad time of day to play, but that was a match I shouldn't have lost. Now they'll put me after her in the ranking list, you'll see, though I've beaten her three times this year. As you know, wins in the spring count for less than wins in the autumn.'

I put the book back on the shelf and turned out the second light. There was enough light in the room from the flood-lighting outside to enable me to see that she was weeping; she was not weeping aloud, but there were tears in her eyes.

'Losing to her in two straight sets . . . how could I allow that to happen?'

But she was young, and I knew that when I woke early next morning I should hear the sound of the skipping rope hitting the floor. I also knew that I loved her, but I was afraid that if I told her so I should lose her.

VIII

The most conspicuous thing about him was his inconspicuousness. He preferred being unnoticed; when others loudly proclaimed their opinions, he kept his to himself. Not that he was afraid of anyone; when we tried to save Julia's life he showed more courage than anyone else. He was inconspicuous even in appearance; he must have been in his late fifties, and his hair was neither light nor dark; so unnoticeable was he that he tended to be overlooked. But he was the first person I ran into that day in the public gardens by the Lech facing the municipal offices.

His name was Josef Zielinski, but he was known to his colleagues and the inhabitants of Landsberg in general as Pigeon Zielinski, because carrier pigeons were his passion in life.

He came from Kattowitz in Upper Silesia, and lived with his mother in a room in a small, narrow house that his father always called the family grave. It was right behind the coking plant that belonged to the Kattowitz Mining Company, where his father and grandfather had worked as foremen; during Whitsun 1920 his father was shot dead at a demonstration of German workers against the French occupation troops in Kattowitz, and after that mother and son went to live with a brother.

His father had bred carrier pigeons too. Carrier pigeons played a big part in the lives of the inhabitants of the grimy

houses, which were blackened with smoke and coal dust and haunted by the lingering smell of the waste gases from the coke works. It was never quite dark in the evening in the back room because of the poisonous yellow flare directly opposite the window. Carrier pigeons were the main topic of conversation in the locality, and the fascination they exercised was not surprising, for they seemed to be the only thing that stayed white there; and, after the cession of eastern Upper Silesia to Poland, the Carrier Pigeon Club remained a kind of intact German enclave, in which German was spoken and the books were kept in German. Joseph Zielinski won his first prize at the age of thirteen, and he was later elected secretary of the club, chiefly, no doubt because of his handwriting, for he used the old-fashioned German script. It looked like a succession of little jabs, interrupted only by the letters with long loops, such as the s, the j and the z.

It was this totally uncontemporary handwriting that first attracted my attention to him when it suddenly turned up in the big ledger at Neuschwanstein in which all the art-objects traffic was recorded; I was told it was the handiwork of the 'Pole'—the 'gentlemen' of the various art staffs looked down their noses at the SS guards who were allotted to them. In 1939 Zielinski, who was already twenty-seven, was drafted to the Waffen SS, and he became a member of the guard company that kept watch over the art objects assembled in the Louvre in Paris, and in 1942 he arrived at Neuschwanstein with twenty-five railway truck-loads of fine art. At Neuschwanstein he volunteered to keep the ledger, because his duties as guard commander alone did not satisfy him and keeping carrier pigeons was obviously out of the question at that time. Then, in the middle of 1944, he was transferred with other men of the SS guard companies to one of the labour camps that were being hastily set up in the Landsberg-Kaufering area; guarding working personnel had become more important than guarding art treasures.

105

After the war, and after being severely wounded, he stayed on at Landsberg, where he found work in the municipal offices; and he ended up in a job that might have been made to measure for him. He became head of the filing department, and it was in this capacity that I met him again. He was proud of his work, which he carried out with immense pride, dignity and devotion; he was a man who believed in what he was doing, and he still sometimes used the old-fashioned German script, which resulted in his petty cash vouchers being sometimes returned on the grounds of illegibility.

I had come from the Lehr estate by car. Julia had offered to give me a lift, but as an estate vehicle was coming to Landsberg in any case—it delivered eggs, vegetables, etc., all produced with the aid of organic manure only, to Fritz's household—she naturally drove straight back to Munich. I was glad of this. When I had had to take photographs in this neighbourhood I had always avoided being driven here by her, to avoid questions I did not want to answer; and after our talk of the previous evening I was particularly anxious to avoid them now. I had asked where the physiology book came from, but Ehrengard Lehr could no longer remember. She and Julia Dressler had been contemporaries at the university, and in view of the shortage of text-books at that time she thought it quite likely that they had lent each other books, and it was noticeable that the *ex libris* she put in all her other books was missing from this one.

The road from Steingaden took us past a number of Lehr works; I had never before realised how many of them there were in the area. Whenever we came to one the driver pointed out the blue square with the white L in the middle. There was a lightweight concrete works, an asphalt works, a cement factory, and a number of gravel pits. The driver had used to work for the firm, driving one of the huge cement transporters, but had had to give it up because of gout in his hands. This was a kind of occupational disease, the result of

driving in summer with open windows, with the drivers hands on the wheel especially exposed to the draught.

I made him put me down near the municipal offices. I wanted to walk the last part of the way along the Lech, which would give me a little extra time before meeting Fritz Lehr. In the public gardens there was a meteorological station, with humidity gauge, recording barometer and thermometer, and Joseph Zielinski was standing in front of the white-painted wooden fence, looking at the readings and then at the sky with an expression implying an alarming disparity between the two. He did not notice me, but it was impossible to walk past without greeting him. When I was close he looked more alarmed than ever, as if a catastrophe were imminent; the sky was a brilliant blue, but the barometer had dropped sharply.

Two or three years had passed since we last saw each other, and at first he did not recognise me. He looked searchingly at my face and my lips, and I had to tell him my name before he realised who I was. He apologised. 'It's always the same, sometimes it's better and sometimes it's worse,' he said, 'I simply can't recognise faces any more. It's to do with my wound, something has gone wrong inside me. I remember voices at once, and after years and years I still recognise people's handwriting, but faces, no. Sometimes I don't recognise people after only a few weeks, and walk straight past them. And it's getting worse.'

He spoke a strange dialect; the Bavarian he had taken on in the course of twenty-five years had combined with his original Upper Silesian to form a remarkable mixture; it was as if the grimy workman's house in which he was born had been adorned with stucco ornaments.

'They had me on the chopping block again,' he said. 'Just a few more splinters, they said it was, and these are the last, they said, but I expect they were lying again. I don't know what they get out of telling me these lies. Those SS doctors were more honest at the time. They were tough guys. Listen,

Zielinski, they said to me, there are three possibilities: (1) You won't get off the operating table alive; (2) you'll survive, but you'll be crippled for life; (3) we'll be lucky and, if you pull yourself together afterwards like Willy Birgel, you'll ride again for Germany. Well, I was lucky.'

He was wounded in April 1945 when a train-load of forced labourers from Camp I on the way to Dachau was shot up by fighter-bombers. He was one of the escort, and was struck by metal fragments; he survived severe damage to his dorsal vertebrae and had had many operations, and the fact that he was not a cripple was due solely to his will-power. When you looked at him you noticed the stiff way he held his head, as if it were in a splint, and I knew that at night he slept in a kind of plaster bed modelled to the shape of his back.

'The important thing is to keep moving,' he went on. 'I must never sit around for long, but be on the move the whole time.'

We had left the meteorological station and were approaching the municipal offices. It was a new building, and I remembered he had talked for years about the happy day when he would at last have enough room for his files; this had been his dream for years. I assumed he was still working, and had gone out for a moment to see about the weather and keep moving in accordance with the doctor's orders, so I mentioned the matter.

'No, I don't work any longer,' he said. 'I haven't worked for the past year, they pensioned me off early, at fifty-seven, because of my disability. Just imagine it. I'd been waiting for the move for more than twenty years, and when it happened I wasn't there. What a shambles the old place was. It was impossible to file anything properly or find it quickly. And now they have that magnificent new building, and I'm not there. You should see the new filing department. It fills the whole basement. There are actually empty shelves. The chief administrative officer was always the only one who had proper respect for the files. He worked his way up from the

bottom, he's not one of these new young administrators who came straight from school and know everything best. He dug his heels in and got it—the whole basement. Nothing but metal shelving. You should see the layout. I go and have a look at it sometimes. Everything arranged clearly and sys- tematically. I've still got the whole thing in my head, you can ask me any questions you like. Fishing and fishing rights, 75-756; animal breeding clubs, 70-700; war cemeteries, 06- 061.'

He turned his head in that stiff way of his and looked at at me. 'You've come about those skeletons they've dug up?'

The question came out of a clear sky, and I was taken aback. For a moment I did not realise what he was talking about, but my body reacted more swiftly and spontaneously than my mind; sweat broke out under my armpits and wet- ted my shirt.

'What skeletons?'

By now I had realised the connection in Zielinski's mind between the files and his question, for it was over the files numbered 06-061 that I had sat for hours, scrutinising page after page and making notes, at the time when I still hoped they would yield some definite information about Julia's death.

'I thought you must have come because of that,' he said uncertainly.

'I don't know what you're talking about.'

'Don't you? Can you imagine anything so stupid as start- ing a gravel pit near the old labour camp? They were bound to come across skeletons. Even if it wasn't generally known, there must have been someone who remembered. Now the chief executive officer is holding the baby.' He spoke hesi- tantly, in a hushed voice, looking round to make sure we were not being overheard. 'What an appalling business it was, simply covering up the bodies with earth in any old place and not even taking the trouble to dig them a decent grave. What an appalling business. And then someone comes

up with the idea of digging a gravel pit there. Simply idiotic.'

He was talking about the old camps in the area. They had been established in May 1944, eleven of them altogether, and traces still remained, remnants of huts and foundation walls overgrown with grass. The continuous air raids in the west and the threatened loss of industries in the east had led to the idea of putting factories underground, and the choice had fallen on the Landsberg area for two reasons; strategically it was relatively safe and its morainic topography yielded the most important building material, gravel, in adequate quantities and with no transport problems. The plan was No. 1 priority top secret, and the object was to construct underground sites for the aircraft industry with a total floor-space of 300,000 square metres, using a labour force of 90,000 on a three-shift basis. The overall organisation was in the hands of the Todt Organisation, and for the actual construction a number of different contracting firms were brought in, the biggest of which was the Lehr concern. The major problem, of course, was where the necessary labour force was to come from. There was no available labour, either in east or west, so it was provided by the SS from the only existing source, the concentration camps. They came from Lodz and the former Warsaw ghetto, but they were mostly Jewish concentration camp inmates from the Baltic, some of them accompanied by their wives and children in order to 'raise their working morale'. It was never possible to establish for certain how many of them there were altogether; when they died, as they did in large numbers, the camps were simply refilled. Post-war estimates varied widely, but the most probable figure was about 14,000 dead, most of them from weakness, undernourishment and illnesses; and, as Zielinski had said, not much trouble was taken over burying them; they were simply shovelled into the earth and covered up somewhere near the camps.

'Where were they found?'

'They're building a new dam on the Lech for a power

110

station on the B17, and they came across skeletons where
they'd made a cemetery. A mechanical digger belonging to
one of the firms involved turned up a skeleton. The chief
executive officer was informed immediately, and that's how
I came to know about it. He sent to the filing department for
the old plans. He's out there now. They've stopped the building work for the time being.'

'What have they found?'

'So far they've found twelve skeletons, I hear. It happened
once before, while I was still working. A peasant turned up
a single skeleton and reported it.'

'And what happened?'

'They're buried as soon as they are released. The police
have to be informed first. They have experts, and they have
to release the remains before they can be buried.'

Near the labor camp, he had said. There were several
cemeteries.

'You mean the one near the former sick quarters?'

For the first time he looked at me directly. There was both
sympathy and reproach in his eyes.

'No, on the other side of the road,' he said. 'Haven't you
given up yet? You'll never find her grave. You know where
she died. I told you at the time, Boettcher was so dangerous
because he was a coward. It was nothing but cowardice that
made him have the people in the sick quarters shot. But you
ought to forget it. We shouldn't be standing here talking
about it. You did everything possible at the time.'

'You did more.'

'Did I?'

'More than others did.'

'Then you ought to stop thinking about it. You know that
everyone wasn't like Boettcher.'

'I've given up thinking about it for a long time.'

'Good. One *can* put it out of one's mind. I have. You remember my wife? She always said one must put it out of
one's mind and forget it. Whenever I started reproaching

111

myself, it was *she* who said it was no good going on ever-lastingly brooding about it, it was time to snap out of it, you did more than enough at the time. Those were her own words.'

His wife was a Pole from Sosnowitz. She had been in Women's Camp No. 1, where she was in charge of the kitchen. Julia Dressler was in the same camp. Zielinski was the guard commander at the women's camp, and after the war he had married the former inmate Hedwig Zeligowski.

'One *can* put it out of one's mind,' he repeated. 'Do you know whom I met recently? Ewi. Do you remember her?'

I nodded, but said nothing.

'I ran into her in Munich.'

'What has become of her?'

'Don't you know? Her husband divorced her; he has some sort of top job in the Federal Railways administration, and he paid up handsomely. At all events, Ewi's O.K. She looked really smart in her fur coat; and that leg trouble of hers, it's completely unnoticeable. She runs some sort of night club in Munich, they say she always has the best-looking girls, the girls with the best legs.'

Again I said nothing, and Zielinski had to bridge the silence.

'You must come and see us some time, you promised to a long time ago. My wife won't talk about the old days, that's one thing you can certainly count on. We shall be delighted to see you, and nowadays I've got plenty of time.'

His observations at the meteorological station must have returned to his mind, for again he looked anxiously at the sky.

'If only the weather holds out till this evening. There are so many young ones . . .' He smiled. 'My pigeons were released at Harburg this morning. That's the longest flight we have in Germany now; Harburg and Flensburg are both exactly 750 kilometres distant. In good weather they do it in ten hours. Mist is the worst thing, you know, it forces them to make détours.'

He was suddenly as absorbed in his carrier pigeons as if we had talked about nothing else.

'With the older birds it doesn't matter so much,' he went on. 'They're the best at finding their way back, they have the advantage of experience, of course. But this time I've five young ones doing the stretch for the first time. Others use tricks, but I don't. I always say nature helps herself. Good food, cleanliness, that's what has always given me the best results. We'd really be delighted if. . . .'

I realised he wanted to go back. He still had many hours of waiting ahead of him, and he would certainly go on worrying about the falling barometer. He certainly knew the route his carrier pigeons ought to be taking, and perhaps he might be able to telephone someone along the way to find out what the weather was like. He turned once more, with that stiff motion of the whole upper part of his body, because he could not turn his head, and smiled. Perhaps he expected me to go with him, and for a moment I was tempted to do so.

I did not have far to go; the Lehr planning office was a new building too. They had demolished the old villa and put in its place a long flat building with a great deal of glass and stone facing. The higher elevation in the middle made the whole thing look something like a ship, and this impression was reinforced by a white painted mast with rigging and pennants that took the place of a flag-pole in the middle of the area outside the entrance. All this might have fitted in well enough in a coastal landscape, but what it suggested to me was that only a very influential personage indeed could have secured approval for such a building in this environment. As I approached a car stopped outside the wide entrance, and a short, thickset man got out; the material of his light, greyish-green summer suit fitted tightly over his shoulders, and he wore the inevitable dark green hat with chamois hair ornament. He was nearly sixty, but took the steps in a few strides. I waited for a short while, because I

113

had no desire to meet the chief executive officer, especially as he might well be coming from the site where they had found the skeletons.

I had never been in the building before. The reception hall was dark, in spite of all the glass, and the concealed lighting in the ceiling was on. In the middle of the oak-panelled rear wall there was a recess with an over-sized self-illuminated globe, and above it five or six clocks showing the time in different capital cities all over the world. It was all very impressive, as it was certainly meant to be. A telephone operator was sitting behind a desk that was big enough to play table tennis on; there was nothing on it except a small bottle of nail polish, which she quickly put away. Next to her was a flat telephone switchboard on which four or five little lamps were alight.

In the ante-room there were two desks and two secretaries, both blonde and both with the cool manner that makes one feel like a supplicant. Both were on the telephone and ignored me. On both desks there was an intercom, one of them with more connections than the other; on this one there was a nameplate, with the name Helga Ziethen, which meant nothing to me. When I touched it I had an electric shock from the thick nylon carpet I was standing on. The blonde looked at me disapprovingly and interrupted her telephone conversation by putting her hand over the receiver.

'Whom do you want to see?' she said. 'Have you an appointment? I'm sorry, but I have no note that anyone is expected.'

I turned and saw Winter, Lehr's chauffeur, emerge from one of the almost invisible doors in the wood panelling. He was carrying a cup of coffee, which he put on the secretary's desk. Then he turned to me, and said: 'The chief is expecting you. He'll be free in a moment.'

'Listen, Winter, appointments are my business,' one of the secretaries protested indignantly, but he ignored her, and the expression on his face did not change. It was a narrow,

serious face, immediately suggesting a jockey or circus performer; in fact his slender frame suggested the traditional jockey. He was about sixty, and had worked for the Lehrs for forty years, but he looked ageless; and, as always happened when I met him, I could not help looking at his feet, which were so small that one wondered whether he could get shoes to fit him, and he always smelt of the same after-shave lotion. The impression that he was a performer was increased by his livery, navy blue trousers with stripes along the seams and a light coloured doubled-breasted jacket with three gold stripes on the sleeves. I had always wondered what they meant, but had never asked; they probably meant nothing at all.

I made a remark about changes that had taken place, and asked whether Fräulein Engels was still there. The secretary again began insisting that only she made appointments, but Winter again ignored her and walked lightly ahead of me down a narrow corridor, knocked at a door, and let me in.

The office was minute in comparison with the vast reception hall and the big ante-room, and was made to seem even smaller by the plants on a stand by the window; even on the big, old-fashioned safe there was a flat plastic receptacle in which cactuses were growing. For a moment Margarete Engels did not notice me, because she was typing and wearing earphones; the grey cord hung down at the side of her head as if she were connected up with something on which her life depended, like a hospital patient receiving a blood transfusion or artificial nourishment.

She too must have been over sixty, and she had been with the firm at least as long as Winter; I knew her from before the war in Berlin, when she was secretary to the old gentleman and used to tip off his sons when he was in a mood in which he might respond favourably to requests for money. She was at her best and happiest when people approached her for advice, when she could act as an intermediary, smooth things over, help someone who had been overlooked

when salaries were raised, or could cause sudden and un-
justified dismissals to be revoked. I had always liked her,
and we had several times played with the idea of her becoming my secretary, but I had never been able to afford her
salary.

'Hans Pikola. Pikola with a k,' she exclaimed when she
saw me. She removed her earphones and smoothed her hair,
which lay in waves as meticulous as if she used curling tongs
every morning. 'You have an appointment with the young
chief, haven't you? You're doing the commemorative volume,
he told me. Well, it's a pleasure to see you. You look a bit
thin, but then you always were. What do you think of our
new building? Building? What am I talking about? It's a
palace.'

She came from Berlin and had never lost her accent, but
her voice had grown husky after a thyroid operation. Papers
and files were scattered all over her desk, and she started
looking for her cigarettes. At last she found a slender golden
cigarette case and a lighter. I took it and gave her a light,
and tried to express my admiration of her new office.

'You'll have to wait for some time yet, I'm afraid. The
chief executive officer is with him, isn't he?' she said. The fact
that she was no longer installed in the boss's ante-room, that
things happened in the building without her being the first
to hear about them, must have been terrible for her, but
perhaps she had her own sources of information; I wondered
by what route this piece of information had reached her so
quickly in this out-of-the-way office?

'Have you heard what happened at the building site?' she
went on, and began looking for an ashtray. 'It's dreadful the
way things keep cropping up again. They're said to have
found twenty skeletons already, and they're still digging.'
She spoke in a hushed voice, just as Zielinski had. 'It's only
right, of course, that they should be given a decent burial.
It was dreadful of course, and we were all involved, weren't
we? At the time we all wanted to win the war, that's what

116

I think now as I did then. It began so splendidly with all those victories, and everyone said to himself keep your eyes shut, when we've won it'll all be forgotten. That's what I thought, I admit it, that's what people are like.' She drew on her cigarette. 'Do you like people? I don't. I always thought that when I was old it would be better, but exactly the opposite is the case. First you're born, and there's nothing you can do about it, nobody asked you, you're just there, and you have to see it through, and at the end of it what happens? They dig you in and the worms gobble you up. Dreadful. Not that I don't want to go on living, on the contrary, I very much want to. I've worked my whole life, ever since I was a young thing of sixteen, and I've ever so many plans. I want to travel, to see something of the world. But I always thought that when I was old I should live peacefully and happily from day to day. But instead one only gets more anxious than ever."

She seemed to have had no-one to talk to for a long time. I said nothing. What was there for me to say? I waited while she lit another cigarette. She had always been a heavy smoker, and towards the end of the war I had given her my cigarette ration.

'Won't you have to retire soon?' I asked eventually.

'I shall be sixty-five in two years time.'

'You're not in the ante-room any more?'

'It got too much for me,' she said, quite naturally, I thought. 'It was my own idea. I can't stand the pace any more. It's better as it is. I'm still there, and can give advice when anyone wants it.' She pointed to the desk and the letter in her typewriter. 'I only do his personal work, private letters, expenses, and that sort of thing, all his private business that's done through the firm. Both of them are incorrigible, the old one and the young one, I've never been able to get them to produce proper receipts that the tax authorities will recognise. But I get on with him all right. I think that to have been with a firm for forty-five years is a good reference

in itself, and in my opinion it's also a good reference for the bosses.'

'How is your brother?'

'Erich, oh, he died three years ago. Didn't you know? He too worked for the Lehrs for years, and finished up working on the old gentleman's estate. But it wasn't the same as when the old lady was alive; his whole pleasure in life was working for her. He was always talking about the villa at Grunewald, the big garden there was his pride and joy. And the old lady never interfered, she let him do what he liked; he could plant whatever he liked, so long as there were no pink flowers. I don't know what she had against them, but she couldn't stand pink flowers, begonias, phlox, primulas, cyclamen and a lot of rock plants. Above all, she hated pinks. And just imagine it, when she died in 1951, shortly before her husband was released from Landsberg—it was worrying about his imprisonment that drove her to her grave —just imagine it, when she was buried at the cemetery here someone sent an enormous, very expensive wreath, and in 1951, you'll remember, there wasn't the superfluity there is now, it was a wreath of hundreds of pink carnations, hundreds of them. Not a single member of the family noticed it, it just slipped in, and it was too late to do anything about it, and my brother went absolutely white in the face. He had spent a whole lifetime taking the greatest care to carry out her wishes, and then that happened. The poor woman. Pink carnations, which she hated most of all, the mere smell of them used to upset her. . . .'

A voice interrupted her. It must have been Fritz Lehr's. But it was distorted by the intercom. 'Is Oldewaage with you?' She found room to put her cigarette down and began searching hectically for the right key of the intercom, which was hidden somewhere under a pile of papers. 'What's up?' the voice said. 'He's always passing the time of day with you.'

'No, he hasn't been here.' She had at last found the right key.

'Oh, while you're there, I want a flight to Madrid tomorrow morning. I've got to be back in the evening.'

'But you've got appointments in Munich tomorrow morning, and the German Commission in Madrid haven't yet told us when the labour . . .'

He cut her short. His voice was harsh and abrupt. 'Once and for all, Fräulein Engels, appointments are not your business. How many more times must I tell you that? Why do you and Winter keep meddling in Fräulein Ziethen's business? Then I have to listen to her complaints, just because you can't get used to the fact that she's in the anteroom now. So please note what I'm saying. And I want the tickets at the Munich office, not at the airport. . . .'

Her calm had suddenly vanished. Her cigarette had dropped over the edge of the ashtray, and when she put it out I noticed her hand was trembling.

'That's the way he always treats me.' As soon as she had said this she looked in horror at the intercom, as if she were afraid she might still be connected. Her whole body was trembling, and I could not bear to look at her, in case there were tears in her eyes.

'I must see about the tickets at once,' she said. 'He's quite capable of coming through in a few minutes' time and asking whether I've got them yet. It was nice of you to look in. I hope. . . .' She had dialled the wrong number. She put back the receiver, and looked at me so appealingly that I had no alternative but to get up and leave her alone.

119

IX

I had difficulty in finding my way back to the entrance hall because of the many corridors and doors, all of which were exactly alike. When I at last found the right door, Fritz Lehr was just saying goodbye to Benno Weegmann, the chief executive officer, who already had his hat in his hand; I could not help wondering how he had managed to get his bald head sunburnt. I realised he intended to take no notice of me, but when he saw that Fritz greeted me in a friendly manner he smiled too.

'Well, Pikola, are you satisfied with your fee now?' he said.

He had published two books about the district under his own name and used photographs of mine without my consent. He then paid me a fee, but such a wretched one that I took him to court, not for the sake of the money, but as a matter of principle. The case ended up in the appeal court.

'Not completely,' I replied.

He smiled at Lehr and then at me, as if to say that Lehr's friends were his friends, we were all friends together.

'No? Then we ought to have a quiet chat some time, as man to man, and clear the whole thing up. And the sooner the better, so far as I'm concerned.'

'So far as I'm concerned, it's settled.'

'But you said . . .'

'I said I was not satisfied with the fee. But I was satisfied that you had to pay costs.'

He produced a sour smile, put on his hat, and shook hands with Fritz Lehr. 'I'll keep you posted about developments,' he said.

'Thank you. And I think you should give very careful consideration indeed to the question of a press statement. In my opinion there's no hurry whatever. You should leave it to the police. They'll make an announcement if they think it necessary. It will be in nobody's interest to make a great fuss about it, you'll see.

He waited until Weegmann had disappeared through the glass door and then made a welcoming gesture. 'Well, now at last I've got time for you.'

His office was almost as vast as the entrance hall. One side consisted only of glass, and you could see a stretch of lawn. There were big, dark leather armchairs, and the same nylon carpeting in varying shades of blue as in the rest of the building. I only noticed now that it was decorated with the letter L. On the walls there were framed photographs of yachts in full sail, as well as some older photographs of warships in which Lehr had served, some of them with the officers' faces superimposed. The whole thing rather suggested the saloon of a ship, and Fritz Lehr moved about in it like the captain.

The two of us were of about the same height; I think the fact that he struck most people as shorter than they expected was simply due to the fact that in photographs he always created the impression of being an unusually big, athletically built man. There was also something else in the photographs that deviated from reality; they invariably showed him in one of those dark blue, carefully tailored, narrow-waisted suits with immaculate white shirt and white-spotted tie that made him look like a successful business man; a man of undefined nationality who was a remorseless working machine and was justified in making heavy demands on others because in the first place he made them on himself. But this was another impression that was modified in his presence.

121

His hair was not so dark as in the pictures, but was touched with grey. His light flannel trousers bulged at the knees, his dark, double-breasted blazer with gold buttons fitted loosely, and he had a silk handkerchief under his open-necked shirt. He looked more like a yachtsman or sportsman than a typical manager type.

I must have been scrutinising him closely, because he smiled and unbuttoned his blazer to show me the excess weight he was carrying.

'I've got to get my weight down again, but I don't know what to do,' he said. 'It started quite suddenly, almost over night, when I was forty-five. But that's a problem you don't have.'

He walked over to the desk, where there were more photographs, some in silver frames, others in removable cases with oval cutouts.

'Christina told me about your meeting,' he went on. 'I didn't know you knew her in the old days. Those are my children. The two big ones are my first wife's. You met her, didn't you? Weren't you at the wedding? Those were the days. Then I really had guts. That American lawyer didn't want to take on the old man's case, so I took refuge behind his wife's skirts. And you know what came of it? I married their daughter. That was a *coup*, in 1948, don't forget; the old man is still in Landsberg, I'm not denazified yet, and I marry the daughter of a Jewish lawyer from California who had been practising in Berlin fifteen years before. It was rather like running a fast motor-boat into an enemy convoy that threw everything it had at you and getting away with a whole skin.'

That, or something very like it, was exactly what he had been awarded the Knight's Cross for doing during the war; he was one of the few naval sub-lieutenants who got that high distinction. But that picture of him also requires amendment. He was by no means a model naval officer. During his training he was sentenced to periods of detention three

times, each more severe than the last, for simply going to sleep in the air raid shelter instead of going on route marches, which he specially detested. His record also included a reduction in rank for insolence to a senior officer; that was the result of a quarrel with an admiral in connection with the latter's daughter. He was simply one of those natural go-getter types who manage to get their own way.

'I saw my first wife again recently, by pure chance. Found her sitting next to me in Madrid, watching Santana play. Jinx her name is. I must confess I can no longer remember what it means. In the meantime she has been divorced again, and I had the feeling she was in Europe looking for a new victim. One shouldn't meet a woman again after so many years, I assure you. Not that she has aged, but she's so American. Everything about her is perfect, make-up, clothes, everything, too perfect, and there's a line around her mouth—those American women are as cold as ice. And I have a daughter at college over there, and a son, though he doesn't bear my name any longer, he's nineteen and he's in Canada, he dodged the draft because he didn't want to go to Vietnam. But I don't want to talk about myself. They tell me you have a daughter named Julia who has completely won the old man's heart. I was talking to him on the telephone this morning. It was the first time in my life that I've ever heard him say anything nice about the female of the species. He asked me to send her flowers from Munich. I don't believe he's ever spent money on flowers in his life before. And her name is Julia? Not after *the* Julia? Why have you never told me about her before?'

He had brought up the subject I had been dreading, but the way he spoke showed that to him it was all over and done with; to him it belonged to the dim and distant past and didn't matter any more.

'Don't take it amiss,' I said, 'but when we met again in Munich that time your whole manner was hardly an encouragement to tell you a great deal. I thought you had

changed a great deal. Actually I once wrote to you because I wanted advice on some building matter, but I never had a reply.'

He looked at me in astonishment, as if he were really seeing me for the first time. Then he slapped me on the back.

'How right you are,' he said. 'Between ourselves—when I put on a show like that I sometimes feel sick with myself. It's the people I have to deal with, there's nothing worse than building contractors, especially those who have grown too big too quickly and are suddenly making a pile. And on top of it there's the fact that the old man kept us short for so long. You may not have realised it, but he grudged us every pfennig. Every wretched little manager in the firm had long since had a Mercedes while I was still going about in a Volkswagen. Until I took charge here, I was earning 1,000 marks a month, not a pfennig more; and if ever I was a few minutes late the old man would be standing at the door with his watch in his hand, and he would tell me off in front of the staff, when I was thirty-six. I'm in charge now, but it took a damned long time, and that's why. . . .'

He was interrupted by the ringing of the telephone, and I had a chance to watch him and think about him while he held the receiver to his ear without replying, half sitting on the desk, but restlessly, continually moving his feet and with an expression of concentration on his face. One could come to no definite conclusion about that face, for the two most striking things about it simply did not fit—a rather passive softness on the one hand and animal strength on the other.

When he at last spoke, he did so with finality.

'Listen,' he said, 'I've warned him once before, and I've had enough of it; and I don't care a damn that there probably isn't going to be a prosecution. The fact that the union knows about it is enough for me. I don't want any trouble with the unions, not at this time of day. You can give him the choice between immediate dismissal or three months' pay if he goes of his own accord. I'm not in the least inter-

ested in where he's to find another job. If you feel obliged to do something for him, that's your affair. And that's the end of the matter. And tell Fräulein Ziethen I'm not to be interrupted. I don't want any more calls put through.' He put back the receiver. 'Too stupid,' he said. 'I can't stand stupidity.'

He looked at me. 'There you have a typical example of what I was talking about,' he went on. 'The building trade. Those works interpreters can twist every personnel officer round their little finger. Some of them simply have to make money on the side, they can't keep their fingers off it. They make foreign workers pay for writing out sick reports for them, and they charge them fees for filling up their tax reclaim forms at the end of the year. Or, as in this case, they simply get them to sign blank forms and then pocket the whole refund themselves. The building trade is the most primitive thing there is. Nowhere else are there so many thugs and crooks. Basically other industrialists look down on us, and in any case people think of developers as high-class swindlers who make their money by fraudulent land deals and charging excessive rents. That brings us to what you've come here to talk about, the commemorative volume, because it's an important point for you to bear in mind. I should like the book to do something to counter that public impression. Once we were a building firm, but those days are over, and we shall be less and less so in the future. At first I was against the whole idea, but I think this volume might contribute to changing the firm's image.'

We were still standing, that is, he was using the width of the room to pace up and down while he talked, but now he stopped and looked at me. 'Have you heard about the skeletons they've dug up?'

I nodded. We sat, and he went on: 'I saw it coming. Oldewaage warned them. He knows all the sites from the old days. He has been in the firm for years, they sent him to us at the time, as they did to all the big construction firms,

I think they called them advisers on ancient remains or something of the sort. His job was to give instructions to make sure that no prehistoric remains were destroyed while sites were being prepared. It was regarded as a highly important matter at the time, and trial trenches had to be dug before excavation work could begin. At all events, Oldewaage was the expert, and while they were drawing up the plans he warned them that they were likely to turn up skeletons. You know about the Jewish camps that were there. That was an appalling business. They were half starved before they got here, and then they had to work like horses. And heaven knows what hopes the poor devils arrived with. Imagine yourself a Jew in a concentration camp at Riga. One fine day you're told you're being sent to Germany to work. You'd think it could only be an improvement. But they went on dying like flies, just as before. And then those people just shovelled them into the earth like animal carcasses. Everyone was indignant, the peasants and the local burgomasters, and the water board intervened, they were genuinely afraid all those dead bodies might pollute the water supply. But my honourable brother-in-law only had to call them grousers and grumblers and threaten to denounce them for causing despondency and alarm by spreading unfounded rumors, and after that nobody dared open his mouth.'

I could hardly bear to listen to him, but what made it tolerable was the completely natural way he spoke. He did not say labour camps, but Jewish camps, and he did not drop his voice and talk in hushed tones like Zielinski and Margarete Engels, and he went on looking at me quite openly.

'The person to whom it's most upsetting, of course, is the chief executive officer. He is terribly proud of his district. He promoted and popularised those "beautify your town and country" competitions, and if he ever hears a lavatory at a country inn isn't perfectly clean or that cats are running about in the kitchen he immediately sends the public health

inspectors to make the owner's life a misery. Now here he is with this beautiful district, with the Ammersee, the Lech, a large number of well-known beauty spots, with a long list of distinguished artists, living and dead, associated with the area, and then, he has those eight Jewish cemeteries in his beautiful district. I don't know what he wouldn't give to wipe out the stain; and I think it also upsets him personally, because immediately after the war he was on the list of those who had to build those cemeteries. That little American lieutenant, Trotta, his name was, had the idea of having the Jewish cemeteries built by local ex-party members. "Turn up at eight o'clock in the morning with a shovel and a good pair of shoes." ' He smiled. 'I was on the list myself, at the same time the firm got the first contract from Military Government for the necessary building materials. I still remember it: 300 cwt. of cement, 200 gallons of petrol, twenty gallons of oil, 180 lb. of nails and, I think, 8,000 bricks. . . . The whole thing had been completely forgotten, and now those bodies have turned up. Though I'm sure he's being over-anxious. Nobody will want to make a great fuss about it, at any rate I don't think they will.'

I am not at all clear what my feelings were while he was talking; all that comes to my mind when I think about it is the grain of the wooden table, the leather chairs, the strange feeling one had when one sat on them or shifted one's position, forcing the air out of the cushion, Fritz Lehr's socks, which had slipped down to the heel of his shoes, and the telephone installation next to his chair, on which plexiglass keys lit up from time to time. He also talked about these things merely as if he were repeating reminiscences, and then came back to the commemorative volume without any transition, assuring me how delighted he was that I was doing it.

'I had rather expected Christina to suggest giving the job to one of her young men,' he went on with a smile. 'Not that they're so young any more, and being left-wingers doesn't

stop them drinking up all my best liquor. And you know what they'd charge, don't you? What fee have you in mind?'

'Do you want to discuss that first?'

'That is what I should prefer. What have you in mind?'

'Five thousand,' I said, and realised at once that Gottfried Lehr had been right. 'Five thousand down and five thousand on delivery.' The thoughtful and slightly irritated expression on his face vanished at once.

'Agreed,' he said.

He put his finger on one of the keys, and said: 'Fräulein Engels, write out a cheque, please . . . 5,000 marks . . . Pikola . . . for commemorative volume and/or public relations work.' Fräulein Engels tried to say something about the air ticket to Madrid, but he switched off.

'Well, as I was saying, a point to which I attach importance is trying to get away from the odium of being in the building trade. The really good times in that trade are over anyhow, and they won't be coming back so soon either. In the past everything was all right if you kept a firm grip on things. Short, seasonal labour contracts that let those Spaniards, Italians and Turks rotate. But when you start building them nursery schools and extra school and hospital accommodation, the law of diminishing returns begins to apply. There's no fighting the trend. And if the Social Democrats win this election the whole process will be speeded up. They want reform at our expense. Protection of workers, protection of nature, protection of the environment. But I don't want to paint things too black, because one can come to terms with them. I'm not one of those who believe that if they win the election it will be the end of the world. Once they're in power they'll acquire a taste for it, and nothing is ever eaten as hot as it's cooked. All I'm trying to say is that this course of development was clearly foreseeable, and that for the past few years I've been doing my best to take it into account.'

He said all this, it seemed to me, without much self-

128

involvement, without wasting much feeling on it, with that face of his that was both sensitive and tough at the same time.

'What I've always preached to my people is diversification and expansion. That's the law of the market and, quite apart from that, of the taxation system. We have shifted a large part of our building activity abroad, NATO headquarters in Brussels, the Keban power station in Turkey, Cabora Bassa in Spain. We have invested in South and Central America. Building elements, growth industries. We have taken over a whole series of businesses or acquired a majority interest in them. We are engaged in four independent fields of activity, of which pure building is only one, and I should like that point to be made in the centenary volume. I'll write it all down for you. So we're no longer the Lehr Building Company, but simply the Lehr Company, and not the Friedrich Lehr Company but simply the F. Lehr Company. Also I want to change the company emblem. . . .'

Once more he was interrupted by the telephone. The vein on his brow swelled visibly. 'I said no-one was to be put through. . . .' But then he started listening intently. This time he made short comments: 'In that case we'll make an application to declare them all redundant. . . . But the liquidation of the firm has been announced. . . . Yes, there's no question about it. . . . There can be no question of a climb-down. . . . What? Listen, don't try that one on me. The chairman of the works council told me himself that they'll take the compensation we're paying them and go round the corner and find another job. . . . No, certainly not. . . . I didn't pay five million for a majority interest and half-a-million for workers' compensation only to draw my horns in afterwards. . . . The devil I will. What have I got a law department for? . . . What? So now you're starting with that one. I don't care a damn what the Augsburg Wool Company once was, I'm interested only in the site. . . . What? Prevent the removal of the machinery? Televi-

sion? You let yourself be impressed by every. . . . Oh. . . .
Yes, I see. . . . No, wait a moment.'

He put the receiver in his lap. I had ceased to exist for
him; nothing existed for him but the problem that had
cropped up and called for a solution. I saw it in the working
of his face; now he really looked like the man in the photographs. All the phlegm had vanished, leaving an almost sen-
sual pleasure, as if what was involved was not a matter of
money and accounts, but an act of passion. He picked the
receiver up again. 'Listen,' he said. 'I want you to talk to
the trade union; or, better still, get someone from the bank
to talk to them. And without my knowledge, you understand.
I have not yet considered the possibility, but the bank *might*
be able to persuade me that the union's own building company could have the site. . . . Then the unions will ensure
that everything goes smoothly. . . . We'll see about that.
. . . If we need them, we've got to do business with them.
. . . Of course. . . . Yes. . . . that's the idea.'

This time he made no comment when he had finished the
conversation. I still did not exist for him. He went over to
the other telephone on his desk, dialled a number and talked
to someone for a few minutes. He jotted something down,
and came back and dropped into the armchair. The air hissed
out of the cushion. His thoughts were still elsewhere, and
he was suddenly in a hurry to end the interview with me.

'I don't know what Gottfried and my father may have told
you, but I don't want to see too much about tradition and
the past in the book. I want it to concentrate on the present
and the future.'

'Your brother. . . .'

But he cut me short. 'All my brother and sister really care
about is how much they can draw from the firm,' he said.
'They want to see plenty of hard cash and have a voice in
the business, but I bear the responsibility and make the decisions. Sometimes I risk my neck and deliver myself bound
hand and foot into the hands of the bank. Especially my dear,

retiring sister, who doesn't want anything for herself. . . .'
He stopped short, and for the first time I had the impression
that he had let his feelings run away with him.

'I'll tell you what I'll do,' he said. 'I'll dictate my ideas on
the subject, and you can use them as you think best. Fräulein
Engels will send them to you. I'll include everything I should
like to see in the volume, and I'll dictate my ideas just as
they strike me, not in any logical order, but as they occur
to me. You'll be getting details about the subsidiaries and
associated companies, statistics, turnover figures and all the
rest of it from Nagengast in Munich. He's what I call my
breakfast-time manager, because he holds forth at me over
the breakfast table, but he calls himself director of public
relations services, and he attaches immense importance to
the full title. He's one of those dour Prussians and, if I know
anything about him, he'll be offering you a complete draft
for the whole job, with a lot of stuff about entrepreneurial
courage and total dedication and that sort of thing. You can
dump all that in the wastepaper basket straight away. But
his facts will be correct, and those you'll be able to use.' He
rose. 'Well, I think we've covered the main points,' he added,
and pressed one of the keys. 'Have you got the cheque? No?
I'll fetch it. Tell Winter he's wanted.'

He went through a door I had not previously noticed and
came back with the cheque in his hand. 'Christina said we'll
be seeing you on her birthday. Do you think you'll have a
draft ready that we could discuss in the meantime?'

'Yes, if I get what you're going to dictate and the information from Munich soon.'

'You'll get them at latest the day after tomorrow. Au
revoir, then. And you must bring your daughter with you.
A girl who made an impression on the old man is a girl I've
got to meet. Tell me, Christina says that you and your
wife. . . . I know, marriage is a funny thing. To think that a
business man like me would ever enter into a contract of
that kind. . . . And how are things otherwise in that area?

Do you remember our first girls at Garmisch? . . . We must talk about all that the next time we meet. Personal things have rather gone by the board.' He escorted me to the door. 'Winter will drive you back to Augsburg. . . . No, my dear fellow, I won't hear of it. I don't need him for the next few hours, there's no question of his not driving you back.'

X

I tried to sit in front next to Winter, but he saved himself embarrassment and put me firmly in my place by pointing out that the boss would have no sympathy whatever for such a thing; he had strict instructions that passengers were to travel at the back, and just as strict instructions not to talk to them. He had driven first the old boss and then the new since 1929, that is, for forty years, apart from the brief post-war interruption, and both the old gentleman and his son were alike in that from the driver's point of view, at any rate from *his*, Winter's point of view, they were ideal employers, i.e., they kept their distance. There was none of that unnecessary, endless waiting in the evening outside theatres, hotel bars or private houses; for that they used other drivers, or taxis. For longer journeys the boss went by air, and if he needed a car at his destination he, Winter, drove ahead and waited at the airport to pick him up. On business journeys he stayed at the same hotel and occupied an adjoining room, but that did not mean that the boss ever asked him to join him for a meal, even at the smallest village inn. He, Winter, always decided the route and which way they should enter a town, and there was never any interference, he was never told to drive faster or not to overtake. And finally, only he drove the boss's car; when he went on leave the Mercedes was left in the garage for four weeks and the

boss used another of the firm's cars. When this wasn't done it led to nothing but trouble among drivers, because when something went wrong it was always the other man's fault.

Drivers and cars were a subject on which Winter talked endlessly; we discussed them again later at the garden party while he was waiting to fetch guests or take them home. He had driven since 1926 without an accident. For the first three of those years he had been a taxi-driver in Paris, as he had been unable to find work in Germany, and it was there that he had been 'discovered' by the old gentleman. Since then he had driven the Lehrs in nothing but Mercedes, apart from a brief period of unhappy memory during which Fritz Lehr, after marrying Jinx Greenberg, had thought it necessary to change, first to a Lincoln and then to a Rolls-Royce. He had driven Mercedes from the outset, always the biggest model. The old gentleman had had the 'big' Mercedes, the twelve cylinder, as early as 1938; even then it had a top speed of 150 miles an hour, though the petrol consumption was enormous. But what did that matter when a gallon cost not much more than a mark? Of course with a car weighing three tons one shouldn't accelerate up to sixty miles an hour from a standing start or when the lights turned green. That was the problem with the *young* drivers of the present day, they mistook a big Mercedes for a sports car, no wonder they then had trouble with the Cardan shaft. He, Winter, drove a Mercedes for 140,000 miles before it was traded in, and it was still in perfectly good condition, apart of course from normal wear and tear. The interlude with the Lincoln and the Rolls-Royce was a time of bitter memory to him; it had nearly caused him to hand in his notice; the Rolls in particular had given him nothing but trouble, in his opinion it was one of the most overrated cars in the world, from the finish to the *electronic* system with which the windows and the boot were opened and shut and the seats were adjusted; it was far inferior to the *hydraulic* system of the Mercedes. . . .

134

But that afternoon we talked very little. We were separated by a glass partition. When I said something he must have noticed the movement of my lips, because suddenly I heard his voice from a loudspeaker behind me. 'Press the second button in the door on your left, then you'll be able to speak,' he said.

I tried again to dissuade him from taking me all the way. 'It'll be perfectly all right if you put me down at the station,' I said. 'I can take the next train, any train, Winter, it'll be perfectly O.K.' But he replied that if I insisted it would only cause him embarrassment; he wouldn't know how to explain it to the boss.

He drove on without even taking his foot off the accelerator. The car moved smoothly and silkily. I had always been surprised at the ease with which this small, delicately built little man handled such a heavy vehicle, but that was only because I did not know enough about servo-mechanisms, power-assisted steering and automatic gear change. He had put on a chauffeur's cap, which was also adorned with gold stripes. There would have been no need to do so for my sake, but it had nothing to do with me, no doubt it was something on which the boss insisted.

I sat at the back, feeling that unless I got out into the fresh air I should suffocate. But it passed away, and I was aware of nothing but the gentle, rolling motion that made me want to go to sleep. The leather upholstery reminded me of the chairs in Fritz Lehr's office, as did the whole interior of the car, the thick carpeting, the grain of the wood under the partition, the blinking lights and switches on the dashboard. I was no more able to think clearly than I had been in his office, as if in both places a screen, a system—whether hydraulic or electronic—had been built invisibly into the walls to make thinking impossible.

We had long since reached the B17 and had passed the underpass and the triangular junction at Kaufering; if you knew the place, you could still tell where Women's Camp

No. 1 had been, and see the siding on which the freight-cars had stood, including the one with the brakeman's box in which Zielinski had let me meet Julia . . . I felt for the button, and pressed the wrong one, because the seat moved. But I went on trying until I found the right one.

'Will you stop, please,' I said.

'Stop?'

He slowed down. I looked out of the window for the turning I wanted him to take. Flat fields lay on either side of the road. I pointed to some isolated farm buildings. 'If you wouldn't mind taking the next turning on the left. Immediately beyond the farm buildings. It's just a track.'

'You mean . . .'

'Yes,' I said quickly.

He seemed to consider the proposal for a moment, but then turned left without making any comment; this was the exact spot where I had been taken prisoner by the Americans. The track was almost too narrow for the car and was full of potholes, but the Mercedes rode them smoothly. There were only about four hundred yards to go. I did not have to tell him where to stop. There was only one spot in which I could possibly be interested, a group of pine trees surrounded by a low wall beyond a slight eminence in the middle of the fields.

I got out, and so did Winter. I felt sure he was going to ask me whether I was going to be long, because if so he must call up his boss and tell him he was going to be delayed; (and in fact that was exactly what he did). I assured him that I should not be long.

I walked past the cemetery to where the sick quarters had been which had been under Boettcher's personal control and in which Julia had been at the end. The foundation walls were covered with long grass, but they were still there, and you could tell where the huddle of wooden huts had been. You could see the foundations of the outer walls and the place where the chimney had been; otherwise there was

nothing but earth. Only one of the huts had had any cellaring, and the traces were still visible; that must have been Boettcher's quarters and those of the guards.

I walked the whole length of the place, to the edge of the deep, disused gravel-pit. It was full of rubbish that had been tipped over the edge; wrecked cars lay there rusting away with empty, staring window frames. This was where the three hundred and sixty inmates of the sick quarters had been shot.

They had been driven down the slope, and the machine-gun on the edge at the top had fired into them until no sign of life remained. But imagination failed, and all I heard was the sound of a tractor in a neighbouring field. I went on gazing down into the pit, and what startled me more than anything else at that moment, more than my memory, was an old bus in the middle of the débris. It too had been stripped and was rusting away but, strangely enough, no-one had troubled to remove the white plate over the driver's cabin. It was grey and dirty, but the word 'Special' was still plainly visible.

I turned away, and went back to the group of pines. The gate in the low wall round the cemetery stuck. There was only a single narrow gravel path, and a memorial tablet stating that 360 people had been killed and were buried here. There were no names, and I stood there drained of feeling; I said to myself that I must tell Julia about this, I should have done so long ago, I had put it off far too long.

There was also something else in my mind, and there was no driving it out—the memory of the days and weeks I had spent in Zielinski's little office, surrounded by files and with files on the desk in front of me. This was something that I did feel, the strange feeling one got in one's hands after a while when one had been turning over sheet after sheet of these old files; it was not only the dust and dirt, one's whole body felt soiled. In my mind's eye I could see the sheets of paper, now becoming fragile at the folds, the tape holes

strengthened by rings, the typing that was faint because of the worn typewriter ribbons, the different type-faces of different typewriters, particularly the one with the big italic type in which the letter 'h' was always cocked up, as in 'honour'. I had all this in my head as if on an illuminated plate.

Lieutenant Trotta's order. Fritz Lehr had made only one mistake; the actual amount of cement ordered had been 400 cwt.; and also he had forgotten the tipping lorry.

In the course of the week the number of workers at the Jewish cemetery has steadily declined. It is essential that those engaged on this work should not make difficulties and should apply to be excused only in cases of extreme urgency.

Handwritten letters, written on half sheets, greying with age and in fading ink or barely legible pencil.

Please excuse me from work on the Jewish cemeteries. I joined the party only in 1937 and never held any office in it, and I was neither in the SA nor in the SS. I was myself subjected to persecution because I did not send my boys for service in the Hitler Youth.

I have to supply 200 bread rolls daily for the Occupying Power and 700 for the civilian population. I cannot guarantee the quality of the bread if I am not present myself.

I have only one apprentice boy, but I have 300 pairs of shoes to repair, though I have not accepted any new work for the past six weeks, and I therefore ask to be excused. . . .

As the potatoes have to be lifted and seeds to be sown. . . .

I am a dentist, and I am very busy, and above all I knew nothing whatever about such things.

More files, with better papers, a new typewriter ribbon and a different type-face.

With the beginning of the holiday season a bigger influx of visitors to the cemeteries from abroad is to be expected, and steps must therefore be taken to clean up the cemeteries and memorial stones; and, if possible, a beginning must be made with a planting programme, as the cemeteries are at

*present in an unworthy condition. Trees damaged by wild
animals must be removed. Some of the gravestones are tilting
and must be straightened. The inscriptions must be fresh-
ened up with black paint, rust must be removed from the
entrance gate and it must be painted (the gate grey, the
handle black, the Star of David gold).*

The surfaces of the graves must be filled up with earth.

*The municipality declines to take part in building up the
approach road to the concentration camp cemetery. It cannot be expected that the municipality maintain a road made
at the time by the Occupying Power across farmers' land.*

*A game tenant has complained that tents have been put
up contrary to regulations, that motorscooter racing has taken
place, and that battledore and shuttlecock has been played
over the cemetery wall.*

*In reply to your complaint we can assure you that the
cemetery cannot of course be compared to the neighbouring
monastery cemetery in which the graves of deceased monks
are cared for by their fellow-citizens.*

*Note has been taken of Herr O.'s statement that the re-
mains of concentration camp victims are likely to come to
light and that the extraction of gravel should therefore be
forbidden.*

I tried to work my way back, to remember how all this
had cropped up again. Who had dragged it up and why?
It had all been dead and buried for years. Even the forgotten
names that had turned up again seemed to have a special
significance. How had it all started? Sylvester Nagengast,
Karl Boettcher, Kajetan Müller-Heydekrug, Heinz Oldewaage
—they struck me as the names of a race of people whom I
had believed to be extinct. Winter, Horst-Dieter. Did anyone have a name like that nowadays? Horst-Dieter Winter?
What nonsense. The telephone books and address books were
full of such names, and no-one thought anything of them.

Winter had turned the car. It was equipped with a telephone, and he had the receiver in his hand. Had I been too

long? He said nothing, replaced the receiver, put on his cap and opened the door for me. I looked at him and remembered the day—it was February 28, 1945—when he drove Fritz Lehr to Augsburg in the twelve-cylinder Mercedes. It was two days after the air raid in which my mother was killed, and it was then that he told me what was happening to Julia Dressler and asked me to help.

Would Winter remember the trip if I reminded him of it? And, if he did, would he remember anything except how difficult it had been to get petrol for a car that gobbled it up at that rate, and how worried he had been about the worn tyres and, above all, how dangerous it had been to drive along the dead-straight Reich main road No. 17 to Augsburg in broad daylight in a car as conspicuous as that, with enemy fighter-bombers about that fired on everything that moved—it had been a fine, almost spring-like, day into the bargain? And wasn't he quite right after all these years to remember such things and not certain others?

We were back on the road. The car slowly accelerated. On the righthand side a notice appeared pointing to the Lech building site. There was a newly asphalted turning leading to it, and there were bulldozers and other builders' vehicles in the distance. A car had drawn up at the roadside, and a man was standing next to it. He signalled to us to stop and, to my surprise, Winter stopped. Without my doing anything, the right-hand window was lowered, and the man put his head through it. 'You can be completely reassured, Herr Lehr,' he said, and stopped short when he realised his mistake. He was a young man in a pin-stripe suit with a white handkerchief in the pocket, and when he put his head in the window you could not help noticing that he wore a toupee. For a moment he said nothing, but then, after looking at the car and at Winter, he must have decided that he could safely entrust what he had to say to someone sitting in the back of the Lehr Mercedes.

'When you see Herr Lehr,' he said, 'please tell him that so

140

far forty-eight skeletons have been found, but the police have found no trace of violence. None of the bodies shows any sign of a shot in the back of the neck, and they all have their gold teeth. I have been able to confirm this myself.'

The young man was a stranger to me; evidently he was from the district executive office. He must have been in his late twenties, and he was keen and competent; no doubt it would be said later that he had worked his way up from the bottom.

I sat back in the cushions. Winter closed the window, and once more the system worked and switched off my thoughts. All I noticed was that the windows suddenly assumed a darker shade because of the thick clouds that had gathered.

Zielinski would be worrying about his pigeons, particularly the young ones. I envied him for it, and I envied Winter too. I wished I could worry about things like carrier pigeons and Cardan shafts and which was really the better, a hydraulic system or an electronic one.

XI

The landing stage was about five hundred yards from the boundary of the estate. I could see the lights of the paddle-steamer, which normally plied on the lake but had been hired for the evening by the Lehrs, and I could hear the music. There were Chinese lanterns on both decks, little white lights dotted the railings, and lines of lights led up to the funnel. The music came in waves, as the wind came and went. It was an east wind, which in this area generally meant good weather; Zgodda had been right about the weather, but the political prophets had been wrong about the election. The weather was fine, and even now, at nine o'clock in the evening, it was nearly 65 degrees; and on the television screens nearly three hours after the closing of the polling stations there was no more talk of a Social Democratic landslide.

I turned away from the bank. The big park sloped gently down to the lake. It had a remarkable stock of old trees. Any expert would have said that they would not survive a single winter in this cold, damp, misty climate. But, whoever planted and looked after them, the Californian pines and Japanese larches had thriven mightily. As in a botanical garden, there were plates in front of them giving their botanical and popular names. The same had been done with the young trees and shrubs, except that in the case of the latter white plastic cards hung in the branches; in the half-

light it looked as if the park were populated with a lot of white birds.

In comparison with the park, the long building, or collection of buildings assembled under a single roof, looked new. The trees, the lawns, and the red paths created a sense of permanence, but the impression the house made on me that evening was that it might have been specially built for this occasion only; and this impression was reinforced by the tents and stalls that had been erected round it by a party catering service. There was a big blue and white striped tent in which we had had dinner, a beer bar, a pretzel stall and a variety of grills in which the charcoal had just been lit. Some men were putting fish on little white sticks. Cats from far and near seemed to be used to this sort of garden party, for suddenly I noticed a good dozen of them in the park.

Only a few guests did not take part in the tour of the lake. The orchestra engaged for the evening preceded the procession to the landing stage, leaving behind three musicians, to whose music three or four couples were dancing on the big terrace; these were older married couples, and they circled slowly on the marble floor under the awning. A few men in dark suits were sitting at the open-air bar.

Portable television sets had been set up in the open air in the most varied places; there were a good dozen of them, and they were all switched on. In these surroundings they were like toys, illuminated peep-shows; the pictures did not flow into one another, but looked like stills being shown one after the other. In the course of the past half hour the tone of the interviews and comment had changed; a mistake seemed to have been fed into the computer; at all events, the latest calculations now pointed to a tie between the two big parties. It was not yet clear whether the National Democratic Party would or would not get into the Bundestag, and the Free Democrats were still in danger of falling below the required five per cent of the vote. Only a few employees

of the catering service were following both programmes on the screens.

The photographer whom Christina had hired was sitting at a table at the edge of the terrace; he had his equipment in front of him on the table. He was a man of about my age, or perhaps a little older, and he looked exhausted, with his hair hanging over his brow. In the early stages of the party he had photographed the arriving guests with his electronic flash equipment, and during dinner he had gone from table to table. He was using a Polaroid camera, a Japanese model, and the idea—it was Christina's—was that every guest should be given a photograph of himself before he left, a finished print in a specially made holder giving the date and the occasion.

The man had done his job with a smile, and the guests had helped him by responding with a smile, because for a moment he was more than just a photographer, he was a wizard, a magician, who stopped time in its tracks and showed that nothing passed away. But now he was just an exhausted, disgruntled old man who infected me with his mood and made me more doubtful than ever about my calling.

There were about sixty guests at Christina's birthday party, and they looked as if they had been assembled by chance. In fact they had been carefully selected, hand-picked, so to speak; they were a mixture of business men, politicians, artists, sportsmen and people whom Christina called distinguished idlers. Most of them were married. One reason for the lack of unmarried men and young people was certainly that the Lehrs' children were not yet old enough for them to matter; Christina would certainly not overlook them when the time came. Her touch was perceptible everywhere; there was a perfection of detail that pointed to long practice. Certainly nobody here knew that she had once watched cars in the Old Market at Dresden

144

for twenty pfennigs an hour, and very likely she had forgotten it herself.

The seating at dinner had presumably cost her a great deal of thought. I had on my left a woman of forty who worked for a polling organisation which had forecast a big win for the Social Democrats. She was not in the least put out by the fact that this prediction had gone badly astray; all she worried about was her husband's appetite; he was a television chief who, she complained, invariably over-ate on these occasions. She did her best to keep her eye on what he was eating three tables away, and gave one of the waiters a ten-mark note to ensure that he should not be offered any second helpings. The girl on my right was wearing a golden dress that was so low cut there was no need for anyone to worry about the men at our table eating too much. Her dress and her bosom struck me as familiar, and then I remembered she had been one of the assistants in a well-known television quiz show. The name on the card on the table in front of her said Karen Blum, which was at least a partial explanation of why she had been put beside me; she was married to the doctor in whose hands I had been for many years. Dr. Blum was just over sixty, and all I knew was that he had married a girl of twenty-three after his divorce two years before. The man on the other side of her was a young racing driver, not quite so successful as his father had been in that profession, but successful all the same. The two of them engaged in animated conversation, and she really was the type of girl that follow drivers from Le Mans to Monaco, go to boxing matches, and wear wide-brimmed hats and a lot of stop-watches round their necks; I wondered what Blum had to offer in the face of all this. I should like to have asked him. I asked myself a great many questions that evening, and I felt out of place.

Once more I was astonished at the ease with which Julia fitted into this company, just as I had been when we called

145

on Fritz Lehr's father. Christina had put her next to the
owner of a big firm of auctioneers. He had already discovered what her job was and assured her that she could
count on work from him if she set up on her own. It was
not only Old Masters that were damaged and had to be
restored. Far from it. Modern pictures were exhibited,
packed, sent away to be exhibited elsewhere, and often
came back damaged. The work was easier and better paid,
etc., etc., . . . Julia told me all this after dinner on one of
the few occasions when we were alone together, and then
Fritz Lehr took her away. I talked to strangers and strangers
talked to me until it was time for the trip on the lake and
Christina came up to me.

She looked better than ever. She wore a long, simple dress,
with long earrings, and had had her hair done in an Evita
Péron style, which made her face narrower and severer; she
really looked like a reigning queen. She certainly was the
ideal wife for Fritz Lehr; Winter, the housekeeper, the
waiters, the staff, turned to her and her only for instructions,
and she gave them briefly and succinctly and she seemed to
be keeping her eye on everything, making sure that everyone would say afterwards that she gave the best parties and
provided the best entertainment and the best drinks that
didn't give anybody a headache. She came up to me with a
fur jacket over her arm that she no doubt intended to take
with her on the boat.

'Are you enjoying yourself?'

Her attitude made it clear that I did not really belong
here, but that special circumstances, whatever these might
be, justified an exception being made. Not that she was spe-
cifically cool towards me; she merely made it plain that
nothing of what there had once been between us counted
here, that she did not want to know or hear anything about
it, and that it conferred absolutely no privileges on anyone,
least of all myself; and she behaved in exactly the same way
with other men who stopped and talked to her.

146

'Have you seen Fritz?' she asked. 'It's time to go on board for the trip round the lake.'

As arranged, I had brought with me the complete first draft of the commemorative volume, and was still expecting to be able to discuss it with Fritz Lehr. I had last seen him leaving the dance floor with Julia and going into the park, but I had no desire to mention the fact.

'Do you think he's going?' I said. 'I really came here because of the commemorative volume. I thought I might be able to look it through with him.'

She looked at me searchingly, as if I deserved her confidence, and then said: 'I must say your daughter is . . . What shall I say? Attractive isn't the right word, she's a remarkable young woman. Now I understand why you kept her hidden. I never imagined you'd have a daughter like that.'

'What did you expect her to be like?'

'Not like that, at all events. Not so . . . interesting.'

'Is that what she is?'

She obviously found this a very absorbing question.

'In her way, yes. She's striking because she's different. Doesn't she care very much about men?'

'I don't know enough about that to be able to answer that question.'

I did not want to talk about Julia, and I could not make out what Christina was driving at.

'But she hasn't had many men, has she? I've got an eye for these things. That's what makes her different, and so attractive to some men. We can talk frankly, can't we?' She walked a few paces into the park. 'You know, I know Fritz. He doesn't enjoy these parties unless he can find someone at whom he can make a pass. To him it's simply a matter of course. He's a go-getter who has to get what he wants, and on evenings like this he has to show he isn't losing his grip. I think he has always been like that, but that's something you know about better than I do, because you've known him

147

longer; all he has ever cared about is knowing that he can get any girl he sets his cap at. Before my time, between his marriages, it was just the same. He hasn't had one-tenth of the affairs that people say he has had, because he's a man who rations his strength, even in sex. Generally there's nothing behind it, or much less than the ladies themselves hope for. He still plays the same game. He makes up wildly to someone for a whole evening, and all it amounts to is taking her into a dark corner and pawing her and making promises. Next day she calls him up at his office and she's terribly disappointed that he's so cool, or is simply engaged and unavailable. And afterwards, as soon as she's got over it, she comes and tells me all about it. It's all extremely harmless; when I look through the list of guests I generally know in advance whom he's going to make a pass at that evening, and I very rarely make a mistake.'

I tried to take all this lightly. 'And who's your tip for tonight?' I said.

'You don't know her, she's the blonde I put next to him. She's sexy *and* she's married, which should have made her doubly attractive. I always seat them next to him, to save him any difficulties with the preliminary approach. But this time I made a mistake.' She stopped and looked at me. 'Tonight I think it's Julia.'

I think I laughed, and said something about paternal feelings. The word stuck in my throat, and she too was quite tense and serious.

'Trust my nose in the matter,' she said. 'I see what I see. Let me be quite frank—I don't like it. I told you a few weeks ago that it took me a long time to get all this'—she made a sweeping movement with her hands that included everything in sight—'and that's why I'm on the qui vive.'

'But Julia. . . .'

'I know what you're going to say, that only makes it worse. *She's the girl that's hard to get.* That's a challenge that's bound to rouse all his sporting instincts. His business, his

148

work, his money, keep reminding him of all the pleasures he's had to sacrifice for them. Others start gambling or something to try and be born all over again, but Fritz sticks to women, and any woman that resists him only stimulates him.'

I looked at her, for the first time it struck me that I felt sorry for her. She had said that she had no more bad dreams, or something of the sort. She had security, more security than others, and to protect it she had to be on the alert, more alert than others, all the time.

I tried to reassure her. 'I think you're worrying unnecessarily,' I said.

'Perhaps I am. But I just wanted to tell you this, and to ask you to keep your eyes open too. Very likely it won't last beyond this evening, and, if it did, very likely I should know about it before you. I'm simply asking you to do something for me. I like knowing where I am. In any case, if she gives in that will be the end of it. I'm not worried about him, but I'm not so sure about your daughter. I know that type, or at any rate I think I do; those rather dreamy ones are just the type that fall for men like Fritz. You know, when one has had an upbringing such as mine one isn't shattered when life doesn't run smoothly and easily. You're used to pulling yourself together to face up to things. It's harder for those who grew up believing there was solid ground under their feet. There never has been, has there? The ground has opened and threatened to swallow me up several times.' She shook her head. 'You still manage to make me say things that don't suit me.'

'Once upon a time they suited you.'

She did not go into this. For a moment there had been something of the old confidence between us, but she reestablished the distance again.

'Please go to the boathouse over there,' she said, 'and tell the two of them that it's time for the trip round the lake.'

I must have looked at her in astonishment, because she laughed.

149

'The boathouse is for the difficult cases,' she said. 'Fritz has a standard attack—direct and head-on. If it fails, he tries a feint. *I'm not the man people take me for, in reality I should like to be living quite a different kind of life,* or something of the sort. You can take it from me, it's incredibly effective.'

The band was forming up, and the guests were coming out on to the terrace.

'I have to go now, please do as I ask.'

She put her hand on my arm. It was a cold, studied gesture, and she stalked off in the same way, walking upright, almost stiffly; and I said to myself that, whether one liked her or not, she was certainly a remarkable woman. Presumably to live with a man like Fritz Lehr one would have to be.

The boathouse was at the edge of the grounds. It looked big enough for several boats. Rails led about fifteen yards down to the bank to enable the boats to be launched. Two sailing boats were moored to red buoys near the landing stage and the bathing huts. Gulls had dirtied the covers, so they could not have been used for a long time. I could see no light in the boathouse, but it was light enough; there was a full moon, and the sky was clear.

There were some steps at the side of the structure, and the door at the top was edged with light. But I was not prepared for the blinding light inside, or for the boat itself, which filled the whole place; it was a good thirty feet long and more than ten feet wide; it was, indeed, no ordinary boat, but a motor yacht, looking even more powerful than it must have done in the open; the superstructure was white, the fibreglass hull green, and there must certainly have been sleeping room for seven in addition to the saloon; at all events, its size was astonishing. It was like being told by a child that it had a favourite toy in its room, a horse, and then finding that it was not a rocking horse but a thorough-bred racehorse.

I stood there for a time. Behind me, through the open

150

door, I heard the band strike up, the brass, the clarinets. Then Julia and Fritz Lehr emerged from the wheelhouse on to the sundeck.

Fritz Lehr wore a blazer with a silk scarf round his neck and Julia was in a dark silk dress with no jewellery except a narrow silver belt. There are dreams that recur over long intervals of time; you see a house, rooms, corridors that you had long forgotten, but they are all immediately familiar, you know you have been there before. That was exactly the feeling I had when I saw the two of them standing side by side on the deck.

'They're waiting for you,' I at last managed to say. Fritz Lehr stepped on to the wooden platform that surrounded the boat at the height of the rail and held out his hand to help Julia. 'Christina said I'd find you here,' I went on. 'The cruise is just beginning.'

'It's a dream boat, isn't it?' he said. 'Only the Finns can build a boat like this. Two wheels, a hundred and thirty feet of sail surface, a Perkins engine good for ten knots. Fuel tanks for a range of 630 sea miles. With that you can ride out any storm at sea.'

I tried to assure myself that he looked slightly ridiculous in his blazer, silk scarf and white shoes in this over-dimensional toy, which was a piece of pure senseless show-off in a place like this. But I had noticed the name of the boat in golden letters on the side of the wheelhouse, *Dange II*. This too was a forgotten dream. Many years ago I had known *Dange I*, a reconstructed coastguard cutter dating from the twenties, when the Memel harbour area was internationalised; there was also a certain external resemblance, for *Dange II* distinctly preserved the cutter's silhouette.

'It reminds me of another boat,' I said. 'It drew too much water for the Dange.' The Dange is a river that runs into the Memeler Tief.

'You're quite right, it's a pretty absurd boat for a lake like this.' He did not follow up what I had said. 'That's how

151

dreams end. All my life I've dreamt of being in a small boat on a big sea. Now I've got a big boat on a lake that's too small for it. For two years I had her at Travemünde, but I never managed to get there, so I brought her here so as to be able at least to dream a bit. One day, I keep saying to myself, I'll simply drop everything and sail away, and after a year at sea I shan't even understand why I found it so hard to make up my mind to do it. She's registered at Lloyds, I could put her on wheels tomorrow and six hours later I could be in Genoa. One day . . .' He left the sentence unfinished, looking at Julia as he did so, and I remembered what Christina had said.

'If you're really serious about it, you ought to do it,' I heard Julia say as we left the boathouse. After the bright lights inside, the night seemed dark. He had switched off the neon lights and locked the door, and we walked towards the house. I reminded him of the commemorative volume, but he shook his head. Not today, he said, for that we needed peace and quiet, he would come and see me about it in the next few days, perhaps actually tomorrow. The two joined the stragglers making their way towards the ship. I remained behind.

'Aren't you coming?' Julia said.

'No, I'd rather stay.'

'Would you like me to stay?'

'Oh, no, certainly not; I simply don't very much want to go, that's all.'

I could feel how very much she wanted to go, how much she was looking forward to the ship, the lights, the people, the music; you could see it in her face, her eyes, her wanting to be young and to be thought attractive; and this too reminded me of something else, of another summer, another party in a garden that had run wild, with red mallows and yellow water flags growing as thick as a hedge in the marshy soil.

'Really I'll stay if you'd like me to.'

152

'No, you go, I shan't be bored, and besides, I want to follow the election results.'

'All right, then, till later.'

Sometimes Julia and her mother were as alike as the two
boats, and I wondered which of them I was really in love
with; perhaps what I saw in Julia was simply her mother; and
now, when the ship cast off, memory suddenly grew stronger
than the present.

But could I trust memory? Many years had passed, exactly
thirty in fact, and I no longer possessed even a photograph of
that time. So little had happened that summer, and at that
other party there had been only a single violinist. . . .

XII

Three houses play a big part in my memory; they are at all events something I can be positive about, so much so that after all these years I could still find my way about them blindfolded

The first is the Lehrs' house at Memel, in the suburb of Schmelz, right on the old timber harbour; all the Lehrs' houses were by the waterside, as they were later in Berlin and now here. It was my first summer in Memel, and the only one, three weeks in July 1939. The trip had been planned since March, since the return to Germany of the Memel territory, but had had to be postponed until the alterations and redecoration were complete. Changes were made only in the interior; the doors and windows were painted, the floors polished, the carpets and curtains were renewed; the outside was still as Johann Wilhelm Lehr had built it after his return from Samoa on the site of an older property destroyed in the big fire of 1854.

I had chosen a photograph of the house for the commemorative volume, and had put it right at the beginning, because it said a very great deal about the family. It directly overlooked the water, as I said, and it formed part of a row of houses and offices belonging to merchant families; but its height and individuality marked it off from the others, and this was certainly not unintentional. A regulation forbade building more than three storeys high, but this had been

154

neatly circumvented by the now wealthy sea captain, who simply built the basement at ground level, thus raising the level of the whole structure, so that a double flight of stone steps had to be built leading right and left up to the big, heavy front door. Two wings enclosed a big paved court-yard at the back, but the real impact of the building was made by the façade, the steps leading up to the heavy door over which, for lack of a family coat of arms, Johann Wilhelm had caused an axe and a trowel to be carved in stone as the emblem of his new trade. Two superimposed wall pillars supported the black roof, from the gable window of which a red and yellow flag was always flying for some reason or other; red and yellow were incidentally the town's colours, and the flag was so long that it touched one's head when one entered the house; as I said, it was a house that said a great deal about the family.

The second house was on the Lehr estate at Friedrichsruh, about eight miles north of Memel at the confluence of the Dange and the Bahne. The railway station was Gaussen, on the line that led to Leningrad by way of Riga, and from there it was nearly two miles, which Fritz Lehr and I covered in a horse and trap. The estate, with sawmill and brickyard attached, was in a dilapidated state. The Lehrs had only just got it back; the house, which had been burnt down by the Russians in 1915, had never been rebuilt; Friedrich Lehr had left the overgrown ruins as they were as a visible sign of his indignation at the loss of his cups, and he still wanted to have nothing to do with it. But he had bought back the property for his eldest son, August Wilhelm, who had married the year before and wanted to live there. Reconstruction had begun immediately in March, and the shell of the new house was complete with roofs and windows, and one wing was already inhabitable. It was due to be finished by Christmas, and in fact it was finished, but by that time the war had broken out, and, though the family went there for the sum-mer, they never lived in it, and towards the end of the war

it was destroyed again, and now it is a ruin. I did not like it at the time, even the shell was too grand, too palatial, and I remember the builders making jokes about the seven chimneys.

The adjoining property, the Bahne estate, belonged to Julia's father. All I knew about him was the story about the cups, which Fritz and I again mentioned on the way from the station. We passed the house, but it was invisible behind a thick hawthorn hedge that had been allowed to run wild. The entrance consisted of two huge stone pillars and a double iron gate, which was overgrown with thick matted reeds growing inside. When I think about the place now it is just as if I were back in the house, as if I had walked straight in, and I could describe every timbered ceiling, the leather sofa in the library, the porcelain in the glass case in the hall, which had a brick floor. The first time I drove past the whole place created the impression that, if anyone lived there, it was someone who wanted to be left alone.

According to all the information that I eagerly snapped up in the days that followed, the owner was indeed an eccentric. Karl Gerd von Dressler did not use the honorific 'von', and no-one in the neighbourhood ever referred to him except as the General. He never received visitors, but was on intimate terms with the fishermen, shepherds and stable boys. He bred singing birds and racehorses for the Karlshorst track. But the whole neighborhood knew about the 'book' he kept in which he regularly recorded his dreams; his special interest was premonitions and predictions from whatever source they came. Whenever he heard of any such thing he went to see the person concerned, especially among the fishermen on the lagoon or the shepherds on the edge of the big moor, who seemed to have a special gift for that sort of thing. He tracked down people who had these experiences and, since it was known that he paid well for them, others came to him of their own accord. Some believed that some of them invented stories, because they wanted to have their

name recorded for posterity in his 'book.' But most took it very seriously; at all events, he did.

The 'book' actually consisted of a number of ordinary black notebooks, and he continued with them even after his recall to active service during the war; in particular, he kept them up right through the siege of Stalingrad, so Julia told me; and my mind used often to dwell on this general who, when inspecting his troops' positions in the morning in that terrible winter in the encircled city, would creep into the men's refuges in the ruins and get them to tell him their dreams. This also interested me because somehow it was a link with Julia; it was the sort of thing she might well have done herself, she was perfectly capable of it. Also I should have given anything to know about her dreams. I was never able to find out what happened to the General's notebooks; whether he destroyed them himself before his arrest in July 1944, or whether they were confiscated or destroyed, they never reappeared.

This was not the sort of thing to attract Fritz Lehr to the neighbouring property; from his description of Julia, who was studying medicine at Königsberg with his sister, all I gathered was that she was a very reserved girl, who wore a brace on her teeth. That summer Fritz had other girls in mind. He had bought an old coastguard cutter, and was busy painting and rerigging it, and our intention was to spend a fortnight cruising in the Kurische Haff with two girls on board. The girls who took part in that sort of trip were of a different type. Ever since our school days Fritz Lehr had been the one who had got the girls. In fact, 'I'm going to find some girls' was a favourite expression of his, and on his return from such expeditions he never had to report failure. His favourite hunting ground was the Labour Service camps, and he also kept a notebook with a large number of names and addresses. His type was always the same: rather plump girls, who were generally taller than he and were good at cooking and bed-making; and, to my surprise, they were all

rather common and consequently rather outspoken. Fritz
Lehr wanted nothing to do with well-educated girls from
good homes, who in his opinion only 'complicated' things.

He went off in the *Dange I*, as he christened his boat, with
two girls, but without me; and he did not take my absence
very much amiss, because on the very first day I had broken
a metacarpal bone in my left hand on the building site at
Friedrichsruh. It swelled up pretty badly, and the nearest
doctor was at Bajohren, an hour away. The estate manager's
wife could not guarantee that if *he* dealt with it the bone
would grow together properly again, and she said it would
be much better if she took me to the Fräulein Doctor; and
the way she said *Fräulein Doctor* made it plain how much
she respected her. I did not know she meant Julia; all I was
aware of was that there was a short cut to the neighbouring
house by way of a path that went a little way down a valley
with a stream in it and a lot of alder trees, then across a field
where horses were grazing and along the side of a field of
flax to some labourers' thatched cottages. The path was well
trodden, and it was evident that in spite of the ban there was
a good deal of contact between the two houses, at any rate
among the staff.

My guide handed me over to another woman, with whom
she communicated in a whisper, which increased the mys-
teriousness of the proceedings. Moreover, they talked Russian; the woman who took charge of me was Nyanya, who
had been Julia's nurse. The Russian element predominated
among the General's domestic staff, perhaps because in the
late twenties he had spent several years in Russia in the
service of the Reichswehr, which had secret training areas
there. They all lived in the thatched cottages, and they were
a motley crew. There were former batmen who worked as
grooms, there was a coachman, Nyanya's husband, named
Davidov whom the General had brought back from Russia,
there were Estonian and Lithuanian housemaids, and there

158

were also one or two Germans who were there only because the General wanted to tap their 'premonitory' abilities. All these people constituted his family, so to speak, for Julia's mother was dead, and otherwise there was only an aunt who was in charge of the household, or rather, was supposed to be, because later I generally saw her sitting everlastingly at the same table in her long dress in the big sitting room, always using the same pair of scissors; her face bore a great resemblance to the General's.

With my left arm in a provisional sling, I followed the nurse through an outer garden that had run wild. There were some stone figures overrun with mallows. Soon the house came into sight; it was half country house, half farmhouse, and the timber was painted a strange pale, greyish-red colour; Davidov later explained to me that that precise shade was obtainable only by painting it each spring with the blood of a freshly slaughtered ox. On the gables over the entrance there was a sundial, and the date, 1744.

Nyanya, in her long dark dress and with a dark handkerchief over her head, which she wore in spite of the heat, preceded me into the hall. Here it was cool. Voices were to be heard on the other side of a door; as it happened, Julia's aunt's birthday party was in progress, and Nyanya said she would see whether she could get the 'Fräulein' to come out. . . . She opened the door and left it open, and then I saw Julia in her long pink dress bent over her aunt's hand. When she noticed Nyanya she straightened herself. Nyanya said something and pointed to the door, and the two of them came towards me, Julia first, and I saw her green eyes. . . .

I am afraid I cannot trust my memory of the next few hours. I was in love with her from the first moment. Is that credible? I knew nothing about her. We never talked about love. And yet so it was, so it is in my memory. Perhaps it was because I was only just twenty, and she was twenty-three

I am not sure even if I can trust my memory of the next three weeks. I am quite sure of only two things, the places we went to together and her face.

I had plenty of time to look at her face, from the very first moment when she made me sit on the brown leather sofa and bent over my hand, felt the fracture, considered whether or not an X-ray was necessary, and finally put it in plaster—until that last night when she danced for herself alone. Her face was always serious, concentrated on what she was doing at the moment; it was an almost unrelenting face, apart from that rather dreamy expression that was always present.

She had thick, dark hair, prominent cheek bones, white, strong teeth, and only if one knew that as a child she had for many years worn a brace on her teeth did one notice that her upper jaw was rather prominent. She was certainly what people call a serious beauty, but there is no point in my describing her, because for me it was the most beautiful and most expressive face I had ever seen.

As I have already mentioned, she was working for a medical exam that summer, and she was totally uninterested in everything else. So it was quite natural that I should go and see her again so that she could look at my hand, and that I should then keep her company, which consisted simply in her handing me one of her books, pointing to a passage— about the tendon sheaths of the hand, for instance—and then saying: *the tendon sheaths, vaginae tendinum, allow the tendons to slide smoothly and protect them from friction against the underlying bones. They are tubes of connective tissues lined with what is called the synovial membrane. There are three different kinds, peritenon, epitenon and mesotenon.*

I can still hear the sound of her voice when she said things like *peritenon, epitenon and mesotenon.* When I heard her, she answered with her eyes shut. Whenever I arrived or wherever we went, she was never without her books. I did not care what she talked about, whether it was about psycho-

sensory cortical centres or intra-ocular pressure, all I cared about was being with her.

Her favourite spot was a seat in the outer garden, just in front of the place where her father bred his singing birds. This was a structure that once perhaps had been a winter garden, but had been adapted for its present purpose. The floor was covered with fine white sand that had to be renewed once a week; when the supply ran out Davidov had to drive a cart to the Baltic coast, which was the only place where such fine sand was to be found. The place was also equipped with small trees, swings with mirrors and feeding troughs, and the big window had been removed and replaced, at any rate in the summer, by wire netting. The spot that I remember best is the white painted seat.

To me it seemed most unsuitable for working, because of the distraction of the continual chirping and fluttering of wings behind us, but Julia said it was the place where she could concentrate best; so there we sat, sometimes till late in the evening. She would fetch a light, and often it was so late that even the birds had grown quiet and only her voice was to be heard:

We differentiate between: (a) a field of perception where perceptual impressions arise without their nature being recognised; (b) a field of memory, where recognition, gnosis, of the characteristics of the perceptual images takes place. Thus we proceed by way of perceptual images to memory images.

And, unless I forgot to do so, because I would be looking at her face instead of at the book, I would tell her she had forgotten something; and she would nod very seriously and say: Of course, *the two fields are connected by paths of association.*

Sometimes, at any rate during the first few days, I would try to persuade her to do something else, to go to the seaside for a bathe, for instance, or go on an excursion or play tennis, but I had no success. Once she showed me how fishermen caught eels at night on the *Dange,* and I remember the fires

on the bank over which they smoked the fish. Once she took me with her when she needed frogs for an experiment, and she explained to me the expert way of skinning a rabbit. But it was all the same to me as long as I could just sit beside her and look at her face.

That was all that happened in those three weeks that summer. Or was it? At all events, I cannot remember anything else. It is like a recurrent dream that one cannot influence, it simply is like that and it recurs in the same way. But of course I also remember my last evening there, which was also hers, because they coincided.

I did not see her all day long. I knew she was packing. In the evening I went to say goodbye and to suggest that in the morning she might come with us to Memel in the coastguard cutter; Fritz Lehr had brought it up the river, and it was his idea. I expected her to say no; indeed, I hoped she would, because I did not want to share her with anyone.

As I passed the thatched cottages I heard the sound of music. Actually it was only a single violin, and not even a proper one; it was merely a fiddle with a long neck and only two strings. I had heard music and the clapping of hands in the distance on previous evenings, and the singing had made me think that many instruments were involved. But it was only a single fiddle to which they were dancing in the light of an open fire and the full moon on the hard-trampled earth between the cottages. The fiddler was Davidov; he was wearing an old uniform jacket that was several sizes too big for him, with shining epaulettes; I suspected it was one of the General's cast-offs.

I should have walked by if someone had not called out my name. It was Nyanya, Julia's former nurse. The men were not dancing, but three or four girls were, each by herself. At first I did not recognise Julia, because all the girls were wearing the same long skirts and simple blouses with their hair loose. I looked at the bare feet under the long skirts. One pair was whiter than the others, a pair of white dove's feet among the

162

darker ones; Julia must have removed her shoes later than the others, for she still had them in her hands while she danced, circling sunk into herself, with closed eyes.

Somebody nudged me, and I found myself looking into Nyanya's face; she nodded to me encouragingly, and said:

'Why don't you dance with her?'

I must have looked at her in surprise. She was always there, always on the alert, but I had never really noticed her. I had taken her for an old woman, if only because of her dark clothing and the dark handkerchief she always wore over her head. But now that I was close to her I saw she was not old at all, hardly over forty. She had been nineteen at the time of Julia's mother's death, since then she had taken her place.

I said something like: 'But she'd only say no. She always says no to everything unconnected with her books. There's no point in asking her.'

She smiled at me from under her handkerchief; it was a smile that radiated charm and sharp wits.

'I didn't say you should ask her. I said you should dance with her,' she said. Then she shook her head, and suddenly looked thoughtful and worried. 'She'll never be happy with a man who asks,' she went on. 'She doesn't like being asked.' And I remember that she whispered: 'Poor Julia.'

Poor Julia? At the time that statement meant nothing to me. A girl who danced like that? How could I? It was impossible. I could not interrupt her dancing, especially in front of all the others, so I just stood there next to Nyanya, who had turned out to be a young and pretty woman, and only half listened to her as she went on:

'Why don't you take her away? You're a doctor too, aren't you?'

'No,' I replied with a laugh.

'No? You're not a doctor? I thought you were. I've heard the two of you talking. Couldn't you talk about something else? So you're not a doctor. All the same, take her away.

Someone has got to, not ask her, but just take her away. This is no place for a girl. A father who writes down bad dreams and an old aunt who has never been happy in her life. You don't understand. The only protection against unhappiness is to let yourself be happy. But I know Julia—she thinks you can protect yourself against unhappiness by shutting yourself off from it. Her mother was the same. She was so frightened of unhappiness that she could never be happy. Poor Julia. How can she ever be unhappy if she's never been happy? Take her away. . . .'

But she spoke into the wind. Julia went on dancing, the men went on clapping, Davidov's uniform jacket had burst open over his chest, and he was extracting music from his two strings such as I have never since heard in my life. Even when he stopped, the music in my head went on. Julia too seemed to have to pull herself together to realise where she was. She came over to us with her shoes in her hand. Her face was glowing, I could feel the heat she exuded, she gave it off like a stone that has been all day in the hot sun. When I asked her whether she would dance with me, she dropped her head and said: 'No, I've danced enough, I'm quite giddy,' and went to one of the wooden benches, where she put on her shoes and stockings.

I took her back to the house and invited her to come with us next day but, as I expected, she said no. When I passed the cottages on the way back I saw Davidov and Nyanya dancing together. He had handed over his fiddle to someone else who did not play nearly so well, but Davidov made up for it by the way he whirled round with his wife in his arms so that their feet seemed hardly to touch the ground. When I passed she saw me. She looked at me, and shook her head. She was still smiling, but it was a sad smile.

It all ended with a surprise, almost a touch of bitterness. I told Fritz that evening that Julia had declined the invitation. I don't know whether this stimulated his interest, or whether his curiosity had been aroused when his brother told

him that nothing had been seen of me for the past three weeks; at all events, when I came down to breakfast next morning with my things already packed he had gone, leaving a message that he would wait for me at the landing-stage. I went there alone, it was not far, and you could see the mast of the cutter from a distance across the reedy shore. When I got nearer I heard voices and laughter, and when the landing-stage came into sight where the boat was tied up I saw the two of them on the sun deck; Fritz was explaining to Julia how to set the sails.

'You see, I managed to get her to come,' he said to me later, and I was pleased at the extra hours we should have together. But when I walked down the narrow landing-stage towards the boat and saw them together before they noticed me, I felt a small stab of pain.

Then I did not see her for three and a half years, but I cannot say they were years of separation. We wrote often, I more often than she, I must confess; in the course of time my letters grew more and more frequent and longer and longer. From a distance I found the courage to write what I felt about her. My feelings for her, so far from diminishing, increased; perhaps the fact that I had met her in the last pre-war summer played a part in this. I proposed to her once or twice; she did not accept, but did not break off the correspondence. As I said, she wrote less often than I, but never let too long an interval elapse; she wrote with the regularity of a well brought up girl who knew what was right and proper. The contents of her letters were the same; they were full of news about what she had been doing, the theatres or exhibitions she had been to. She had passed her medical exam with flying colours; her only brother had been shot down in a Stuka over Warsaw and killed; she had passed her qualifying exam; her father had returned to the active list, and she had followed him to Berlin, where she was working in a military hospital; she was going on working

165

with a view to specialising in surgery. The Bahne estate was deserted, even the birds had had to be released. . . . It was titbits of factual information of this kind, most of it communicated quite unemotionally, that made me feel that after all these years I really knew very little more about her, in spite of the accumulated bundles of letters. Occasionally she mentioned Fritz Lehr; she had seen him briefly, had had dinner or gone to the theatre with him; these were just items of news, like the rest. At the end of January 1943 I saw her again for the first time.

I had a short convalescent leave after an attack of dysentery in Africa. On previous leaves I had never managed to see her; either she was not in Berlin or something else cropped up. It seemed possible that she was avoiding me, so this time I simply telephoned and asked her whether we might not meet, as I was passing through Berlin. But of course we could, as I was just passing through, she said, she would be delighted to see me, when was I arriving? Very well, then, she would wait for me in the first class waiting room, that was the best place, as the trains were so often late nowadays.

January 21 was a cold day, and the train was more than two hours late, because of snow drifts on the track and jammed brakes. When it at last drew into the Anhalter station I wondered whether she would still be waiting, and whether I should see her at all. I knew from her last letters that she was very worried about her father, who was in Stalingrad, where a major Russian assault on the surrounded armies had begun two days previously. Everything was so different from the old days that it seemed as if not years but whole decades had passed.

I was still full of gloomy thoughts while the Military Police examined my papers at the barrier. But then, as soon as I caught sight of the revolving door of the waiting room, I forgot them all and made a dash for it, crashing into people and making them look round at me and shake their heads.

I spotted her at once. I can still hear the sound of the

rickety revolving door behind me, and I know that the waiting room was overcrowded, smoky, and hot after the coldness
of the train. She was sitting at a table near the door and,
though she had been waiting for more than two hours, she
had not taken off her coat or fur hat. A moment passed before she noticed me, so I had a chance to look at her closely.
Her face was more serious than ever and her eyes more deep
set, but I had already done this for her in my imagination,
so that the intervening years suddenly vanished; the only
surprise was that there was a reddish gleam in her hair, or
what was visible of it under her fur hat; I had always believed
it to be quite dark.

I remained standing at the table, expecting that she would
rise and we should go off together; I had never been to her
Potsdam flat, but I visualised it; I imagined she had laid the
table and put candles on it, and in one of her letters she had
mentioned that the district railway ran right below her windows, which had given me the idea that we should be awak-
ened in the morning by the noise.

'Won't you sit down? she said. 'What sort of journey have
you had?'

One chair was still vacant at the table, and I sat down. A
woman in a turban was asleep with her face resting on her
left elbow on the table while her right arm hung down; in her
sleep she was still grasping the handle of her trunk, which
was tied up with thick string. A very young soldier with a
pale face and army spectacles suddenly looked very disappointed. I don't remember the others.

'I'm sorry you had to wait so long.'

'Why? Two hours' complete peace, with nobody knowing
where I am and nobody to worry me. I don't know how long
it is since the last time that happened. I ought to come and
just sit here more often.' She looked at me, and smiled. 'Are
you disappointed?'

'Why should I be?'

'At the way I look.'

She felt the lapels of her coat, and I noticed that under it she had on her doctor's white coat. Her hands were noticeable because of big white moons on the nails. She seemed not to mind our not being alone, and I was beginning to forget it myself.

'You're beautiful,' I said.

'When is your train going on?'

'You're as beautiful as ever.'

'Really?'

'Yes. Couldn't we go somewhere? I can stay longer, as it happens.'

'It will be difficult to meet. I'm on duty for practically twelve hours a day, and afterwards I'm no good for anything, I'm practically wiped out.'

I tried to give her time, and asked about her work, and I know I was surprised that there was an undertone of mockery in her reply, for her work had always seemed to me to take precedence over everything. 'I do what is expected of a woman in these times—I do my duty. How long have you got?'

'Three days. Three times twenty-four hours.' To me it sounded like an eternity.

'I'd ask you home, but I'm only a sub-tenant, it's practically only a single room.'

'I could go to a hotel somewhere near.'

'It's very difficult to find a hotel room, they're all so over-crowded.'

This time I smiled.

'I'll find a room somewhere. You can always get a room in one of the big hotels. May I?'

'What?'

I bent forward to take off her fur hat, but she leant back and would not let me.

'Please take it off,' I said. 'You have such beautiful hair, take it off just for a moment, please. I like your hair.'

I had totally forgotten our surroundings. She removed her

168

hat and held it on her lap. The edge had left a mark in her hair. It was freshly washed, and I remembered Nyanya always complaining that she washed it much too often.

'How are things at home? Have you been back?'

'No, not for a long time.'

I realised that she did not want to talk about it.

'And your father? Have you news of him?'

'He's alive. They flew him out a fortnight ago. Didn't I write and tell you?'

'No. Lucky for him.'

'I don't know; I mean, I don't know whether it was a good thing for him or not. He was one of the officers who pressed for permission to break out of Stalingrad while it was still possible. He says it was a crime to stay there, totally senseless and a crime. And he doesn't just think it, he says so, I've never known him so beside himself. He's risking his neck by talking like that, or if he's lucky they'll just send him back to his estate. But I don't dare go on hoping that. We're an unlucky family, and we bring bad luck to others. You don't believe there are such people? But it's true.'

Once more she spoke in a tone that was new to her; there was a bitterness about it that, for all her seriousness, had never been there before.

'But that's nonsense,' I said. 'You're tired and overstrained, and it's natural you should be worried about your father.'

'My mother . . . Did you know she committed suicide? No, you didn't, that's something that was never talked about. The reason was absurd. She believed father had had an affair in Berlin. Too absurd, because all he was ever interested in was horses, singing birds and dreams; and, even if he had had an affair, that was all it was, and in any case it was long since over. Someone told her about it, and she worked herself up about it and committed suicide. But she was my mother, you see, I'm always afraid there may be something of her in me.'

There was nothing I could say, and I was again suddenly

169

aware of the surroundings, the waiting room, the people, the bespectacled young soldier who was listening open-mouthed.

'Before my brother took off on his last flight he wrote me a letter,' she went on. 'It was practically a letter of farewell, full of gloomy forebodings. It was dated the day of his death. Do you still say we're made for happiness?'

I remember what Nyanya had said on that last evening. *How can one ever be unhappy if one has never been happy?* She had also said: *Take her away.* I suddenly knew what I must do, and that only I could do it, and that I must do it now, before it was too late.

'But Julia, how can one talk like that? Do you know what we're going to do? You're going to take three days leave and we'll go to the estate. Even if we can only spend a day there. You said you haven't been there for a long time. Wouldn't you like to go back and see the house and Davidov and Nyanya?'

'No!' she exclaimed violently. 'No!'

The woman in the turban started, and people all round us turned their heads. Julia sat there as if turned to stone, and it suddenly struck me that in her letters she had never mentioned her former nurse; this was strange, as the two had been so close. But I was not prepared for what came next.

'But why? . . . What has happened to Nyanya?'

'She's dead. Both of them are dead, she and Davidov, and it's probably lucky for them that they are dead.'

Again she spoke in that bitter, mocking voice.

'But what happened?' I asked quietly, in a whisper, to avoid attracting still more attention.

'They give no information about that,' she said, and laughed bitterly. 'If on top of it they gave information, that would cap everything.'

'They?'

170

She looked at me searchingly, as if she must first make sure of me before replying.

'Yes, *they*. They killed them both. Those murderers killed them both.'

The woman at our table was now completely awake and was looking at us. I noticed that the soldier in the spectacles got up and made his way towards the exit, and I also noticed that he left his luggage behind. I took Julia by the arm and led her away from the table. A waitress pursued us and began upbraiding us, until I realised that it was only because Julia had had a cup of coffee for which she had not yet paid. I took her into the other waiting room. We climbed over piles of luggage that blocked the free space between the tables. Then at last we reached the crowded station concourse, and I felt better, though in my mind's eye I could still see the young soldier and the change that had come over him—the tense interest with which he had listened, then the shock, and then the grim determination that came over him and, strangely enough, made him look younger than ever.

'What happened? Tell me what happened. Who would want to kill them, and why?'

'I'm sorry, I didn't want to talk about it, I was determined not to. It doesn't change anything if we talk about it. What made me start talking about it?'

She put on her fur hat. The fur was reddish, like that of a fox. Her coat was rather short, and the white doctor's coat was visible underneath. She wore black flat shoes and thick, dark stockings. That time she had danced with bare feet. Perhaps it would be better if she didn't talk about it. Perhaps I didn't want to hear about it. Davidov had held Nyanya in his arms and whirled her round so that their feet hardly touched the ground.

'We were all away,' she went on. 'Father, I, my aunt, none of us were there when we were needed. I think perhaps we

171

might have prevented it, perhaps father might have been able to prevent it. He certainly would have tried. He knew, he was one of the few who knew, but he never expected anything would happen to her. She was my nurse. She was practically one of the family.'

The crowds milling round us were like a stream that carried us to the entrances to the platforms and away again, and sometimes we seemed to be caught up in a whirlpool, so that I had the feeling we were going round and round. A voice on the loudspeaker announced the late arrival of trains.

'She was simply Nyanya, Russian Nyanya, nobody worried about her being a Jewess, as if it were impossible for a Russian woman to be also a Jewess; and, as I said, hardly anyone knew she was a Jewess. There were many Jews in our area, some had always been there and others had fled there. My father knew them well, he always said they understood horses, and also he liked dealing with them. We noticed what happened after 1939, of course, suddenly so-and-so and so-and-so were missing, and it was worrying, of course, but basically not more than that at the time. And none of us worried about Nyanya, particularly when more than two years passed and nothing happened.'

She adjusted her fur hat. She wore no gloves, and two fingers of her left hand were numb because of the cold. I took her hand and held it in my coat pocket.

'They came for her six months ago. We don't know who, but someone must have denounced her. They arrested her and interrogated her, and she's said to have admitted immediately she was a Jewess. They sent her to a camp at Riga. I heard about it only afterwards, bit by bit, and I went to Riga. I really thought I should be able to do something for them there.'

'And Davidov? Was he too a . . . ?'

'No. But when they came to take Nyanya away and he couldn't stop them—I know he had a gun, the shot-gun he

172

shot rabbits with—but there were too many of them, and I was told he raged and shouted that they should take him too, because he too was a Russian Jew. It would have taken more than two men to overpower him, and they told me that he calmed down only when they said, very well, then, he could come too if he wanted to. So they took him to Riga too. I don't know whether they were left together. I don't know where they died, or when; I don't believe that story about their trying to escape. My father telephoned and sent telegrams and stormed and raged as only he can, until someone came to see him and gave him to understand that he had better show more restraint, and in any case it was too late to do anything about it, because both of them had been shot while trying to escape.'

I sought for something to say, and the strange thing was that I could not get out of my head the memory of Davidov in his old uniform jacket with the shining epaulettes that had burst open at the chest with Nyanya in his arms; even the sound of the fiddle was in my ears, and the tune, which was gay and light and rather jerky. I felt indignation and guilt, but the fiddle went on playing in my head, and I saw it and its long neck and two strings and the bow, from which the white horsehair stood out, so wildly did Davidov play.

They were dead, both of them were dead, and yet this seemed as good a moment as any other to tell Julia I loved her. I put my arm round her and kissed her. We were at the station, and there were many round us who were saying goodbye and doing the same. She did not seem surprised, she did not try to stop me, she put her arms round my shoulders and we kissed, and then she looked at me, almost incredulously, and said:

'Is it true? Do you really love me?' Her hat had slipped from her brow, but this time she did not try to straighten it. *Take her away.*

'Yes,' I said. 'It's true, and it always will be. Will you marry me?'

This did not seem to surprise her either. She did something remarkable. She took my hands and put them to her lips.

'My darling,' she said, 'my friend, my dreamer. How can it still be possible? How can one still live in dreams? Was it my Nyanya who put the idea in your head?'

'Will you?'

'What?'

'Marry me?'

'In these times? There's too much pain in the world already.'

'In that case no-one could get married any longer.'

She looked around, as if the answer lay in what she saw.

'You've got to go again. You say you've got three days, and then you've got to go again. Something might happen to you, it might even happen tomorrow. People get killed in war, and many who have not been killed wish they were dead. I see it every day, I'm reminded of it every hour of the day in my work. Something might happen to me too . . . and one of us would be left, with three days to remember.'

'But you do love me?'

'Yes, I love you.'

'Then I don't understand.'

'Please try. I wish I were different. I wish I could be different and could forget everything, but I can't.'

She glanced at the station clock.

'I must go now,' she said.

'When shall we see each other?'

She had said she loved me, which was more than I had expected.

'It will be better if we don't see each other again.'

'But we could at least go out this evening. We could go and have dinner somewhere. When do you come off duty? I'll fetch you.'

'No, please don't fetch me.'

174

She mentioned a restaurant where we could meet, and then I took her to her train. Her fur hat was still out of place.

I found a room in a hotel in Potsdam, near her flat. I slept a few hours, because I had been travelling all night. I dreamt about Davidov and Nyanya, and woke up bathed in sweat. In the afternoon I could no longer stand it and took the district railway out to Werder, where her hospital was.

I had been to Werder once before, in spring, when the trees were in blossom, for which it was noted, but today it was bitterly cold. There was no snow on the ground, but the trees were full of hoar-frost from the dampness of the lake and the mist. I asked the way to the military hospital, and had to go through narrow alleyways and climb steps until I found the converted school. I discovered that Julia worked in the neurosurgical unit; she had not mentioned this in her letters, but it was typical of her to choose such work.

They sent me down corridors with wax-polished floors to the operating theatres, where I waited for more than an hour, surrounded by hospital smells and noises. I watched the lights going on and off over the doors. Lift doors were opened and shut. Medical orderlies and nurses passed, pushing stretcher-trollies, with shaved heads lying under the white sheets and others with blood-soaked bandages; in many cases the bandages left only the eyes, nose and mouth free. The smell, the noise of the stretcher-trolley wheels, the murmur of voices, and the thought of what was going on on the operating tables behind the swing doors made me feel ill. But I did not regret having come. Sitting on the bench and waiting for her, I understood a little more about the life she was leading. I realised what she meant when she said at the station, under the impact of her daily work,

175

that she could not marry someone who would be leaving her after three days. When she did not appear after an hour, I left without seeing her.

That evening I did not mention I had been to the hospital; and we did not mention Davidov and Nyanya again. I don't know what we talked about, it was nothing but trivialities. I know she was tired, dead-beat, and also I remember what she said when I took her home and we said goodbye at the door. Once more she asked me to go and not come back again.

'I know that if you stayed, if you came with me now, I should change my mind, and I don't want to, please try and understand,' she said.

Should I not have listened to her? I should certainly not have gone out to Werder that afternoon.

Next morning I telephoned her at her flat, but she had already left for the hospital. I tried to call her there, but could not be put through. I was told to try again during the midday break, which began at one o'clock. So I went out to Werder again, and the first thing I saw was the black Mercedes parked outside the entrance. There were few such cars with a civilian number at that time, and the chauffeur at the wheel was Winter. I suspected what was going to happen, and watched from a side street opposite. I did not have long to wait. Fritz Lehr came through the doorway, with Julia at his side. He was in uniform, a brand new, tailored naval uniform, and he had a naval dagger in his belt. Winter jumped out of the car and opened the door for them. I could of course simply have emerged from my hiding place and gone across and greeted them. I don't know why I didn't do it. Instead I stood there as if rooted to the spot. He looked so distinguished and smart in his new uniform and, who knows, perhaps he might have expected me to salute him, as he was my senior in rank. I heard him telling Winter to drive to a well-known restaurant, and then I watched them get in and drive away.

I left Berlin by the next train. In her next letter she mentioned that Fritz Lehr had unexpectedly come to Berlin for a day, and that she had seen him. The letter was nearly three weeks on the way. By that time I had long since been back in Africa, where Rommel had had to give up the Buerat position and Tripoli and withdraw to the Mareth Line on the Tunisian-Tripolitanian border. In the middle of February he counter-attacked in the direction of Tebessa. We took the Casserine Pass, Faid, Hafsa and Feriana, and outside Thala there was one more big tank battle. Those were the last victories of which I took pictures. They were excellent pictures; I have been told that I never took better in my life. But then there were no more victories, but only rearguard actions—and the second-lieutenant in the British 11th Hussars who pumped three rounds into me with his sub-machine gun and nearly killed me. But it was not to be, and for some undiscoverable reason one last aircraft turned up, and in Athens Dr. Blum removed the bullets and fragments, and two months later I married Thea.

XIII

The three musicians who had been left behind had long since given up playing, and the couples had withdrawn under the awning on the terrace. It was cooler now, and the electric radiators had been switched on. The smell of grilling meat and fish came from the barbecues. Every now and then snatches of music came from the steamer that was still cruising on the lake. Slow pictures were still following one another on the television screens. A thriller was being shown on one programme and there was singing on the other; the catering staff audience was now bigger. Soon after ten o'clock it was announced that according to the latest calculations the Social Democrats and Free Democrats together were four seats ahead. But no-one seemed very worried.

Three men were sitting at the bar. One of them was Blum, whose wife had attracted so much attention at my table. The second was the television chief whose wife had been so anxious about his over-eating. He was drinking and, no doubt stimulated by drink, was demonstrating a strange adroitness in throwing salted almonds into his mouth three or four at a time. As soon as the plate was empty the bartender refilled it without being asked. The third was a well-known television film maker. He too was drunk, and was uninterruptedly making speeches at the television chief I could hear what he said.

'The trouble is that it's people like you who are sitting at the controls. *We're* the people who know something about the job, but it's people like you who have the say-so, have no understanding of the medium but throw their weight about and make decisions. It makes me sick. People like you make me sick. People like you are the last people I want to talk to.'

But he went on talking to him, and the television chief quietly went on with his game with the almonds. I almost envied them their drunkenness.

I sat on an empty stool next to Blum. The barman asked me what I wanted, but Blum answered for me.

'Don't bother, he doesn't drink,' he said. 'That's his trouble, he sticks to his principles, he knows too much about what drink would do to his liver. Those are the most ungrateful patients. I cut out two-thirds of his stomach, and you'd never believe the interrogation he put me through afterwards.'

⸺ I had never imagined Dr. Blum, that distinguished professor of surgery, drunk, but apparently I had a weakness for drunks that evening, because I nodded to the barman and said:

'Give me a drink.'

'What would you like?'

'The same as he.'

He put down a glass in front of me and refilled the professor's.

'To your liver,' he said, raising his glass. 'It'll stand a drop.'

'If you think so.'

I drank the Greek brandy, and was surprised at being able to swallow it. I had another, and felt a slight sensation of giddiness, but it was not a disagreeable sensation.

'You haven't let me examine you for a long time,' he said. He leaned towards me, swaying slightly, and pulled down my eyelid with his forefinger. 'Tongue out. Dreadful!' he said, and smiled. 'It's really time you came to see me again.

179

It's more than a year since I saw you in my consulting room.'

'I've been intending to make an appointment.'

It was good to see him like this. At the hospital he was a tyrant and a star, as he had already been in Athens, where he went about only in snow-white uniforms. He was then married to a German opera singer, a coloratura soprano who often appeared in Athens. Not that I cared, or resented his prima donna behaviour. He was a virtuoso, and when he operated on me in Athens he saved my life. Not that I attached much importance to living, either then or tonight, but all the same his skill, the way he did his work, deserved respect.

When the famous Herr Professor paced the corridors of the hospital, followed by a swarm of young doctors, and went to the patients' bedside and told them to put their tongue out, it was certainly a sight to be seen. The fact that a specialist of his eminence bothered about the state of their tongues, just like an ordinary general practitioner, inspired the patients with confidence. Perhaps the whole performance was carefully calculated, but why should it not be? People, sick people, want to be impressed, and how he impressed them. Perhaps that contributed more than anything else to his enormous reputation.

I liked him; perhaps most of all because he had a wife who was forty years younger than he and was now out in the steamer on the lake while he sat here worrying what she might be up to. He was worrying, and how. I could tell, without pulling down his eyelid. Normally I should never have asked the question, but now, sitting on the uncomfortable bar stool with a third glass in my hand, I included myself in the fraternity of the drunk.

'You've got a marvellous wife,' I said. 'I sat next to her at dinner, she's really marvellous. Do you just leave her alone like this?'

He turned his back to the bar. Through the trees you

180

could see the dark surface of the lake and the lights on the opposite bank. Some of the lights must have been those of the steamer.

'You've never been very good at concealing your real thoughts,' he said. 'You're wondering why she married a man forty years older than herself, aren't you?'

I emptied the third glass.

'Yes,' I said.

'She's a lovely girl, isn't she?' he said.

'So I've noticed. Nobody could help it.'

'Everyone wonders, the nurses at the hospital, my secretaries, all my colleagues' widows who were after me. They all want to know why the devil she married me. I'll tell you. It's my grey hairs. No, really, believe me. Grey is in, as they say. Young women nowadays are all for grey. The cult of youth is over and done with. The young men make the foam, but we make the waves. All those young firebrands have had it. They've lost their mystique, and it's we ancient patriarchs who are now in possession of the secret doctrine, it's we they enthuse about, and only we can grant them absolution.'

He looked at me, smiled tipsily, drank, and said:

'I'm talking tripe. Absolute tripe. Between ourselves, I'm sitting here feeling quite sick at the thought of what she might be doing at this moment.'

He looked out into the night as if he could see through it. Perhaps he could, which was why he needed another drink. I sympathised with him.

'Then why did you marry her?'

'Why? Yes, why? I hardly have any time for her, the hospital and the practice take up all of it. When I come home in the evening, I'm done for. There she is, sitting and waiting, and I'm nearly dropping off to sleep. It was the craziest thing I could have done, but people do crazy things. We live to do crazy things. Don't tell anyone. Don't tell anyone that *I* said anything like that. A doctor shouldn't say

things like that. But it's the truth, the whole truth. . . . Of course I've got something to offer her; I'm invited everywhere. I'm on every guest list, I get invitations to first nights and receptions, and she enjoys that; she can wear her new clothes, and I go because I see how much she enjoys herself. One must be fair. She gives me the feeling that I'm still capable of doing crazy things.' He drank, and went on: 'What do you think was the matter with me before? I was deadly serious. My sons and daughters were grown up, and I had a good wife. When I came home in the evening they all crept about on tip-toe and were full of concern for me. My house-jacket. My slippers. *Please keep quiet, father's home, he's had another exhausting day.* With her I come home all in, my head full of problems, furious with my colleagues, and before I've taken my coat off there she is, looking radiant and wanting to know where we're going tonight. You feel more dead than alive, but she twitters round wanting to know what she's to wear this evening, and you go with her and feel very much better. It's crazy, but marvellous. You should try it.'

'I'm thinking of doing so.'

He looked at me in surprise. I was no less surprised at having said it. Perhaps it was the drink.

'Then let me give you a thorough examination first.'

'Next week?'

'Ring for an appointment. I shan't keep you waiting. I've got a marvellous new thing, a computer test, I brought it back from America, you're just the right case for it. But I'll give you a piece of advice straight away, free of charge, a piece of advice you'd never get from me in my consulting room. How old is she? I mean, how much younger is she than you?'

'Twenty-six years.'

'You're fifty, aren't you? Well, your problem isn't as big as mine, but all the same. Forget everything I've told you. The situation is much simpler.' He bent forward, and was

suddenly completely serious. 'The whole secret, Pikola, is having money,' he said. 'All you need is a great deal of money, and the greater the difference in age the more money you need. Money attracts them, and it's money that keeps them. . . . Damn it, man, don't look at me so indignantly. It's the simple truth. I'm not drunk. I'm never soberer than when I have been drinking and see her enjoying herself with young men. It's simply a fact you've got to face. There's nothing wrong about it, it's not immoral. I'm happy with her, but it's the money that attracts them and keeps them, and don't you forget it.' He turned to the bar and pointed to the empty glasses. 'Give us another two, please.'

The thriller on the television was over. The leaves on the trees over the sets might have been made of metal. The latest news was that the Social Democrats and Free Democrats combined were eight seats ahead, and a professor with a classical German name and a bundle of papers under his arm said to a reporter: 'If that is the majority, I should say that we should do it.' He did not say what it was that they should do, but perhaps that had been anticipated in the reporter's questions. The steamer was now quite close in, the band on board was playing, and the skipper gave the signal for drawing alongside. The charcoal grill attendants switched on the electric bellows. The air was full of the smell of burning fat, and I saw more cats prowling about than ever.

XIV

The first thing I saw were the photographs of the garden party that Julia had left on the table. There were two of them; one showed Julia and me, and the other Julia and Fritz Lehr. In both we were looking at the camera and, as so often in flashlight photographs, the faces looked distorted, almost deranged. I no longer remembered their being taken, I was no longer even sure that they dated from the evening before. When I looked at them I felt nothing, remembered nothing; I had to look at the date to convince myself that they had been taken yesterday. But *yesterday* meant something quite different. I had been much further away, and I still was.

On the way back with Julia I talked about that summer. What interested her most was the 'book,' the collection of notebooks in which the General recorded his and other people's dreams. She asked what had happened to them, but I did not know. I could have told her more, but did not. I could not, I was not yet ready. I was not yet ready even to remember it all myself. I had buried it, wiped out the place it occupied in my memory, but it had been resurrected.

Julia went on to Munich the same evening. She wanted to finish her Holbein, and also she wanted to look at some flats; she would telephone if she found anything that looked suitable. And I had to make an appointment with Dr. Blum. Also I had to have things out at last with Thea.

I woke up late, long after she had gone to work. I fetched

184

the post, and looked through it at breakfast. It consisted of the usual circulars, and a telegram which had been sent the day before; a newspaper wanted photographs of children's fashions for its weekend coloured supplement. It was the sort of job I hated, and I decided to refuse it. But then I remembered what Blum had said last night, so I telephoned the office in Hamburg and asked what fee they were offering. They told me, I promptly asked for double and, to my surprise, they agreed without arguing; this had never happened to me before, but then I had never asked for double before. I rang up an agency and told them how many and which children I needed; I suggested taking the pictures in the Munich zoo, with the enclosures in the background, elephants and zebras and flamingoes, and also outside the big monkey cage. I had suggested this rather as a joke, but they thought the idea *simply brilliant*. Afterwards I felt like taking my cameras and smashing them once and for all.

I had brought the material for the commemorative volume back with me. There was nothing more for me to do with it. I tried telephoning Lehr, but he had gone out and had left a message saying he had not forgotten and would be getting in touch with me. I tore up the photographs of the evening before, and went into the other room and stood in front of the grey filing cabinets containing the thousands of photographs I had taken in the course of my life. I pulled open the drawers and took out some of them, but they meant nothing to me; I was looking at people and places that had withdrawn, dissociated themselves from me.

Once I must have believed that by photography I was preserving experiences, documenting them, but now just the opposite seemed to me to be the case—by preserving these people in pictures I had dissociated myself from them, pushed them away from myself. What was the point of turning experience into paper, reducing it, enlarging it, cutting it out and touching it up? Once more I felt a strong desire to destroy it all.

There was an old-fashioned writing bureau in my room. I opened it up and looked for an old sealed envelope. It had lain there for more than twenty years. I tore it open and took out the three negatives. I felt a strange pain in my hands as I touched them; these three photographs, I thought, were perhaps the only ones in my life that counted. It was true, at any rate at that moment. They marked a break in my life, as if I had had two lives, one before I took them and one afterwards. At all events, they had certainly changed my life.

I laid the negatives side by side on the retouching table. They were overexposed and shaky, but they had been taken with trembling hands, for it was fear, sheer unadulterated fear, that I felt when I crept under the trucks in the siding to take photographs of the camp. It was early morning, and the inmates were drawn up for roll-call in front of the huts, surrounded by guards with rifles slung on their shoulders. There were perhaps two hundred human figures in the photograph, and one of them was Julia, and I wondered whether it would be sensible to try to make an enlargement and eliminate all the other figures so as to be able to show her daughter the last and only picture that existed of her mother.

But that too was only photography—of an event, of sufferings, that were unimaginable and incommunicable; even I, who had taken these pictures, at that moment felt only what *I* had felt, the fear, the sharp gravel that cut into my knees, the sweat that broke out all over my body in spite of the coldness of the morning, the fear in my hands clasping the camera. . . . While I stood there bending over the pictures it all came back. Between me and the past there had always been a barrier, a protective layer, a security cordon. But in the past few weeks it had dwindled and dwindled and grown more and more porous, and it was now a thin membrane, so thin that henceforth past and present were in almost direct contact.

186

At the time of my wedding Julia had sent me a greetings telegram with her congratulations, and her letters continued to arrive, the same letter as before. But then, in the summer of 1944, they had grown rarer, and the tone changed; they were more reticent, and then they stopped completely. One day I telephoned her at home and actually heard her voice, which seemed unchanged, but what she said to me was not. She said only a few words; 'Don't ring again, and don't write. You'll hear from me when it's all right,' and then she rang off.

I waited, but heard no more from her. My letters were returned unopened, marked 'Addressee gone away, present address unknown.' I tried telephoning again, but a strange woman's voice that sounded nervous and frightened said that no Fräulein Dr. Dressler had ever lived there, and then I was cut off. I rang the military hospital at Werder, and there I was passed from one person to another and ended by getting no information whatever. I could think of no possible explanation, until I saw in the newspaper the first sentences passed by the People's Court on the 'scoundrels, traitors and cowardly murderers' involved in the attempted anti-Hitler *coup* of July 20; I immediately spotted the name of Karl Gerd von Dressler; they had put in the honorific *von* to which he attached so little importance. He had been condemned to death and the sentence had been carried out on 4 September 1944.

Such sentences were said to involve confiscation of the deceased's property and the arrest of members of his family, but no confirmation was obtainable. I did not find out what had happened to Julia until the day Fritz Lehr came to Augsburg.

They gave me eight days special leave; such a thing still actually existed in February 1945 if one had a good and sufficient reason, and the death of a parent counted as such a reason. The raid on Augsburg was carried out by about a

hundred four-engined Flying Fortresses, and there were about two hundred deaths in the city.

It was a possibility on which one had always had to count. After these raids I always tried to telephone my parents at once, but on February 26 it was impossible to get through, and not till next day did I hear from my father what had happened. Two bombs had reduced the house to rubble and killed everyone in it. My father owed his life to the fact that he was out in the country trying to scrounge some extra food—a task for which he was ill-fitted, for he generally came back practically empty-handed.

The funeral took place on February 28, the first warm day, a real foretaste of spring; one reason why I remember it so well is that I arrived at the cemetery much too early and overheard the conversation of two men who were digging a mass grave; they were greatly relieved at the change in the weather and were congratulating themselves on the fact that the soil had thawed; they kept reminding each other what a business it had been after the raid of January 16, when there had been many deaths and the soil had been frozen solid.

I shall not go into the details of the funeral, the speeches and the handshaking. At last my father and I were left alone by the graveside. The cemetery was in the middle of the city, and eventually we left too. Just as we walked out into the street the big, long, black Mercedes drew up and Fritz Lehr got out, came up to us, expressed his condolences to my father, and then looked at me and asked whether he could talk to me. He was in civilian clothes; after the death of his eldest brother he had been exempted from military service. Everything about him, his shirt, tie, pullover, jacket, was smart, expensive, of peace-time quality, and I still remember—as if it were of any importance—that he wore shoes with crêpe soles; I still have in my ears the sound they made as he walked beside me between the graves. He himself suggested that we should go back into the cemetery

after my father had insisted on going off alone, which he said he had been intending to do in any case.

I noticed that Winter was there, which was some sort of an omen; and so we went back into the cemetery and walked between the graves, and I realised that he thought it an excellent place to talk, for no-one would take any notice of us there or listen to what we were saying.

'Tell me,' he said, without beating about the bush. 'Do you know what has happened to Julia?'

This took me completely by surprise. I told him I knew what had happened to her father, but had no news of her. He walked to a bench and sat down.

'She's alive,' he said, and it sounded exactly as if he had said she was dead. I froze in my overcoat. He wiped his brow, as if he were sweating. A Fritz Lehr who was afraid was something new to me, but he must have been afraid, because he kept on looking all round to make sure we were alone, and he stopped talking whenever anyone went by.

'She's alive,' he repeated. 'I've known it only for a few days. I've been trying to get in touch with you. Gottfried told me . . .' He then started talking about my mother, remembering things of long ago, as if he did not realise we had just buried her. It was all very strange and confusing, he spoke of Julia as if she were dead and of my mother as if she were alive.

'What has happened to her?'

'I know no details. Her father was put on the unemployed list after Stalingrad and went back to the Dange estate. He's said to have belonged to the inner ring of the plotters. . . . I mean the resistance. At any rate, that's what I was told, and there's no way of confirming it, but he must have been initiated into their plans, because he was at the top of their list. They arrested him in Berlin. Julia was on the estate, and they arrested her there.'

'Did she turn to you for help?' I suddenly remembered him, in his brand-new naval uniform with that ridiculous

189

dagger, coming down the steps with her by his side and saying to Winter *to Horchers*. 'Did she write to you?'

'No. I heard all this at Friedrichsruh. I went there once from Libau after I was released from the service. People were naturally talking about it. She was said to have been taken to Riga.'

'Riga?'

'Please, I beg of you, there's no reason why we shouldn't talk quietly. Yes, Riga, there must be a camp there.'

Riga reminded me of many things, including what Julia had said about her family. Now they were all dead, but she was alive.

'You said she was alive.'

'Yes.'

He sat back and let his shoulders sag; he still had his silver cigarette case in his hand. He looked tired.

'Where is she?'

'Here.'

'Here?'

'Yes, here. In a camp. Please, let me explain. The Todt Organisation has been constructing underground bunkers to be used for aircraft production. It's all too late, but you must look at it from the point of view of last spring; when it was decided on, it was just about the most important construction site in the Reich. A whole series of firms is involved, ours among them. The idea is to provide floor-space for the aircraft industry. . . .'

He went off into a lot of technical details, flew off at a tangent, and started telling me about the aircraft to be produced there. This was top secret among top secrets; he seemed to derive satisfaction from risking his neck by revealing state secrets to a third party. I did not press or interrupt him, for I too needed time.

'The main problem from the outset was where the labour was to come from. First they were going to bring in Italians, then building squads from the Atlantic Wall, then workers

from western or eastern Europe, but in the end there was no alternative to using what was still available.' He sat up and looked at me. 'The individual firms involved had nothing whatever to do with it. It was decided at the top. They're evacuating all the camps in the east and bringing them here in train-loads, and she must have come with one of them.'

'When was that?'

'At the end of September last year, I believe, but I can't be absolutely sure.'

'Why not? Haven't you talked to her?'

'How could I possibly do that?'

'You said she was in a labour camp.'

'Yes, in a camp. But we have nothing to do with the camps. They're run by the SS. They're taken under guard to the working sites, and they're kept under guard all day long. The firms involved do not have the right to inspect the camps. Nobody is admitted except a few men who deliver the rations, and the guards. I told you, the camps are run by the SS.'

I could not help thinking of what Julia had told me about Nyanya.

'What are they—Jews?' I asked.

'Listen, it makes no difference to me what they are. They're not allotted to the firms involved as Jews, or enemies of the state, or anything else, but simply as labour, and I've always said they must be decently treated, I mean, if there's ever any chance to do such a thing. What's the use of people who collapse from hunger on the construction sites?'

'She's working on a construction site?'

'If she were, it might perhaps be possible to get into contact with her; it would be difficult, but perhaps it might be possible, though I don't know how it would help her. No, there are two women's camps at the triangular junction at Kaufering. Women work on the building sites too, but she looks after the sick. During the winter the situation has

badly deteriorated. One train-load from the east introduced typhus into the place. There's a great deal of trouble about disposing of the dead, but that I'll spare you. In practice we're working with one-third of our nominal strength. New train-loads keep arriving, but the state they're in . . .'

He was off at a tangent again, talking about restrictions, procurement difficulties, the petrol shortage, and again I was grateful for the respite and let him go on. But he came back to the subject quickly enough.

'You know Oldewaage? You met him once in Berlin at a lantern lecture, you remember? At all events, he's concerned with the burials, and has been deputed by the firms to introduce a bit of system into it. He has been trying for weeks to get a mobile crematorium, you'd never believe the amount of paper warfare involved, and on top of it he exposes himself to the charge of interfering in things that don't concern him. . . . Well, he has no access to the camps, but at one of those conferences he saw her. He's absolutely certain it was she, even though he knew her only fleetingly from before the war. But he swears it was she.'

'When was that?'

'Three weeks ago. But he didn't come and tell me immediately. He says he first had to get over the shock of seeing her among all those Polish and Jewish women. Whether what her father did was high treason or not, she's still a German and a general's daughter. Well, Oldewaage was utterly shattered. He says we must do something, we must get her out.' For a moment he fell into the role of daredevil, as if he were suggesting some adventure, rather as in the old days when we raced the firm's cars on the closed Avus speedway outside Berlin, or even when he said in the evening after a tournament, well, now I'll go and organise us a couple of girls.

'Well, we've simply got to get her out,' he said. 'That's why I'm here.'

'How do you think it could be done?'

192

He helped himself to another cigarette, and tapped it on his cigarette case. He did not light it.

'I don't know,' he said.

'What about your father? He's a powerful man. He knows the right people. He has influence. A word from him. . . .'

He shook his head, so I did not continue.

'He wouldn't lift a finger. At first I thought of talking to him, but he would do nothing, he's the last person who would do anything. On the contrary, if I tried to drag him in, it would be utterly hopeless. He has no use for the men of July 20; to him they're all traitors and wreckers, or at best they're lunatics and bunglers. His only comment on the sentences was that in his view one couldn't hang enough of those blue-blooded swine. And on top of it she's a Dressler, the daughter of the man who didn't save his cups. I think the execution gave him pleasure, he thought it a just retribution. . . . At all events, the one thing I'm sure of is that we can't count on him. We've got to think of something else.'

It had ceased to be so quiet near us. A funeral procession was coming down the path. The coffin was made of light wood, which reminded me how difficult it had been to procure a coffin for my mother; even coffins were subject to official controls, and those that had not been used by the city after previous air raids had had to be surrendered to other towns.

We waited until the procession had passed, and then he went on:

'There's something else that I've got to tell you. I tried talking to my brother-in-law, my sister Ehrengard's husband, Karl Boettcher, he's a doctor in the SS, and he's the camp's medical officer. That chemist's son from Königsberg hasn't spent a day at the front, but has always found himself cushy jobs. He's a coward through and through. I saw him in Berlin after an air raid warning; he spent his whole time sitting by the radio and was the first to dash to the

basement, never mind what his wife and children were doing, and he sat there trembling before a single bomb had been dropped; it was intolerable to look at him. As I was saying, he always got himself cushy jobs. He became medical officer at the Krupp foreign workers' camp at Essen. Then, in 1943, when the heavy raids began, he moved heaven and earth to get away from there, and he found no peace until he got himself something safer. Finally, with my father's help, he got himself transferred to south Germany. Now he's in charge of the camps here.'

'Have you talked to him?'

'I tried to. After all, he's responsible for the health of the inmates. He's supposed to inspect them and procure them medicines. He decides who's sick, that is, who's fit for work and who isn't. I thought that if anyone could help, he could. There's a camp for sick prisoners, and he's in charge of it. I thought that as she's a doctor he could have her transferred to it; he could make sure that nothing happened to her, and that she survived.'

'And?'

'The fellow does nothing at all. He's just frightened. On the one hand he submits long reports to his seniors in which he tries to show that everything is in order in the camps, that he has noted an increase in weight among the prisoners, and that productivity has improved. The numbers of deaths that he reports are too low, all for fear that they might send him to the front. On the other hand, he does nothing at all. He's terrified of catching typhus. How dare I try and tell him what to do? he yelled at me. Was I intervening on behalf of that scum? What did it matter if some of them died? There were plenty more where they came from, and we would get the labour force we needed. It was all that scum's fault, and ours, that is the building firms, who expected him to supply a healthy building force. Fear makes him schizophrenic. He sees the end is coming, and he's

194

afraid of what will happen when the Americans arrive and discover the conditions in the camps. But he does nothing. When I went to see him he showed me the cyanide capsules he has to kill himself with before the Americans catch him and bring him to account. . . . Fortunately Ehrengard knows nothing about this, my father took her to Steingaden, and there he doesn't dare behave like that. . . . Nothing is to be hoped for from him. He'd rather denounce me, or simply keep his mouth shut. You never know what a coward will do. I need your help.'

In the course of years this scene—two men talking in a cemetery and hiding their true feelings from each other, because that was the situation, at any rate on my side—has grown more and more unreal in my mind. Later, many years later, I imagined I dashed to help Julia when Fritz Lehr asked me to; I nourished the idea, it comforted and consoled me, but now, when it all revived in my mind and I again felt confronted with the decision, I was aware that I wondered why he had turned up and was dragging me into this.

'What can I do' I asked.

He made a helpless gesture, let his cigarette case spring open, and there was something final about the way he snapped it to again.

'Perhaps I only wanted to talk to someone about it.'

I suddenly remembered Zielinski, who had been a guard at Neuschwanstein and had then been transferred to one of the camps at Kaufering.

'Which camp did you say she was in?'

'Camp I. In the triangular junction at Kaufering.'

Zielinski, if I remembered correctly, had talked about Camp I, or at any rate about a women's camp. I did not mention the fact.

'I've thought of the possibility that it might be possible to get round someone with money,' he said. 'If it were a matter of money, the amount at my disposal is not unlimited, but

195

a certain amount is available. If it can be done with money, it needn't fail on that account. Do you see any way of doing anything?'

I wanted to think. I needed time to think, but he interpreted my silence differently.

He stood there, frowning, looking at me with a hesitant, searching expression.

'Can I rely on you that all this will remain between ourselves?' he said. 'I'm sorry, it's crazy, one no longer knows whom one can trust.' He put his cigarette case back in his pocket, and made a gesture in the direction of the graves. 'Again, my sympathy,' he went on. 'Your mother was a fine woman. It must be a heavy blow to your father. If there's anything I can do. . . .' He held out his hand. 'At any rate, it was good to be able to talk to a friend.'

We shook hands, and I watched him walking down the path. He stopped and looked round, evidently not knowing the way out. I followed him and caught him up, and said:

'Tell me, why are you doing all this?'

'What do you mean?'

'Are you in love with her?'

The question gave me away; it must have revealed to him what my trouble was, but he seemed not to notice it. But the question for the first time relieved the tension that was in him; the nervousness and anxiety that was so unusual with him suddenly vanished. He laughed aloud, and said in his normal voice:

'Oh, no. She was not my type.'

'Was there anything between you?'

Again he laughed quite unconstrainedly.

'I've had affairs with so many girls without their meaning a thing. No, you're on the wrong track. There's nothing whatever between us. She's too serious for me. The times are serious enough, what would I want with a girl like that? When I took her out I always felt rather sorry for her. Such an attractive girl, digging herself in and saving herself up

196

for the devil knows what, for a great love affair, no doubt. No, really, there has never been anything serious between us. It's simply that. . . . Well, I shan't start all over again.'

'All right,' I said, and walked with him to the exit. When we said goodbye I said:

'I'll think it over. Perhaps there might be a way. I'll let you know if I think of anything.'

But now I had made up my mind. Why should I deny now, after all these years, that my making it up was connected with his answer? I was alarmed and terrified by what he had told me, but above all I was relieved by what he had said right at the end.

I went there next day. I can hardly remember the journey. The train kept stopping along the open stretches of track, and twice we had to get out because fighter-bombers were about. I had barely slept all night, and had dreadful dreams about Julia, Nyanya, Davidov, my mother, and of graves talking to each other across the frozen ground. I was tired, dead-beat, and kept dozing off in a corner of the compartment; and I remember the strange mixture of feelings I had: relief, determination and fear. And I know that in the end only fear remained.

XV

All that was left of the sign over the door was EWI's BEER
B. . . . The hut was painted green and had a tarred roof,
and a stove pipe emerged through one of the windows. The
smoke that came from it was as grey as the sky. Some rusty
cigarette advertisements were hung on the walls, and there
was another on the door. The hut was quite near the station,
and its trivial ugliness was made worse by the dirty snow
that had been swept up against the side; it was yellow from
the urine of the men who came out and relieved themselves
every now and then. It was their uniform that gave me the
idea of going to the place, taking my suitcase with me.

I had no idea of how I was to get into touch with Zielinski
without asking anyone, so I had stood undecided outside the
station until I noticed the green painted hut and the SS uniforms; the men generally arrived in pairs, and other pairs
inside the hut made way for them and went off with their
carbines slung over their shoulders along the railway em-
bankment; it was a well beaten path. In the end I went over
to the hut, feeling nervous and uncertain.

I know I spent the whole afternoon there, but I have no
idea how the time passed. In my memory it was the most
hideous place imaginable, but I also know that afterwards,
when I went back to it after seeing and talking to Julia,
everything seemed beautiful.

Inside there was nothing but the counter at which the

198

men were standing, a hat stand, and two tables with dirty red check tablecloths at which nobody was sitting. The salt and pepper pots were empty but, curiously enough, the tooth-pick holder was full, and once one of the men came over, leaned over the table, and helped himself to a toothpick. It was hot inside, and I took off my coat, and I remember the look on the face of the woman behind the counter when she spotted the black band on the left sleeve of my uniform. It was the only time that anything like interest appeared in her eyes, but she made no comment, and it was presumably the visible black crêpe that protected me from questions, for when the men glanced at me and noticed it they left me in peace at my table without talking to me.

I sat right by the window. Narrow strips of the red check material of which the tablecloths were made hung at either side of it. There was something strange about the window pane; sometimes I could look out and see the path along which the men came and went along a siding on which a long row of trucks was standing; and sometimes I could not see through it at all; it reflected my face as in a mirror. Per-haps it had something to do with the way the light was falling.

The woman behind the counter made no move to serve me, and eventually, when the place was nearly empty, I got up and went over to the counter. She was a big, heavy woman with a florid face and dyed hair. I asked her what I could have.

'What you can pay for,' she replied monosyllabically.

'Beer?'

'The beer's no good.'

'I'll have some.'

I watched her fill the glass, using only one hand. I had al-ready noticed that she always kept one hand on the counter. Under the radio on the wall in the corner there was a pair of wooden crutches, but at the time I did not connect her with them.

199

'Are you waiting for someone?'

She had a coarse voice and spoke with a slight Saxon accent.

'Yes.'

'A bereavement?'

I nodded, and she seemed satisfied. I went back to my table, and she took no more notice of me, except that later, when we were alone again, she asked me whether I would like something to eat. I said I would, but I can't remember what it was, except that it came out of a tall glass container on the counter and I had trouble in getting it down. But I managed it, because I did not want to attract attention. We were not alone very often. Men, all in the same uniform, came and went; Ewi's customers seemed to consist exclusively of SS guards from the camp; I hoped that this was so and that I was not mistaken. None of them sat down; they rested their carbines against the wall, kept their coats on, stood at the counter, talked and drank and went off again, making room for others. One or two of them glanced at me and then leaned over the bar and asked the woman something; with a motion of her head she indicated the black band on my sleeve, which legitimised my sitting there and not talking to anyone. Only once or twice did civilians come in; they came in quickly, put a small parcel of something on the counter, took another in exchange, and made off as quickly as they had come; it was done silently and smoothly, and I concluded that the woman was conducting a flourishing black market business on the side.

I waited like that the whole afternoon. Perhaps it was pointless, perhaps Zielinski would never appear, but I did not have the courage to ask after him, or perhaps I was just sitting there to gather together enough courage. I sat there clasping the glass on the table in front of me in my hands, and sometimes they trembled. I told myself that this was because of the vibration that was noticeable whenever a train passed through the station, but the two did not always co-

incide. There was no clock in the room. The small brown people's radio set on a shelf on the wall was permanently on, but I always seemed to miss the time signal. On the back wall behind the counter there was a big mirror in front of which there were three rows of bottles. They were empty, but someone had rinsed them with a brown colouring substance, which made them look full. In the mirror I could see the door and the men who came in, and in the course of many hours I came to recognize some of the faces, men who came in for a second or third time, downed their *Schnaps* and went off again, and they were beginning to grin at me on the way out. It must have been *Schnaps* they were drinking; the woman served them from bottles she kept under the counter. Most of the men were young. They looked older when they came in and younger when they went out; this dreary drinking den seemed to give them back something they had lost outside. A cigarette, a few minutes' talk, a few glasses of that white fluid, seemed to restore, renew, replace something, so that sometimes I felt I was really watching some mysterious form of medical treatment.

I first saw Zielinski in the mirror behind the counter. He too had that tired, older, look when he came through the door, and he went straight to the counter, where the woman put a glass in front of him without his having to ask for it. By now it was nearly dark in the room, but then he must have noticed a strange uniform and an unfamiliar face in the mirror. He turned, with the glass half raised to his lips. For a moment he looked uncertain and worried, as if he had seen something that was not permitted. He looked at me and then at the woman, who shrugged her shoulders, and then, still hesitantly, he came over to my table, looking grey and worried. Then, when he smiled, it was like a dirty grey mask breaking up.

'What are you doing here?'

I looked at my hands, which were still clasping the glass.

201

I think I was as frightened as I had been at the beginning.
I had hoped he would come, I had been waiting for him and
wanting him to come, but now I was afraid. It reminded me
of those moments in action when one crept forward on one's
belly with a camera in one's hands to get a picture and suddenly realised that one might well be killed while engaged
in that inherently peaceful form of activity. I clasped the
glass on the table firmly and said:

'I've been waiting for you.'

'For me?'

He said nothing. Then he noticed my glass, with some beer
still left in it. 'Is that all you've had? Hi, Ewi, what's the
meaning of this? This is a friend of mine!'

He dragged me to the counter, and the woman put a glass
in front of me. 'He didn't tell me,' she said, and filled the
glass from a plain white bottle without a label. On the neck
of the bottle there was a piece of plaster, and on it the name
'Zielinski.' I realised that the other bottles she kept taking
from under the counter were marked in the same way.

'He's a friend of mine, I tell you,' Zielinski said, raising his
glass. 'Here's to friendship. Here's to this lousy life and
friendship. The lousier it is, the more important friends are.
Isn't that right, Ewi? So let's forget about life and drink to
friendship.' He emptied his glass in a single draught, made
the woman refill it, and noticed my black band. He frowned.
'A bereavement?' It was what she too had said.

'My mother.'

'In the raid on Augsburg?'

I nodded, and was astonished at the woman's reaction.
During all the time I had been there she had not eaten or
drunk anything, but had smoked uninterruptedly, one cigarette after another. But now she dropped the cigarette she
had between her first and second fingers, which were stained
with nicotine, her mouth remained open, and her whole body
trembled as if she were having a fit. She grasped the counter
with both hands. The surface was wooden, and the edge was

202

covered with burn marks where she put down her cigarettes. The whole thing lasted for only a few seconds. The trembling stopped, and she shut her mouth and bent down and picked up the cigarette, and I noticed for the first time that she had only one leg; the other had been amputated above the knee. That explained the crutches, and why she had not moved from her place behind the counter.

When she stood upright she was smiling again. She picked up a photograph from the mirror, where it was half concealed by bottles. 'Do you know who that is?' The remark was not addressed to anyone, and she did not show the photograph to anyone, but just looked at it herself; all I could see was that it was of a girl holding a placard with a big number on it. 'That's supposed to be me,' she said. 'Just imagine that. That's what I looked like once.' She put the photograph back behind the bottles. 'He didn't say anything about being a friend of yours. How was I to know?'

'All right, Ewi, all right, everything's perfectly all right. I tell you he's a friend of mine.'

He picked up the two glasses and the bottle and carried them over to the table. We sat down. I expected him to make some remark about the woman and the scene at the counter, but he said:

'Well, how are you getting on? Surely by now you must have photographed everything? Those were the days when we were at the castle.'

'I've got to talk to you.'

'Carry on, then. Did you say you'd been waiting for me? That was the life. Who would have supposed that I would ever live in a castle? And what a castle. Here you're at the other end of the world, at the world's arse. You came here just to talk to me?'

'Can I talk to you alone?'

He looked round. Suddenly he looked uncertain and worried again.

'We're as good as alone here,' he said. 'No-one bothers

about you here. Ewi's O.K.' He looked at me searchingly. Whatever he saw in my face, he went on: 'All right, then, but let's have another one first. Those were the days. . . .'

I put on my coat, but left the suitcase under the table. It was quickly getting dark. Zielinski led the way, and automatically took the path along the railway line. The path was just wide enough for the two of us to walk side by side. He was not wearing a greatcoat. He too was armed; a heavy pistol in a black leather holster weighed down his belt.

'Well, what's the trouble? Where's the fire?'

I was at a loss how to begin. I looked back at the hut; the light was now on inside, and one of the uniformed men was putting up the wooden shutters. I wished it were darker still. I felt sick and ill. Perhaps it was the *Schnaps*, perhaps not. I had buried my mother the day before. Had it been the day before? I had not slept all night, and the endless waiting all the afternoon had got on my nerves. I did not know what to say. Two SS men came towards us. They moved to one side and saluted smartly. When they had passed I said;

'It's a delicate matter. I don't want to drag you into anything.'

'Drag me into anything?' he exclaimed bitterly. 'Drag me into anything? Good heavens, man, you've no idea how deep I'm in already. I'm right in, up to over my ears. What do you imagine goes on here? Why do you think those fellows go out for a drink every two hours? You can't be deeper in anything than I am.'

'It's about someone in the camp. A woman. If I tell you the name. . . .'

'The name? Listen, how do you expect me to know names? They come and go, at the moment we're having thirty deaths a day, how do you expect me to notice names? Names. Thirty deaths a day. Since the end of December we've had typhus in the camp, but do you suppose we get any medicines? Yes, we get fifty tablets of aspirin a day for seven hundred persons—if there are still seven hundred left. How can I tell

how many there are? No medical records are allowed to be kept, and lists of names are forbidden. I had it all properly organised, but now it's sheer chaos; they're half dead when they arrive here, but that swine of a doctor doesn't even turn up when the trains come in. Do you know what it's like when the trains come in? They cram eighty of them into a freight-car, they're the oldest French cars, and they're on the way for days without food, and when they get here there are four or five dead in every car. But into the camp they come, it's up to us to see what we do with them. Camp I is supposed to provide construction sites with a work force of seven hundred and when I say I can only supply three hundred, the others are sick—sick? he says, who certified them sick, Zielinski? The swine simply doesn't turn up any more, he just watches his films and sends us fifty aspirins a day, and that's that. Fifty aspirins for seven hundred. . . . If anyone had told me that, Pikola. I'm in it up to the neck. What am I talking about, up to the neck, I'm eating shit already, I swallow my portion of shit every day. What was that you said about a name?'

He stood there with sunken head, just a figure in the dark, but I could feel his relief, as if he had at last come out with something that had been bottled up inside him.

'It's as I said, Pikola,' he went on. 'I don't know any names, I really don't. There are too many newcomers and too many deaths. At first I noticed names, but that was at the beginning, and it's over now. It has been getting worse all the time, and you've come at the worst moment.'

'She came here in a train-load from Riga.'

'There were a great many who came from Riga, but now they've stopped. I don't know where they still manage to find them. There are fewer and fewer of them now, and one day it'll be over. One day it will all be over. I can't imagine it, but one day it's bound to be over. A woman, you said? And what was the name? What was the name you mentioned?'

205

'I haven't mentioned a name.'

I hesitated, not because I did not trust him, but because I still clung to the hope that the whole thing was only a bad dream. Perhaps Oldewaage had made a mistake, perhaps the woman he saw was not Julia. The thought had kept me going, I had clung to it, though I was afraid of having too much faith in it. But surely it was possible that he had made a mistake. I remembered the tone of voice in which Fritz Lehr had said *she's alive*, how terrifying it had sounded. Saying the name aloud meant doing practically the same thing, there was a finality about it.

'The name's Julia Dressler. She's German, the daughter . . .'

He had been walking ahead of me, a grey outline broken only by the pistol, but now he stopped in his tracks and turned round; I could only guess the expression on his face.

'She was a doctor?' he said slowly. 'Is that what she was?'

I could only nod. His using the past tense meant nothing. I don't know whether he saw my nod.

'Yes, I know Dressler. I didn't know the Christian name. Julia, did you say? In the camp they simply call her Dressler, or the doctor, she does sick-bay duty, or what passes for it here. She has divided off a part of her hut, and she tries to keep it clean, and helps where she can. But what can she do with fifty aspirins? She has to share them out, and I don't envy her the task. What do you want me to do? Give her a message?'

'Would you do that?'

'Why not? It couldn't be in writing, but I could give her a message. But think it over again first. I'm not trying to get out of it, but. . . . How am I to explain it to you? I don't know if you would be doing her a service, if you understand me.'

'Couldn't I see her?'

'See her?'

Strangely enough, it was lighter now, and I could see his

206

face better. I thought my last question would alarm him, but it wasn't that, he looked calm and thoughtful, and when he started talking again he seemed to be not so much answering my question as trying to clarify in his own mind something that had long been preoccupying him.

'Assuming it were possible,' he said, 'are you sure that she would want to see *you*? You won't believe it, but it is so, you wonder how it's possible for them to have such pride, and where on earth they get it from. That's what I wonder the whole time. I don't understand it. There are others, of course, there are some who creep to all the guards, who would do anything for a cigarette-end, but most of them are so damned proud. I don't know what they're so proud of. They die off like flies, and they're proud. They walk past you without seeing you, they just look right through you. They're in rags and tatters, but they keep their head high, it makes me angry every time. . . . I tell you quite honestly, it's the only time when I might be capable of forgetting myself, because they manage to look at you in such a way that they make you feel a pig. She's one of them, you feel like creeping away into a corner when she looks at you. Do you know what I sometimes think? It's crazy, but I think she looks at you as if she were sorry for you.' He paused before going on. 'That's why I'm not sure she'll really want to see you.'

'Would you try. . . .'

I had the feeling he was entitled to an explanation, and I was about to set out on it, but he cut me short.

'Do you really want to see? Do you really want to talk to her? Afterwards she'll have to go back. And who will be the better for it, you or she? I don't know how you found out she's in the camp. I don't know whether I haven't told you too much. Perhaps it will be better for you to go away and forget the whole thing. Better for both of you. Good heavens, Pikola, do you think I shall ever get out of this shit?'

'Might there be a way of getting her out?'

207

Once more his reaction was different from what I expected. He was far calmer and less anxious than I. He calmly returned the salute of two guards who went by, and did not seem to mind being seen with me here.

'Possibly,' he said, as if it were a problem he had long considered. 'We might get her out in a coffin. We have thirty deaths a day, we no longer count them, we just submit a number for the ration strength, but it's never correct, either before or afterwards. Yes, that way it would be possible. But it would cost you something, because I couldn't do it alone. I should need two helpers, who would have to be let into the secret; it would be risky, but not too risky if they were paid well enough. I know two men who might do, not Germans, but Latvians.'

It struck me that I had heard a great deal of broken German in the hut, as well as some talk in a foreign language. I repeated what Fritz Lehr had said to me:

'Money is no obstacle.'

'They wouldn't do it for money. They'd do it for coffee, silk stockings, cigarettes, say five pounds of coffee each and two hundred cigarettes; I might perhaps have to offer them more, I'll see what I can do, there's no sense in offering them too little.'

He spoke as if the whole thing were already settled.

'Where am I to get those things?'

'From Ewi. Have you got all that money? She won't ask more than she has to, but she can't reduce her prices. She does it for her husband, and the fellow checks every cigarette.'

'When can I see her? I mean, I shall have to talk to her first to prepare her for it.'

He thought for a moment. He looked towards the freight-cars which were standing darkly near us. There were twenty or thirty of them, shunted into a siding. I had seen the men who were guarding them through the hut window. They were in Luftwaffe uniform, and came from a hut surrounded

by a slit trench. Zielinski had walked back a little way with me and pointed to one of the dark rectangular shadows.

'You see that car? Note where it's standing. It's the only one with a brakeman's box. Do you see it? I could take her to it, and you could talk to her inside.'

I looked round. 'Isn't it dangerous?' I was thinking of the guards who continually patrolled up and down.

'It's the safest possible place. Nobody would notice. Apart from that, I don't know anywhere else.'

'What are those freight-cars?'

'Those cars? That's a Reichmarschall train, if you know what that is. It's been here for four weeks, twenty-six sealed cars, packed full of stuff, and they don't know where to send it. Two of them are full of brand new people's radio sets, and do you know what's in the others? *Ersatz* coffee, cigarettes, even if they're only Deutscher Wald, textiles, materials, bales of them, flour, noodles, sugar. . . . They've been here for four weeks, but do you think anything is taken out of them? People have nothing to eat, but only Göring himself has the right to decide personally what happens to them. Let him stuff himself to death with them, I say. Meanwhile the train stands here with six men to guard it. But you have no need to worry about those Luftwaffe boys.'

I remember seeing what happened to those cars later, at the end of April. I came here because I had heard that the Americans had taken Landsberg, which was premature, because they were only advancing towards it, but the local people had heard the rumour, and they advanced on the train, about which there had been a great deal of whispering. The most fantastic stories had gone the rounds, and I saw them coming, with empty wheelbarrows, suitcases, baskets, rucksacks, and also with cudgels and iron bars, because the guards were still there. They advanced hesitantly, but there were so many of them, and those behind pushed them on. The guards fired in the air, but whoever was in command told them to give way, because the crowd was unstoppable.

They used their cudgels and metal bars to batter in the doors, and chaos ensued. Men fought, women tore each other's hair, bales of white linen were unrolled and dirtied by the boots that trampled on them, sacks of peas were thrown out of the windows and burst, in many places the gravel on the permanent way looked like big crystals because of the sugar scattered over it. I saw one old man who got away safely with his barrow full of loot. When he got to the underpass he at last dared to stop and examine it, and I saw his dismay when he opened the first sack and tried the contents with his finger, licked it and tasted it, and then, growing more and more dismayed, slit open sack after sack, only to discover that his booty consisted of nothing but cheap baking essence, not even real baking essence, but *ersatz*.

I was worried by the presence of the Luftwaffe guards, but Zielinski reassured me. He was calmness and confidence personified.

'It's the safest place imaginable,' he said. 'You'll be actually under guard yourself, so to speak. I'll take her there myself. The camp is just on the other side of the track. You will wait at Ewi's. When I come and say. . . . No, I shan't say anything, you'll be able to tell whether everything's O.K. Then you'll simply go and find her there. I'll be waiting at Ewi's, and I'll take her back myself. It'll be perfectly O.K And tomorrow's Sunday, the best day of the week.'

'Tomorrow?' I said. It seemed impossible to wait as long as that, to go through another twenty-four hours. 'Not till tomorrow?'

'What are you thinking of? I've got to make preparations, and in any case Sunday's the best day of the week. It's a busy day at Ewi's, and by the time I fetch her they'll all be well away.'

'And what am I to do for twenty-four hours?' I could not face another whole day in that hut, apart from the fact that my leave pass was valid only for Augsburg. 'Where shall I go all that time?'

'I'll talk to Ewi. You'll be able to stay with her.'

I remembered her bending over to pick up her cigarette, when I discovered she had only one leg. Even at the front, dead bodies had not frightened me so much as persons with missing limbs, but all I said was:

'Is that safe?'

'She's alone at the moment. Her old man is away.'

'She's married?'

'Yes, why not? Because she only has one leg? Do you know how old she is? She's thirty, or not even quite that yet. She was once damned attractive, the prettiest number girl in the Hansa Palace at Leipzig.'

'How did it happen?'

'In an air raid. She was buried in rubble. They dug her out, but they couldn't save her leg, it had to be amputated. Since then she has gone about on crutches and has been dependent on that fellow she's married to. He's in charge of the trains that bring the prisoners and, if you ask me, he's a . . . but never mind that. You needn't worry about her. She hears a great deal and she sees a great deal, and if she sees us together and you buy stuff from her no doubt she'll think things. But she won't ask any questions. All the same, it will be better if you don't tell her anything. It will be better if you don't tell anybody at all.'

We were walking back towards the green painted hut. No light was visible, but you could make out the outline and smell the smoke. We were walking side by side when he said:

'You never told me about her. I always thought you were heavily married. Is the child yours?'

For a moment I did not understand.

'What are you talking about?' I said.

'Her child. I've been wondering the whole time why you were doing it. Obviously, I thought there was something between you, and that the child was yours. Otherwise why should you do it?'

'What child?'

I don't know whether I seized him by the shoulders or simply stood there, looking at him incredulously.

'But I thought you knew about it. When she arrived here at the end of August or the beginning of September she was pregnant. Some of them were, there was nothing exceptional about it. Children keep being born and dying in the trains on the way here, Ewi could tell you all about it. When that husband of hers comes home he tells her how they throw the dead babies out of the trucks. She has to listen to that sadist of a husband of hers telling her all the details. . . . Hell, why do I have to keep on talking about it, why don't I keep my mouth shut? I'm sorry, ... Well, she was pregnant, and the child was born some time in December, about Christmas. I'm supposed to know nothing about it, they try to keep it secret, but I know all about it. There's a Polish woman in the camp, she comes from Sasnowitz, near where I come from, she's in charge of the kitchen, that's an important job in the camp, Hedwig Seligowski her name is. Sasnowitz is only a stone's throw from Kattowitz, where I come from, and that Polish woman's a sly one, she's one of the proud ones, you understand. She fixed it, she protects the child, so to speak, and if there's any milk or anything it vanishes at once. They are incredibly careful, they put it in a different hut every night. Officially, of course, I know nothing whatever about it. . . . So it's not your child? I felt sure it was yours.'

I think I felt nothing at that moment; I tried to take in what he had said, and perhaps also I tried to work out when it must have happened if the child was born at the end of December.

I know he said: 'Do you still want to see her?' and I said yes, or simply nodded.

XVI

I can't remember everything that happened in the next twenty-four hours; or rather some things I can remember and others have faded from my mind: there are gaps, blanks in my memory. Of course I thought a great deal about the child, it occupied a large part of my mind; and when I thought of the moment when Zielinski told me about it, it was like an insult, a slap in the face. I tried to reconcile myself to the idea of her having a child by another man. What did it matter to me who he was? I didn't want to know, I wouldn't even ask. A child by another man, surely that was enough.

I also remember following the woman home that evening; this was another painful idea; a woman with crude wooden crutches under her armpits, preceding me in long, swinging strides, so that I had difficulty in keeping up with her carrying my suitcase. She closed the hut at about eleven o'clock, simply putting a primitive padlock on the door. She wore a Persian lamb fur coat, and later, when it was hanging in the hall, I noticed that it was badly worn under the armpits.

We did not have far to go, only a few hundred yards past the station and then down a side street. I was astonished when I saw the house, because of the contrast with the shabby hideousness of the hut; it was a single-storey villa in the middle of a garden, and it still had a lawn and flower-beds, though all the other front gardens had been dug up and were used to grow potatoes. It looked quite a big house, and it was inconceivable that only two people should be living in

it, that there should be only one nameplate on the door and not the many additional little cards and nameplates that all the other houses had; because of all the refugees, you had to be pretty influential at that time to be able to live alone in a house like that.

But she really lived alone there, you could feel the emptiness of the house as soon as you set foot in it. She did not turn on the light immediately, and I heard her bumping into something when she went on ahead to fix the blackout. I followed her, and the first thing I saw when she put the light on was her husband's photograph. We were in a big living room, and the photograph was in a big, silver frame, on a heavy buffet; my only memory of it is of a short, thickset, balding man, and she remarked that he had taken it himself.

Did she tell me that straight away, or was it later? She showed me to my room, and I heard her moving about the house, relatively quietly where there were carpets but noisily on the tiles in the hall. Motionless though she had been behind the counter, as soon as she got home she seemed to be seized with a restlessness that made her go from room to room. She knocked at my door and asked me whether I would like to keep her company for a meal, and I found her sitting on a couch in the big living room.

On the table there was a tray with things I had not seen for a long time, as well as a bottle of real champagne. She had changed—how had she managed it alone?—and now wore black trousers and a black blouse that made her look thinner and fairer. Her hair was upswept and curly over her forehead. I could not see the crutches, and later, when she fetched another bottle of champagne, she moved about without them, holding on to the furniture and the backs of chairs, which seemed to have been specially arranged to provide handholds at definite distances apart.

She ate nothing at all, but only smoked and drank and, yes, it was then that she told me about the photograph.

'He thinks himself a great photographer,' she said. 'That's

214

how we met. He took the photo of me that you saw. They wanted to confiscate his camera and throw him out of the Variété because it was forbidden to take photographs there. . . . Does this surprise you? I mean, the house and the champagne and the coffee?'

I had told her that I wanted to buy coffee and cigarettes from her, and she had said I could have them. She told me what they would cost, and said I could have them whenever I liked. She seemed to have ample stocks, but I did not bother my head about the matter. Why should I? I had my own problems, and didn't want to listen to those of others. I suspected what was coming. I only had to look at her to realise that she wanted someone to talk to. The best thing for me to do, I decided, was to say nothing, but that did not stop the flow.

'Look at him,' she said, pointing to the photograph. 'Doesn't he look a nice, simple, straightforward railwayman? Do you know what my mother always used to say? Railwaymen, she said, are the quietest and solidest and most dependable men there are, you can always rely on a railwayman.'

I looked at the room, the carpets, the couch trimmings, the lace curtains which were gathered cross-wise, the plants in tubs that looked like palm fronds; it was presumably exactly the kind of living-room that her mother had wanted for her.

'She worried about me when I became a number girl in a variety show. My father comes from an old music hall family, he was an impersonator, especially of women's voices, women singers in particular, his Zarah was his show-piece, and Rosita Serano was another. But my mother went on and on at me about railwaymen, and she gave me no peace till I married one. . . . I'd have gladly charged you less for the coffee, but what do you suppose would happen if I did? If I didn't get the right price, there'd be the devil to pay. He remembers every single detail. Those two bottles of champagne. Before he's been back in the house for an hour he

215

has checked everything and spotted that I didn't enter them immediately. But what can I do? I'm secure with him. I ought to be glad to have him, oughtn't I? Such a good man. A man who never lets his wife down, never, even though she has lost a leg. Would you sleep with me? You certainly wouldn't would you, and nor would anyone else. How old do you think I am, fifty?' She had drunk the champagne almost alone. She laughed. It sounded like an imitation laugh. 'At any rate I look like fifty, don't I? Did I show you the photo of me as a number girl? Perhaps it will be better if I don't show it to you.'

She kept on smoking and staring straight in front of her. Her eyes continually returned to a place on the wall near the door, where there was a small table with a film projector, and next to it a stand with a rolled up screen.

'Do you know where he gets all the black market stuff I sell for him? Has Zielinski told you what he does? Do you know that he escorts all those trains from the east?'

How could I stop her? Everyone had a story to tell, but did they all have to tell them to me? All these stories—Fritz Lehr's and Zielinski's—made me sick. I had no-one to whom I could tell mine. Who was there who would listen to me?

'Would you imagine those poor devils had anything but the rags they were standing up in? But you'd be surprised at the things he comes home with. Brooches and rings and pendants. He's got a sharp eye for gold and diamonds. Who knows where they hide them and what he promises them in return? He must promise them something, mustn't he? And they must believe him. He's got such a candid face, you can't help trusting him. I ought to ask him about it, oughtn't I? I shouldn't watch him unpacking the things here on this table, his face beaming with satisfaction. . . . Would you ask him? *Tell me, Klemens, where did you get it from and what did you promise in return?'*

I sat there and tried desperately to get up from the soft couch, but could not. I could feel the pattern in the velvet,

216

the slight projections and recessions; it might be a flower pattern; yes, it was a stylised flower, five leaves with a dot in the middle. How can one possibly remember such a thing after such a long time? But I remember it. It's only a memory, it was a long time ago, I only need tell myself it's a memory. But I can't escape from the past into the present. The present is suddenly closed, just as the past used to be. The voice is there beside me, and I can't get her to stop talking, or to talk about something else. Why don't I ask about her father? Voice impersonators were always my favourite variety act; the good ones not only imitated the voice but actually slipped into the role. . . .

'. . . . but worst of all are his films. How can a man film such things? How can he take films of those poor devils and then sit here and look at them afterwards? How can a man do such a thing? How can he enjoy it, and actually feel proud when a film comes out well, and tell you how difficult they were to take, particularly the delousing films, the shots of women being deloused before being put in the train and standing naked in the shower room? . . . . and then the two of them sit here, and. . . .'

Suddenly she had one of her fits. Her whole body trembled, and her cigarette dropped from her fingers. But it did not last long, she bent over and picked it up, and again looked at the rolled up screen.

'And then the two of them sit here on the couch in the darkened room and watch the films, they gloat over them. Sometimes I hear them when I come home early. They laugh, and make filthy remarks, and shout for me when they've nothing left to drink, and go on shouting until I take them something. I have to go into the room, and they take no notice of me, because they've got eyes only for the screen, and they don't realise I have to be sick as soon as I'm outside again. . . . That doctor he invites to join him, that Boettcher, is even worse than he is.'

'Boettcher?'

I think this was the first and only thing I said to her all the evening.

'Yes, Boettcher. If Klemens is away only a day or two longer than expected he rings up here every morning and wants to know whether he's back and when I expect him. And he's a doctor, just imagine that. Klemens is tremendously proud of being a friend of his. You ought to ask Zielinski what sort of doctor he is. Zielinski's a friend of yours, isn't he? He said you were friends. You won't tell anyone what I've told you, will you?' But she was not unduly worried by this question, for her thoughts were elsewhere. 'Do you know, when I sit here alone in the evening. . . .'

I don't know how long it went on, how long she went on talking. It was a nightmare, and I could not look at the screen for fear of seeing it had been unrolled and that pictures were appearing on it. I don't know when I at last got to my room, and I know nothing about the night, or what I dreamt, and I know very little about the following day.

I stayed in the house and hardly left my room. She was there the whole morning, and sometimes I could hear her. The telephone rang several times, and generally someone called a quarter of an hour later; at all events, I heard voices, and realised that black market deals were in progress.

We ate together in the kitchen, and I managed to get her to talk about her father and tell me where he had appeared and whom he imitated in addition to those she had mentioned; all she knew about him now was that he was in the surrounded fortress of Brest. She had lost her mother shortly before the war; she had been killed, of all things, in a railway accident, at a place called Oschatz.

She went out at about four o'clock, later than usual, but it was Saturday, when the hut stayed open late. She gave me a key.

I don't know how I passed the rest of the time. Presumably I lay on the bed and slept, or tried to read. I did not go into the living room again, and I was glad I had enough money

of my own to be able to pay for the coffee and the cigarettes. I might have telephoned Fritz Lehr, but did not. What could I have told him? That I was afraid? I was afraid of something going wrong, and I was also afraid of seeing Julia, of seeing her without knowing what to say, of not being able to find the right words, if, indeed, such words existed.

XVII

I went much too early. The hut was crammed, and SS guards were even gathered round the tables, playing cards. I stood in the doorway for a moment, hesitating whether or not to go in, and someone shouted at me: 'Come in or go out.' But then I realised it was because of the blackout. I went in, and found a place at the counter. Ewi smiled at me, and served me from Zielinski's bottle.

'I must have talked a great deal of nonsense last night,' she said. 'I'm sorry.'

I handed her back her key. She noticed the fur hat. I had been thinking what I could take Julia, apart from the cigarettes and the chocolate I had bought from Ewi, and on the way I had remembered the fur hat I had in my suitcase; it reminded me of the hat Julia had worn in Berlin. It was made of lynx fur and had earflaps, and it was a man's hat, but I thought she would not mind that.

Ewi said nothing when she noticed it, and I was grateful to her for that. The photograph she had picked up the day before was right in front of me, and I asked her to let me have a look at it. She picked it out from behind the bottles. It was an old print, brownish and spotty, and showed a blonde in a top hat standing in front of the curtain, holding a board in front of her with a big 7 on it.

'Very nice,' I said. 'You look very nice on it.'

'You don't have to be anything out of the ordinary to be

a number girl,' she said. 'They make up your face, and they see very little of your figure behind the big board. The only thing they look at when they choose a number girl is her legs. They want girls with good legs, two good, long legs.'

She was right. The girl in the photograph had good, long legs. I handed her back the print, and said to myself that seven was not a lucky number, at any rate it had never brought me any luck. I never started anything on the seventh, and if I did it went wrong, as, for instance, on 7 May 1943, when I was wounded in Tunis. And I was born on the seventh, but obviously I couldn't do anything about that.

I know very little about the next four hours. The men talked, and Ewi was kept busy. I had put the fur hat on the counter, and one of the Latvian guards saw it and started talking to me in broken German. He was a huge, broad-shouldered, fair man with a broad face, and he was at least a head taller than me. In the end I realised that he wanted to buy the hat.

I told him it was not for sale, but he was not to be put off. He said he had wanted a hat just like that for ages, and the more flatly I refused his offers, the more he increased them; eventually he offered me no less than three pounds of coffee. Then he switched to pleas and appeals, and when at last he realised there was nothing doing he asked whether he might at least wear it for a few moments if I wasn't going to sell it to him.

By this time we had attracted so much attention, so many men were listening to us and watching us, that I did not dare say no, and he put it on. It was too small for him, but that did not worry him. He tried it this way and that, pulled it over his brow, pushed it back, tilted it, and Ewi had to move some bottles to let him see himself better in the mirror. He was beaming, and insisted on my agreeing how well it suited him, I simply must let him have it, he put his face close to mine and the black collar patches with the lightning flashes on them were right in front of me. Eventually he took it off,

handed it back, and made his final offer—five pounds of coffee, because it was exactly like the hat his father had given him when he was a boy. . . .

He kept coming back to it as long as I was there; he cast covetous glances at it, and could not understand how anyone could possibly refuse such an offer; just imagine it, *five pounds of coffee*. The room was hot, and so full of smoke that I could hardly see the door in the mirror. I wondered where Zielinski could be, and imagined all the things that might have gone wrong. He would come in and say, sorry, it can't be done, or she wouldn't see me; or perhaps he had just lost courage, realised what he was letting himself in for, and reported everything. . . .

At all events, when he came in I didn't see him. I first saw him standing at the bar, being greeted by his pals. Ewi had already given him his glass of *Schnaps*. He took no more notice of me. I waited, but nothing happened, and he went on with his lively conversation. I was at a loss what to do, until at last he looked at me. He looked anxious, and I realised he was worrying about me, fearing I might do something stupid at the last moment that would ruin everything.

I picked up the fur hat and left, and this time I did not forget and shut the door quickly behind me. The weather had changed that morning. First there had been some light rain, which had then turned to snow, but it was not cold enough for it to lie.

I stood there, drained of strength and courage by the effort it cost me to walk out of the hut into the open air. I just stood there, sweating, unable to move. I believe that if guards had suddenly appeared at that moment and taken me away because everything had been discovered, I should have gone with them unresistingly and with a sense of relief. But nothing happened. Behind me I could hear voices and laughter from the hut, and in the distance in front of me I could see the cars waiting in the siding.

I walked down the narrow path beside the railway track.

222

The cars looked all alike. I walked on, looking for the one with the brakeman's box, but could not find it. I began to run, and suddenly reached the end of the train. I saw a human figure—one of the Luftwaffe guards. He was holding a blanket round his shoulders and took no notice of me, but just looked past me. He was stamping his feet because of the cold. I turned back, and this time I found the car with the brakeman's box.

The railway line was about a yard above the path, and the car towered high over me. The small window at the side was misted up. It seemed impossible, inconceivable, that inside that cage there was someone who had been waiting for me for a long time and had heard footsteps outside. I pulled myself up to the side of the truck, took the cold handle and pulled, but could not open it. But I went on, until it suddenly swung open. And then I saw her.

For a moment I was too petrified to know what to do. I hung there, half in the air, until she seized my hand, and it was she who bent forward above me and pulled the door to. Inside it was dark and there was hardly any room, and all I knew was that I was panting, while she was breathing quite normally. But in the few seconds during which the door had been open I had seen the whole of her, and three things in particular, her cut-off hair, the thin grey coat that hung from her and, above all, her boots, which had been at the level of my eyes, a pair of worn old boots, laced with frayed white packing string; they were the boots of an old man.

Inside the brakeman's box there was just room for two, and hardly enough for them to move; even when both of us pressed into the corner, our bodies touched. Her face was close to mine, I had to look at her, there was nowhere else to look, and in spite of the dark you could see her shorn hair, her cheekbones that protruded more than ever, and the hollows where her eyes were—they were too deep-set to be visible. There was no way of concealing from her how shocked I was. I could think of nothing to say. If I had come to give her strength, I was the one who was now in need of

it. I saw her lips move. She said something, but it took me a long time to realise the voice was hers.

'You see, you shouldn't have come. You're running a great risk, and now you're wondering what for.'

I still had said nothing. My tongue might have been paralysed. I had something in my hands, the hat the Latvian SS man had wanted so badly, it gave me my first clear idea and I seized on it.

'I've brought you something,' I said.

She smiled. I could not see it, of course, and yet I knew she smiled at me.

'It's old,' I said. 'I've worn it, but it's warm.'

She did not take it, and I didn't know what to do with it, but just held it, and once more I broke into a sweat.

'Please take it,' I said. ''I'm sure it'll suit you. It's lynx.' I was talking like an ass. 'I thought perhaps you could do with it. Do take it, please.'

'It's very nice of you, but I couldn't possibly wear it.'

'Why not? It's old.'

'It's much too noticeable. Everyone would want to know where I'd got it from.'

She shook her head, as if it were hopeless to try and explain the inexplicable.

I remembered the things in my coat pocket and, as it was better to say something, to hear my own voice, because anything was better than that silence, I said:

'I didn't know what to bring you. I've brought some chocolate and cigarettes.'

Again she shook her head.

'How can I explain?' she said. 'I wouldn't know what to do with them. I should be afraid. Can you understand that? I should be afraid of having something the others hadn't got. Cigarettes, good heavens. If I knew someone in my hut had cigarettes under her straw sack, I wouldn't know what to do; I shouldn't be able to think about anything else. And if I had them, I shouldn't be able to sleep, because I should be think-

ing they knew where I'd hidden them and would be coming to take them as soon as I dropped off. Please give me just one.'

'What do you mean?'

'Just one cigarette. I could do with it.'

'But you used not to smoke.'

Again she smiled, and this time I was sure of it, because for a moment I saw her eyes.

'I'm sorry,' I said. I put the hat on the brake-wheel and took out the packet of cigarettes. It took an agonisingly long time to tear it open, and then some fell on the floor. I picked them up and gave her one.

She held it between her fingers and waited, and I wondered why she didn't light it. Then she said:

'Have you a match?' Again I muttered an apology and began searching in my pockets, which in that confined space was not so easy, but I could find no matches. I started all over again, and again hunted through the side pockets and breast pockets of my jacket and great coat. I was wet through with perspiration, and I hunted through my pockets as if my life depended on it, and in the end I had shamefacedly to confess that I had none. She had asked me for a cigarette, *one* cigarette, and it was the only thing she wanted of me, the only thing I could do for her, and I had no matches. It was absurd, but because of it the universe collapsed over my head. I had failed her in the only thing she wanted of me.

'Oh, Julia,' I said. 'Julia.'

She suddenly looked at me quite differently. She had been holding her head down, so I had not been able to see her eyes. Now I saw them, and when she spoke it was with her own voice.

'Please say it again.'

'What?'

'The name Julia. It's . . . the way you said it, it's as if I hadn't heard it for a hundred years.'

I repeated it, and she said:

225

'I'm glad I came for that alone.'

'Listen,' I said quickly. 'I came because. . . .'

'Don't tell me. It's good that you're here. It's good now. I was terribly afraid. Everything dwindles and vanishes, but not one's fear. I was afraid of seeing you, and I was afraid it was only an excuse.'

'Didn't he tell you I. . . .'

'They tell you a great deal, but you can never be sure what it means.'

'I can rely on him.'

'All I know is that he wears that uniform. Perhaps you think it better to hope, but it only makes it worse. There was a time at the beginning when I had hope, and it was dreadful. Now that I've given it up, it's better. So don't tell me anything.'

Outside there was the sound of footsteps, the sound of nailed boots crunching on the gravel, but it faded away. The small window was steamed over by our breath. She put out her hands and touched my face, as if her hands could tell her more than her eyes. I felt her rough hands and forgot everything else; the only thought in my mind was that I loved her, always had and always would.

'How long have we got?' she asked.

I had not asked Zielinski that. I did not want to be reminded of time, of having to say goodbye, of her having to go back.

'I'm going to get you out of here,' I said. 'He's going to help. We've discussed everything. He says it can be done. Do you understand? If you've got to go back now, it's only for a day or two. There's a way. We can rely on him. He'll help me to get you out. He. . . .'

Her hands were no longer touching my face, her arms were by her side, and I felt her body stiffening. She looked at me as if I had said something appalling.

'I think it would be better if you went now,' she said.

'But Julia. I can trust him. You've seen. The fact that we're here. . . .'

'Please go.'

'Why? I don't understand. He'll do what he says.'

'And why?' Her voice was cold. 'Why is he prepared to do it? Because I'm not a Jewess? Did you tell him that? Is that why he risked his neck by bringing me here? Because I'm something better than the others, because I'm German and a general's daughter? Even if my father was a traitor and a wrecker, I'm not one of those dirty Jewesses, after all, and I'm not a Pole either, am I? Do you for one moment imagine he would lift a finger for a Jewess or a Pole? No, I'm a German woman, so one can shut one eye. So he's willing to get me out?'

'Yes,' I said. 'And he will.'

'And the others? What about the others? Would he do it for them too? Ask him.'

'But please. He's running a tremendous risk. I don't know anyone else who would have done it. All I know is I can rely on him. I know nothing about his reasons. I'm not interested in them so long as he helps us, and there's no reason why you should be interested in them either. What does it matter what he thinks? Please, Julia, let us talk about it sensibly.'

I know that I went on appealing to her, and that she did not understand. My words did not seem to reach her; I often think they were the wrong words, but I knew no others.

'You remember my Nyanya,' she said in the end, 'and Davidov, who insisted on going with her? I didn't understand him at the time; I mean I admired him, but I didn't understand him, because it didn't seem human. He loved her, of course, but what does that mean when you know it will cost you your life? It's human to be afraid and to cling to life, and that's why *you* don't understand now. I understand him now. I understand how he despised them. If they killed her, very well, they must kill him too. To him the only terrible thing

would have been surviving her. When things got specially difficult it was he that always reminded me to despise them and not lose my pride. That's all you have left. Of all the things I thought might help me, pride is all that's left. I was always afraid of losing it, and I still am. I had it when I heard they had hanged my father, and many other times as well, and I have it now, and I want you to understand what you are asking of me. Perhaps it's unintelligible, but I can't help it. There are others in the camp. We've been together since Riga. Not many of us are left, but none of them would understand if I left them now. Quite apart from the fact that for my own sake I couldn't do it.'

'He can't help everyone.'

'I know. That's why he can't help me.'

'I don't understand. In any case it will soon be over. The war can't last much longer.'

'Then I can wait like the others.'

'But how does that help them?'

'Let us stop talking about it. I know you don't understand. Perhaps I don't understand myself. One clings to life, doesn't one? Perhaps it's really connected with my father. He managed to smuggle a message to me, a note scribbled on a scrap of paper, and the priest who brought it to me knew what it said, and I know he was shocked, and brought it to me only because it was written by a man under sentence of death. It was bound to upset him, because in it there was nothing about God and love and forgiveness, it consisted of only three words, *I despise them.* That was what my father had to say before he died, and he thought it mattered enough to write it down for me . . . And now let us stop talking about it. Forget it. Forget you have seen me. I shall try to forget it too.'

I did not know what to say. Certainly words were no use. I was no Davidov; if she died, I should survive. But that was a thought that I think came to me only later. I remembered the child about which she had said nothing; I should have

said nothing about it either if it had not struck me that by doing so I might be able to persuade her to change her mind. So I said:

'And the child?'

She was not so much frightened as suddenly on her guard.

'You know about it? Who else does? Does he?'

'Zielinski? Yes. Doesn't that show you that you can trust him?'

She was absorbed in her own thoughts.

'And we were so careful,' she said.

'What is it?'

'What do you mean?'

'I mean, he mentioned only a child. Is it a boy or a girl?'

'A girl.'

The way she said this revived my hope.

'What does it look like?'

'What babies do look like. There's a Polish woman who works in the kitchen, she's . . .' But she stopped, as if she must be on her guard against me too.

Once more I had a feeling of the senselessness of it all; I felt all this was not really happening, we were not really saying these senseless things, and yet I clung to them, because they offered the only hope.

'Isn't it dangerous?'

'She's a quiet baby, thank heavens. She never cries. That makes everything easier. But of course . . .'

'You mean if it were possible to get the child out?'

She listened to me as if she were listening to a foreign language she was learning. I left her time.

'The child's different.'

'What you said certainly doesn't apply to the child. If we get it out I promise to look after it.'

'How would you do that?'

'One of my father's sisters is in a convent.' I had only just thought of this. 'She'd be safer there until you . . . Severa would do everything for the child, and I would look

after it, I promise you. We should all look after it. Severa would treat it kindly.'

'Yes, she would. You should see what a lovely baby she is. She has long dark hair and green eyes.'

'Then she must look very like you,' I said.

She dropped her head, and I could no longer see her eyes. When she spoke it was barely in a whisper. 'You haven't asked who the father is,' she said. 'Or do you know?'

'No, and it doesn't matter.'

Of course it mattered, but the only thing in my mind was that once the child was out of the camp she might think differently. The child in the camp was something I could not imagine, but if I once had the child I should get her too. At the time I still believed that.

'If it comes off—will you promise me no-one will find out who the father is? You must promise me. I don't want any-one else to know but you and me. He must never find out, and neither must the child. Promise me.'

'Of course.'

'No, swear it. Do you swear it? Good. Then I'll tell you.'

'You don't need to, it doesn't matter.'

'But I want to tell you. I want you to understand. It's a very simple story. It doesn't say a great deal for me, but I'll tell you how it happened.'

'There's no need for you to talk about it, really there isn't.'

'You remember when we last met in Berlin. Everything I told you then was true. I loved you. But I couldn't marry you. For the reasons I told you, and also perhaps because I had forebodings about what was coming. Father always collected all those dreams and premonitions. I might have told him mine. I told you we weren't made for happiness. I think I knew what was going to happen. I loved you, really I loved you.'

'Please. . . .'

'All the same, I was lonely. Sometimes more and sometimes less, but I was lonely. And when one is lonely, a man always

turns up, except that he's always the wrong one. I knew he didn't love me. He didn't even find me particularly attractive. He came to Berlin from time to time, generally only for a day, and if a girl had let him down he rang me up and took me out. Afterwards he wanted to sleep with me, and when I said no he was always terribly surprised. Not that it really mattered to him so much, but being refused upset him, it was part of his day in Berlin, and I spoilt it. That happened three or four times. In between I never heard from him. We never wrote, and he never rang me up except at the last moment.

'That's what happened the last time, at the end of April. He was in Berlin, he had just been awarded that medal, and he wanted to celebrate with me. I went out with him, and he wanted me to stay the night at his hotel with him, and that time I said yes. It was the last thing he expected. I spent the night with him, and his train left very early next morning, which was a great relief to him. He rang me again the same evening, and you could tell how anxious he was; he was terribly afraid I might be taking it too seriously and might be expecting something from him and, when he realised I wasn't, it was a tremendous relief to him. That was the last I heard of him. When I discovered I was pregnant I didn't try to get in touch with him, he knows nothing about the child, and I don't want him ever to find out. I think there's no need for me to tell you his name.'

'No, there isn't.' Something of the old jealousy returned. I knew when Fritz Lehr had received his medal.

'It was crazy,' she said. 'It was crazy to do a thing like that, as crazy as everything else, as crazy as the times. I really love you. Crazy isn't it? I love someone and say no—and then sleep with someone else. Women are always doing that, they're in love with one man and go to bed with another. I don't expect you to believe me, but that's how it was. It had nothing to do with the fact that you had married. That was as unreal to me as the night at the hotel. That shows you what sort of

a family we are. It will be a good thing for the child to get into other hands . . . You think he'll help?'

'I'm sure of it.'

'And you don't mind? I mean, that it's by another man? You'll never give it away? The father will never worry you. He knows nothing about the child. It's my child only. You've sworn never to tell, haven't you?'

'Yes.'

'Then try it. She's a good baby. She never cries. You'll have no trouble with her. She's very quiet. She's used to strangers and she won't cry, she won't even murmur, and she eats everything, you'll like her.'

'I'm sure I shall.'

'And tell him not to worry. If he's worried about the child, tell him I promise she won't give the game away by crying. She'll be perfectly quiet, and when she's taken away she won't be frightened. She's used to someone suddenly coming and taking her somewhere else. She won't cry . . .'

But Julia cried. I could not hear it, but I felt the tears when she did something she had done once before, among the crowd of people waiting at the station in Berlin. She took my hand, put it to her lips, and kissed it. Then she said:

'I'm sorry. There's no reason for tears. Don't forget that. I think you had better go now.'

I don't know what I said, or whether I said anything. I know I went, without knowing I should never see her again.

There were fewer guards in the hut than before, and I had to knock before they let me in. As before, I did not talk to Zielinski; he was just leaving the counter when I went in. Perhaps I had been too long, but there was no clock there to tell me.

The huge Latvian was still there, and when he saw the fur hat he started telling me all over again that he simply must buy it from me. He was drunk, and mumbled that he just had to have it, it was just like the one his father had

bought him, the winters were hard in Latvia, it was *impossible* to go out without a fur hat, and he would give *anything* for it. When I told him he could have it for nothing, he suddenly quietened down. His huge, unsteady frame suddenly grew still, and he came over and stood threateningly over me, knitting his brows and glaring at me as if he thought I might be pulling his leg. But then, when he realised I meant what I said, he grabbed the hat, put it on, flung his arms round me and gave me a bear-hug that nearly crushed the life out of me. I let him. All I could see was his two black collar patches.

He ordered *Schnaps* for everyone present, and I couldn't help it, I was glad to be there. I knew I had done everything wrong; if only I had found the right words I might have been able to persuade her, it was all my fault. But then I couldn't go on thinking about it. Being here meant I was safe again, with firm ground under my feet. I can't help it, but that was how I felt, and I remember that when I looked at the dirty red check table-cloths and curtains and the trodden cigarette ends and the dirty slush from the men's boots on the floor, and smelt the air heavy with stale smoke and men's sweat—I thought it all marvellous, the surroundings, the drunken guards, the woman with curly fair hair and a flabby face—it was all marvellous.

There's not much more to say about Julia. Zielinski smuggled out the child and, as she had promised, it was quiet and did not cry. I got myself a car and a special permit, nominally to go and photograph some of the art treasures stored at Lauingen, and the child lay very quietly in the middle of all the photographic and enlarging apparatus at the back. I left it in the care of Severa, who found a priest, who christened the child Julia, and a woman registrar official, who filled out the birth certificate in my name; but all that was much later.

I had hoped that, once the child was in a place of safety

and she missed it, Julia would change her mind. So I went and tried to see her again, but she refused; all that Zielinski came back with was a pencilled note scribbled on the torn-off corner of a newspaper, saying thank you, thank you for everything, Julia. I could not understand it, and then I did a strange thing. On the day after I received the note, before driving away again, I got up very early, took my camera, and walked past the hut and down the path beside the siding where the freight-cars were standing. I carried the camera quite openly. It was crazy, because I knew that if there was one thing they didn't want and punished accordingly, it was the taking of photographs; it was a suicidal idea.

It was very early, soon after half past six, it was not light yet. I crept under one of the trucks and saw the camp at the foot of the steep slope, five huts in a row with hardly any space in between, and seven rows in all, surrounded by barbed wire. I had not come too early, because I saw the area in front of the barracks filling up with poor wretches with drooping heads assembling for the morning roll-call, and the guards with their slung rifles.

I was perhaps a hundred yards away when I took the photographs, and I was afraid. Sheer fear made my hands tremble as I held the camera. What I did was pointless; it was a senseless gesture. But all I was capable of was pressing the shutter-release and muttering come and get me, can't you see what I'm doing, come and get me—and yet being afraid that that was exactly what they would do.

Later I came back twice, in the middle and at the end of March, both times in vain. She sent me the same answer through Zielinski, and wrote no more notes. At the beginning of April, on about the fifth, Zielinski telephoned to me at Neuschwanstein. He was speaking from a public call office at the post office, and did not mention his name, but there was no need for that. He sounded agitated and nervous and somehow helpless. He said there were rumours that all

the camps in the Landsberg-Kaufering area were to be bombed by our own aircraft before the Americans arrived and found anyone there. He was convinced there was more in this than mere rumour. Someone from the Gauleiter's office in Munich had confirmed that the plan existed, and pressure was being exerted to have it carried out, though so far it had been possible to keep putting it off, with pretexts such as bad flying weather, the petrol shortage, and the shortage of bombs. There were other rumours to the effect that the inmates were to be sent to the Tyrol, on foot if no transport were available. Something was going to happen. The camps would not be allowed to fall into American hands as they were. This might be his last chance of getting in touch with me.

At this I got into touch with Fritz Lehr. I said nothing about having seen Julia, but told him only what I had just heard. I said he must talk to his father, and he promised to do so. For two or three days I heard nothing, but then he telephoned. He sounded confident and in good form. No, he had got nowhere with his father, he said, but he had talked to his brother-in-law again—and Julia was now there. Where? In Camp 4, which consisted only of sick quarters, nobody in it had to work. Karl Boettcher had got Julia out of Camp I and installed her as a doctor in the sick quarters. Everything was now all right; in any case, the whole bad business would soon be over, it could be only a question of days.

I was not reassured, because I remembered what Zielinski had said about Boettcher, and also what Ewi had told me about him. I rang Ewi's number, but put back the receiver when a man's voice answered.

I counted the days, and never left the radio. The Americans were already in Bamberg and Hof, but this area they had left behind. I could not get away from Neuschwanstein; because of the Military Police and the mobile courts-martial that were all over the place and picked everyone up, no-one

dared leave his unit. But of course nowadays my feelings have changed; I now think nothing should have held me back.

On April 22 I could stand it no longer. It took me three days to get there. The Americans were in some places, and in others the Germans were still holding out. Landsberg was not yet occupied, but the Americans were said to be in Kaufering. I arrived there just when the local people were battering in and looting the trucks in the siding. Camp I was empty; the huts were still standing, but the barbed wire had been trodden down.

Beyond the underpass I came across the old man with the barrow, and I asked him when the camp had been evacuated. He looked at me in alarm, and said he knew nothing about a camp, he had never heard of any camps, and then he went on slitting open his sacks.

The green hut was closed, and I did not want to go to the woman's house. Eventually I found someone who told me that the camp had been evacuated four days before. The occupants had been taken away by train, and the train had been shot up by those damned low-flying aircraft. *American low-flying aircraft?* Of course, what else would they be? They fired at everything. My informant was a railwayman, and he got quite carried away in telling me exactly where it happened—at kilometre stone 46.9, on a flat, straight stretch of track, ideal for the fighter-bombers, which had carried out three or four attacks at their leisure; the train had consisted of a lot of battered old freight-cars and an old locomotive. They took their time, attacked from behind, and then—*tack, tack, tack;* he accompanied the sound with the gesture of closing three fingers and pointing his index and little finger. . . . It was hard to divert him from his vivid description, and he became reticent only when I asked him about Camp 4. *Camp 4? Never heard of it;* and about camps in general he could give me no information whatever; there was a great deal of talk about them, but it had

all been kept secret, after all, and he was a railwayman, on the move most of the time, keeping the wheels turning for victory, as I knew, and *a fine victory we now had* . . .

From Fritz Lehr's description I knew roughly where Camp 4 was. I walked towards Augsburg, surrounded by people taking home their loot in baskets and rucksacks. They gradually grew fewer and fewer. Small arms fire was audible in the distance. I got as far as the farm buildings beyond which the track led off the road. An American tank was standing nearby. There was a slight eminence about five hundred yards off, and I saw a jeep going in that direction—it was open because it was a fine sunny day. It had a tall waving aerial. Other tanks were visible in the distance. I don't know what made me follow the jeep, I did, as first the jeep and then the aerial disappeared behind the eminence.

When I went over the hillock I saw the hut of Camp 4 but there was no one left. The jeep had gone beyond it to the edge of the gravel pit. The two Americans had left the jeep, and they stood there frozen against the clear shining sky, looking down. I was still hopeful at that moment, clinging to the thought that Boettcher had taken her in his care. But then I saw the two men in their uniforms move back, slowly, step by step; for a moment they seemed not to know what to do. But then one of them picked up the receiver of the radio-telephone. That's when I saw.

They didn't let me see much. I don't know why; they should have. I saw, for those few seconds, before they got over their surprise, and came to me with weapons in their hands, both of them, as though I seemed very dangerous to them. Maybe I was, maybe it was all in my face, those bodies down there in the pit, grey, already human stones after a day.

They shouted at me, and then, just as the thought was rising in me that Julia's body was down there with the others, one of the men grabbed me and used his rifle to push me back, still shouting at me.

They drove me back to the farm buildings where there were several lorries in which a number of German soldiers were already sitting. They took me there, still with the weapons pointed at my back, and I remember hands which were stretched out, and I was pulled up and someone pressed a cigarette into my hand, and I realised I was surrounded by tired but laughing faces.

I don't remember much beyond that, only the radio-telephones buzzing suddenly in all the open jeeps, and the place full of voices, and jeeps hurrying down the track, stirring up dust. Someone gave an order, and the lorry in which we were sitting started up and was driven on to the road. The men around me were singing.

It was not till later that I learned the details of the shooting and, by the time I was released, the bodies had been buried, all in a single grave. I went to see Joseph Zielinski, who had been severely wounded when the train was shot up at kilometre stone 46.9. I later gave evidence for him at his trial, and it was then that I found out that Karl Boettcher had disappeared. I was full of hatred and a craving for vengeance, and those were the weeks and months during which I read through the files, then and later, so that my hatred of a man I had never seen in my life should not cool off, ever.

Then, nearly two years later, at the end of 1947, I heard that Karl Boettcher's body had been found. Apparently he had managed to be taken prisoner in the uniform of a Luftwaffe lance-corporal. He was taken to a camp at Garmisch, from where he escaped, because one of the prisoners recognised him. He must then have remained hidden in a lonely, pathless wood near Steingaden; at all events, that was where the body was found in an isolated log cabin.

The hut had been burnt down, and the two bodies that were found in it were consequently in a condition that made identification extremely difficult. One was never identified; the other wore a wedding ring that provided a clue. Two

persons, his wife and the chauffeur, Horst-Dieter Winter, declared under oath that the body was that of the thirty-nine-year-old Karl Heinrich Boettcher, a judge added his signature, the bodies were buried, and Karl Boettcher was declared to be dead.

The newspapers barely noted the fact. I know that at the time I had my doubts, not based on facts, but only on a hunch. My doubts derived from my hate and my determination to have revenge, and his death deprived me of their target.

XVIII

There was no more for me to do on the commemorative volume. I had had the text and captions typed at a typing bureau; the typescript was still in the envelope in which they had returned it, and I had not looked at it again. Taking everything into account, I had made a pretty good job of it; it was concise and factual, and amounted to not more than twenty typewritten sheets altogether, and in essentials covered all the points suggested by Fritz Lehr. All the same, writing it had caused me a great deal of trouble and had taken up most of the time.

But what I liked about the job was the layout, at which I had another look—I had had a dummy made of all the 120 pages of it. The placing of the text—in three columns, for the three languages—was indicated on the first page with specimen type and on the others was shown by lines. The layout of the illustrations was shown in the same way; the positions of the black and white illustrations were drawn in with a black felt-tip pen, and the coloured ones with a red one; and the whole thing was divided into three parts of different colours. Copies of the tables and statistics which I had had drawn up were pasted in. The sizes of the illustrations and full instructions for the blockmakers were in a separate envelope. I liked the thing in this unfinished state; it left plenty of scope for the imagination; like this it was perfect and said everything, much better than the finished

product, which in comparison with the dummy was always disappointing.

At last I heard the car drawing up outside, and the slamming of the door. Fritz Lehr had telephoned from the car on the way here. I went to the window, and saw him standing and talking to Winter on the pavement. Then he walked towards the house.

He looked tired and worn. He said nothing about the garden party, ignored the chair I offered him, and showed no interest in the things I had spread out on the big table in the middle of the room. He stood there with his hands in the side pockets of his close-fitting suit and said:

'Let us go somewhere in the car.'

I looked at him in surprise, and pointed to the table.

'Aren't we going to discuss this?'

'Pack it all up, we'll take it with us.'

'But we need space for it. I've got everything ready. It won't take long if you're in a hurry. You can have a look at the text later, but I want to show you the layout of the whole thing, and for that I need space.'

But he seemed to have lost all interest in it. He looked round the room as if considering whether it were a suitable place for what he had to tell me.

'Do I have to have another look at it?' he said eventually. 'I assume it's all perfectly O.K., you're the expert, after all.' He leafed through the dummy. 'It all looks very good to me. Pack it all up. I've got to talk to you. It's important.'

'Why can't we talk here?'

'I should prefer the car.' He smiled. 'It's a fad of mine, but I can talk better in the car. I dictate all my mail in the car, I'm used to it. Wait, I'll help you.'

I'm not sure why he wanted to have this talk in the car. The partition separated us from Winter, but I wondered whether he could not overhear at least something of what we said. Perhaps Fritz Lehr wanted him to, perhaps he wanted a witness. I don't know, and it no longer matters.

241

I kept having to look at Winter's back, the back of his head between his white shirt and his chauffeur's hat. There was a straight line where his hair began, as if it had been cut by his wife.

'You remember my telling you I met my former wife in Madrid,' Fritz Lehr began. 'You remember, Jinx. It was at the Chamartin Tennis Club. I was there on business and I didn't have much time, but I wanted to see Santana, I like his style of play. Unfortunately he had a weak opponent; he won the first set easily and was leading in the second when a boy came and told me I was wanted outside.'

I could not imagine what he was leading up to. By this time we were on the Autobahn. Fritz Lehr had not told Winter where to go; apparently this had been arranged beforehand. I asked no questions and left the talking to him.

'Outside the club a car, an old Dodge, was waiting, and a man. . . . Well, to cut things short I went with him, because I suspected what was coming. Do you know Madrid? No? Well, it was only a short way, two or three miles along the National Road No. 1 to Burgos, and then he put me down at a motel. All he said was that his instructions were to take me to Señor Clemente Stoeber.'

Fritz Lehr did not look at me. He sat beside me, bending forward, with his hands on his knees. He really looked tired, short of sleep, older than fifty.

'The name was unknown to me, but it told me everything, of course. In the past he had used many names, and they all sounded the same. A Spanish Christian name and a German-sounding surname. Absurd, isn't it? He wouldn't have had any difficulty in procuring a forged passport under a Spanish-sounding name; it would have to be forged in any case. At least it would have been less conspicuous. But that is what he has always done, he has always kept to those German surnames that give the game away. So I had no difficulty in imagining who it was. The only surprise was that

242

he took the risk of leaving South America. It was the first time in twenty-one years.'

'Can the heating be turned down?' I said. I don't think I had yet taken in what he had just told me, but my body seemed to have done so before my mind. Fritz Lehr pressed some buttons. But I only felt hotter than ever.

'You know whom I'm talking about?' he said, and added: 'Yes, he's alive.'

'How can he be alive?' I heard myself say. I looked at the back of Winter's neck. I was sitting behind him. I looked at the back of his neck, the skin between the shirt and the hair. I thought I could smell the aftershave lotion he always used. I remembered he was one of the two persons who had identified the body. I must have repeated my question. 'How can he be alive?'

Fritz Lehr leaned back in the leather cushions.

'He left Germany at the end of 1947,' he said. 'He crossed into Switzerland near Lindau, from Switzerland he went to Italy, to Bari, and from there he went to South America. He has lived there ever since, first in Argentina and for the last few years in Paraguay, on the frontier between the two countries. I shan't pull any wool over your eyes, we helped him, the whole family was involved.' He paused for a moment, and then went on: 'At the time his name kept cropping up at a trial in connection with that horrible business, you know what I mean; some men whom he ordered to do it were caught, and of course they pleaded they were merely carrying out his orders. We had to protect ourselves. He was dragging us into something we had nothing whatever to do with, Ehrengard, who really had not the slightest inkling about it, her five children, and above all our name, the family name. My father was in Landsberg fortress, the firm was in the hands of a trustee, it was a critical time, and we couldn't afford to have our name linked with his. That's why we spent the money. It was all fixed by that man in Lindau, it was,

so to speak, the luxury route for hunted members of the SS, with a complete stock of admirably forged papers. What could we do but pay up? We paid up later too. That was the agreement between us, so to speak—we paid up, and he disappeared from our lives for ever.'

'And whose were the two bodies?'

'What do you mean?'

'You know what I mean. The two dead bodies found in the burnt out log cabin in the wood.'

'Oh, that. That was a lucky chance, a gift of providence we made use of. One of our woodmen found them, and told us about them first. Gottfried and I went and had a look, the place had not been burnt down yet. The bodies were of two SS men, we could tell from the tattoo marks showing the blood group. Otherwise there was nothing whatever to show their identity, no papers and no clues. The only thing was they had taken poison, and Boettcher had always loudly proclaimed he would never fall alive into American hands and shown everyone his cyanide capsules. That gave us the idea. The only thing we did was to fetch his wedding ring—he was hiding in the neighbourhood—and put it in the ashes.'

I remembered a remark that Gottfried Lehr had made when I went to see him about the commemorative volume. So he too was in the know.

'And Winter and his own wife swore the body was his?'

'Helping him to escape was a problem in itself,' he said, 'but it didn't mean they would stop looking for him. We had to stop them looking for him, and people stop looking for a dead man. Yes, they swore affidavits that the body was his. I think we were all surprised at how smoothly it went. I remember that the body we picked on actually had a fractured collar bone, just like Boettcher.'

I looked at the back of Winter's neck. I could imagine why he had done it and kept silent all these years. But Boettcher's wife? I tried to remember the evening on the verandah when she had shown me the photograph.

'And she, his wife, was willing to do that?'

'She had to, it was the price she had to pay. She believed nothing of what he was accused of. She simply shut her eyes and refused to believe any of it, but all the same she was afraid that if he were caught he would be found guilty. Also she knew that unless she agreed she could expect nothing more from us. She had to choose between him and the family and her share in the business. And she cares about money and the family. She married him, but she was a Lehr, and she knew that the Lehrs come first. Our family sticks together in such situations. Now she hates us, because we were all against her and forced her to do what we wanted, but at the time she had no choice. Later she was interrogated several times by the CIC, and she was very convincing. To an outsider who doesn't understand what the family and the name mean to us, all this is very difficult to understand.'

Was I listening to him? Did I realise what all this added up to? I don't know. My only thought was that Boettcher was alive. I realised that I had never reconciled myself to the fact of his death, and consequently I was not really surprised. But it was difficult to connect Boettcher, the man I hated with the man in a motel on the road to Burgos. Clemente Stoeber and Karl Boettcher—what had they to do with each other? And why was Fritz Lehr telling me all this? What was his purpose? I looked at him and tried to read his face. He looked tired, but very calm and composed.

'And now he wants to come back,' he said.

'He wants to come back? Here?'

'That was what he told me in Madrid.'

'When was that?'

'Three weeks ago.'

Were we still driving? All I knew was that we were inside an airless, sealed capsule, moving. He had said three weeks ago; that was when Christina had turned up and told me about the commemorative volume project. The whole thing had begun with her, it was with her that the past had begun

to come back, first in tiny fragments and then in bigger and bigger ones until it overpowered the present, and then I knew everything had been leading up to this.

'As long ago as that?' I said.

'We searched for a way out. My first idea in Madrid was that all he was after was money. We have never had direct contact with him during all these years, but from time to time he has made demands. Someone would turn up at one or other of our branches abroad and leave a message for me. This happened every three or four years, and sometimes the intervals were longer. The sums of money he asked for were large, but not shameless, and I quickly paid up. It's now obvious that it was a mistake. But he kept his side of the bargain and never tried to get into direct contact with us. Until three weeks ago.'

He waited for a reaction from me, but when I said nothing he went on:

'He was waiting for me at that motel. He's now sixty-one. I thought he looked older. I don't know whether he's ill, or whether it's simply the fear in which he must have lived all these years. I don't know. I had the impression the past no longer existed for him, and that the only thing in his mind was that he wanted to come back. He's got the idea firmly fixed in his head. He wants to come back. He wants to see Germany again, and he wants to see his wife and children. . . . My first idea was that this was only a new way of extracting money from me.'

'But he'd immediately be. . . .'

'No, he wouldn't. The situation is that he could probably come back without anything happening to him.'

'You think nothing would happen?'

I could not think clearly; all I knew was that my hate was growing.

'Immediately after my return from Madrid I had a talk with someone. Let us say, I was confidentially given an offi-

246

cial view. In the first place, his passport is in order, and he can enter the country and stay here. Secondly, Karl Boettcher is officially dead, and invalidating a death certificate, though of course it's not impossible, is not so easy. A prosecution would follow, but it's doubtful whether it would end in a conviction. There are no survivors to give evidence, and the prosecution would have to depend on the evidence of men who were guards at the camp. Those who were tracked down at the time were sentenced to death. In some instances the sentence was commuted, but how many of them are still alive and, if they are, would they stick to the evidence they gave then? But, no matter what the outcome might be, that trial must not take place. The family couldn't be kept out of it. Just imagine the situation. The whole thing could not have happened at a worse moment. A fine centenary it would be for the family. Sending out the commemorative volume would be pointless. We've got to find another way out.'

I listened, and asked no questions. I suddenly realised that he was still holding back the most important thing. Fritz Lehr was not a man to tell such a long story without a motive. Winter drove on quietly and steadily, keeping to a constant speed. Once I saw him lift the receiver of the car telephone and speak into the mouthpiece, but he did not put anyone through or tell us who the caller was. Other cars overtook us.

The car had its own bar. Lehr snapped it open and poured himself something. He did not drink it, but held the glass in his hand.

'The main problem is my sister Ehrengard,' he went on. 'She has somehow reconciled herself to the idea that he might be dead. If she found out he was alive, she'd insist on his coming back and on his being rehabilitated. She has never realised what he is. To her he has always been a man with a heart of gold, and now, after all these years, he's more so than ever. I know he's counting on her aid. He wrote to her from Madrid, but the old man intercepted the letter. He

might write again. He might telephone. There he is, in Madrid, two hours away by air. I reached a kind of standstill agreement with him, but now it's running out.'

The smell of the cognac spread through the back of the car. He emptied the glass and put it back.

'Yes,' he said, as if I had asked him a question. 'I have discussed the matter with the old man. Before that I didn't trouble him with it, but this time I had no alternative. It was he who built up the whole thing, and it's his name and reputation that's at stake. He has his own views on the matter, and attributes the blame to me. And in retrospect I must say he was right. It was a mistake on my part to go on giving him money. So long as he had money, in South America he was all right; South America isn't Europe. So long as he was able to pay for it, he could get everything—passports, protection, security. If his money ran out they would simply have dropped him, and there he would be, stranded somewhere in a tropical rain forest. The old man's quite right, it certainly was a mistake on my part. He said it would have been better to have tipped off somebody, the Israelis, for instance. He didn't mean that seriously, of course; what he meant was that someone should be put on his trail who had reason to hate him, which would be far, far better than any amount of money.'

These last words gave me the first inkling of what he was driving at. The strange thing was that I still felt totally uninvolved. He could not drag me into anything against my will.

'All the same, there's no getting away from it, what it ultimately all boils down to is paying out money again,' he went on, speaking with a note of regret in his voice about a painful necessity to which he had reconciled himself. 'There's no alternative. I've been to Madrid twice and tried to persuade him of the senselessness of his idea of coming back. I made no impression on him whatever until I told him that none of us would accept him, that even Ehrengard wouldn't, and certainly not his children, to whom he was dead. He must

have had second thoughts, particularly when he got no answer to his letter. That was as far as I got the second time I
saw him. As I said, in the end it boiled down to a question
of money, as it was bound to. I offered him $250,000 to leave
us in peace, and eventually he agreed. But I don't feel happy
about it. It's a great deal of money, and perhaps he now
realises that there's no future in his plan to come back. But
it's not a solution.'

I know that I said: 'Why are you telling me all this? You
must have a reason for it. You're telling me something that
your whole family wants kept absolutely secret. Why?'

He looked at me as if the question surprised him.

'But it does concern you, doesn't it?' he said. 'It concerns
you more than anyone. He caused Julia Dressler's death. If
anyone has good reason to hate him, it's you.'

'Certainly, it concerns me.' I said cautiously. 'But what
does that amount to after all this time?'

He nodded, as if in agreement. 'Yes, what does it amount
to? You're quite right. All the same, she's dead—and he's
alive. Doesn't the fact that he's alive change everything?'

He leant forward and tapped on the glass partition. Winter
did not even turn his head. I saw him nod slightly, he seemed
to know what was expected of him. He accelerated, no doubt
to turn off the Autobahn at the next exit. Then he said:

'Would you take him the money?'

He spoke casually, as if asking just a favour of a friend. To
the drivers who had overtaken us we must have been a very
ordinary sight; two men talking business in the back of a car.
Perhaps we were talking about business and not about feelings. Somehow I was infected; perhaps I already divined the
opportunity that was presenting itself: the opportunity of
acquiring $250,000 and, after all these years, to have my hate
avenged.

'You want me to take it to him in Madrid?'

'I should be glad if someone took the task off my hands. I
don't want to meet him again. I left it open whether I should

hand over the money personally or through a messenger. It has to be in cash. No cheques, or anything of that sort.'

I did not argue, but merely said:

'How would it be done?'

He felt behind him, and put a flat, black briefcase on his knee. He took a sheet of paper from it, as if we really were discussing a business project.

'He expects the money at latest on October 7.'

'When?'

'At latest on the 7th. That's next Tuesday, a week from today. The arrangement is that I either take it to him personally or send a messenger. So he won't think that there's anything strange about it if you turn up. He has never seen you before, and there's no connection between you and him You realise that, don't you?'

'How would I get to Madrid, and where would I pick up the money?'

By now I was almost impatient to be told the details. He looked at the sheet of paper.

'You'd take the Trans-Europe express from Munich to Zürich on Sunday, spend the night in Zürich and fly next day to Madrid, where a room would be booked for you at the Hotel Fénix. It's at 2, Paseo de la Castellana, only a few yards from the bank, the Banco Español de Crédito at 7, Paseo de la Castellana, which is right on top of the Metro station. You would take the Metro to the Plaza de Castilla, and from there you would go by a No. 29 bus to Chamartin, from where you would take a taxi to the junction of the Avenida de Burgos, which is National Road No. 1, and the Avenida Manoteras. It's in a pretty depressing area, an industrial zone with gas works and oil depôts and a great many car workshops. If you go down National Road No. 1 away from the city centre, you'll find a Renault works two hundred yards down on the left. You can't miss it. The motel is just beyond it.'

'And the money?'

'It's in a safe at the bank. All you have to do is to fetch it, take it there, hand it over to him or. . . .'

'Or what?'

He ignored the question and looked at the sheet of paper in his hand.

'I shall pay all your expenses as well as a fee, let us say $5,000. I hate the idea of paying him such a sum, perhaps all for nothing. I wish there were another way out.' He shook his head, and again he seemed to be thinking aloud. 'It's a shame,' he went on. 'It's a shame about the money. Two hundred and fifty thousand dollars—if only there were another way out. I would gladly sacrifice all the money for it. I've written it off in any case. If there were another way out. . . .'

The car had left the Autobahn at one of the exits, and we were now driving back on the other side. Lehr put the piece of paper back in his pocket.

'I assume you have a valid passport?'

'A photographer always has a valid passport.'

So far I had not agreed to anything, but he seemed to regard the matter as settled. I think I now understood him. Perhaps I was trying to test him, to try and find out how far he would implicate himself, when I said:

'Let us assume there were another way out.'

He merely shrugged his shoulders.

'To me it would be worth the money. But I don't see one. Perhaps you'll think of something. So you'll take him the money?'

'Can I think it over?'

'Of course.' He handed me the black briefcase. 'You'll find everything there, flight timetables, addresses, money for your out-of-pocket expenses. You'll find confirmation from the bank and the safe key waiting for you at the Hotel Fénix. If you decide not to go, simply return the briefcase to me, let us say, not later than Friday. If I don't hear from you, I shall know you're going, and there'll be no need for any

further discussion. Oh, before I forget, here's the cheque for the outstanding 5,000 marks due to you for the commemorative volume. I'll have a look at the whole thing quietly later, but I'm sure it'll be perfectly satisfactory. What I've seen of it looked very good and convincing. It was a good idea of Christina's to suggest you.

I don't remember anything else that passed between us on the way back. He dropped me at the front door, and I waited till the car had driven away. I remembered Christina's car, the silvery-grey Mercedes, at the same spot. Had that really been only three weeks ago?

A man was pasting a cigarette advertisement on the big hoarding. The rusty-red posters of the Social Democrats and the black and white ones of the Free Democrats were already covered up. Only half of Kiesinger's face was left; the other, the left half, had vanished behind a basket of tobacco leaves. The man had put a ladder against the hoarding and was brushing over the poster with his paste brush; the surface was still wet, and the outline of the face still showed through.

How much had Christina known? And Gottfried? And the old man? Had the whole thing been planned from the outset, or was that a figment of my imagination? But what did that matter now? Did anything matter now except vengeance on Boettcher—and suddenly laying hands on a fortune?

I remembered what Dr. Blum had said at the garden party. *The whole secret lies in having money. All you need is a large amount of money.* Here was the money, $250,000. My mind dwelt on a handsome, rectangular safe of dull gleaming metal, and the bank notes inside it. I did not know the dollar rate, but $250,000 must certainly be a million marks. Was there room in a travelling bag for a million marks? In my old bag there'd certainly be plenty of room. And I wouldn't break my head about the best way of investing the money, countering price increases, depreciation, revaluation losses,

252

etc., about which there had been such a fuss on the election posters; people like me could never manage that sort of thing. I should simply put the money in another safe deposit and take what we needed, what Julia and I needed, when we needed it. If we spent $25,000 a year, it would last for ten years, and beyond that I refused to think. . . . I might take her to Tunis. At this time of year the temperature would certainly be about seventy-four, and the water would be nearly as warm, about seventy-one perhaps. Tunis was a good idea. When she landed at Carthage airport I should be able to show her the spot where I lay on a stretcher on 7 May 1943 with three bullets in my belly, attached to a lot of tubes; no-one had believed the blood transfusion they gave me would really be of any use. It was only logical that I should now try to begin a new life at the place where I really should have died.

Later, alone in my studio, I took the sheet of paper from the black briefcase. It was impeccably typed on an electric typewriter. I read it, and I visualised myself following the instructions. Though I had never been to Madrid, the names were already familiar to me; the Hotel Fénix, the Banco Español de Crédito, I walked down into the Metro, I got into a bus at the Plaza de Castilla and changed to a taxi at Chamartin. There were the gas-holders and the car workshops, and finally the motel. . . .

And then my mind stopped working. Beyond that point I could not think, my imagination failed. The pictures in my mind simply stopped, and I got no farther. I simply marked time. There was the motel, but I got no nearer. But I felt something I had not felt with such clarity before, even during the drive with Fritz Lehr when he told me Karl Boettcher was alive. Hate, pure hate, drowned everything else, like a flame that drew nourishment from itself.

XIX

I had had the bag for many years. It was not the one I had
bought in Tunis in 1942, though I sometimes said it was
and sometimes almost believed it myself; I had had it made
in the fifties, and it was an exact replica of the old one, made
of the same coarse-grained pigskin with strengthened sides
and special compartments for the cameras and lenses. It was
now old and worn in its turn, and I always had it ready
packed, so that all I had to do was to put a few films in; my
passport was always in one of the side pockets, together
with the international certificate of vaccination and a time-
table of international flights.

I had decided to take nothing but this bag, but it took me
some time to do so. I packed various suitcases, took things
out and put others in, but decided in the end that I needed
the bag only. I took out the cameras and lenses, and left in
nothing but my passport, washing and shaving things, a
change of underclothes, a spare shirt, a second pair of light
shoes, a pullover, and two black notebooks containing these
notes. I packed it and left it on the bed, like a promise that
had at last been kept; everything else had ceased to matter.

I still had to talk to Thea, but after what I had done during the last two days I was no longer afraid of it. I felt as
if I had been disposing of the property of a dead man; I
had sold the photographic equipment and the postcard publishing business, given instructions for the collection of clocks

254

to be sold by auction, prepared all the documents required by the tax authorities, written out standing orders for the payment of various insurance premiums, and signed a form giving Thea authority to handle my bank account. In the past all these things had seemed to be insuperable obstacles, and yet I had dealt with them in only two days. I had forgotten nothing. I put everything in a single folder, bank statements, insurance policies.

I laid my coat beside the bag and waited for Thea to come back. It seemed pointless, and I remember thinking I might as well go without doing so, but I decided it was her due that I should talk to her and not just leave a letter behind. She had a right to hear from my own lips that I was leaving her. It changed nothing, but it was her right. I had betrayed her from the beginning, after all, and she had never had a chance—against a dream no-one has a chance. It had been unfair of me, unfair from the beginning.

On the day when the trees at Werder were white with frost and I left Berlin after seeing Julia coming out of the hospital with Fritz Lehr by her side I had felt sick to the point of wanting to die—and I very nearly managed it.

I was never one of those daredevil press photographers who were always risking their lives in the most exposed positions in the front line. In more than two years in Africa I had never had anything worse than an attack of dysentery, and after my return everyone was surprised at the way I suddenly no longer avoided danger. During the last battles in Africa nothing happened to me until the very last day, when our tanks made one last counter-attack near Tunis— and I can still see the astonishment on the face of that British second lieutenant of the 11th Hussars when I emerged from the cover of my official press photographer's vehicle, it was a Horch with four-wheel drive, with my camera slung round my neck . . . though he was not so taken aback as to forget to pull the trigger of his sub-machine gun.

I don't know how I was brought back. The first thing I was aware of was the sun overhead, the bottles with the blood plasma and the tubes to which I was attached. I was lying on a stretcher in the shadow of a Nissen hut at the edge of an airfield.

I seemed to have been forgotten. When I raised my head I could see the airfield, the shimmering heat over the runways. I could see hundreds of soldiers, but not a single aircraft. I thought I had reached the place where I was going to die, at the edge of the Carthage airfield, four miles outside Tunis, in the sunshine, pumped full of morphia and other people's blood that was of no more use to me. I also remember that there were many days on which I was afraid of dying, but that day was not one of them.

I felt rather well—particularly when *she* came and bent over me and held my hand. She had on the doctor's white coat she had worn under her overcoat in Berlin and a close fitting white hat from which her hair bulged out, and I heard her voice saying it was absurd to think of dying. She stayed with me the whole time, and she said that if only I had the will to pull through everything would be all right, and afterwards she would look after me herself. But that was not so important as something else; she bent over me, blushed, and whispered that soon we should be getting married, the nearest register office was at Bajohren, and Davidov would play for the dancing.

Davidov? But surely he was dead?

Rubbish. Why did I always talk such rubbish? Who on earth had told me that? Davidov played his fiddle better than ever, and Nyanya would make her wedding dress, and. . . .

Two men picked up the stretcher. *Careful* she said, and walked beside me, holding my hand. An ugly, ungainly Junkers 52 was waiting on the runway, its engines spattered with oil—but what a wonderful sight it was. They lifted me in, and I said *please don't let go of my hand*. The engines

started up with a loud, ugly stutter, and then it grew quiet.

I hardly remember the flight. Later I discovered that that Junkers 52 was the only aircraft that left Tunis on 7 May 1943 and that it was the last to do so, and there were more generals and senior staff officers on board than wounded. That I can remember, because they put the stretcher down in the middle of the gangway, and I had all those trousers with red piping down the sides in front of my eyes. The next thing I remember is looking at a glass container full of a dark red, almost black fluid, which was blood plasma, and a voice saying:

'But that's something you've got to tell me—who is she?'

It was the voice of Dr. Blum, who was the chief medical officer of the Lykabettos military hospital in Athens. I had been talking continually in my fever, and all he had been able to make out was the name Julia, and this already interested him more than the operation. It seemed that my tough old Rodenstock had saved my life. The bullets struck the camera first; this made the external wounds bigger, but considerably reduced the force of impact. I lost two-thirds of my stomach, but not my life, which was perhaps what I hoped for. But that was not the sort of thing one told a chief medical officer at that time. And I met Thea.

Ten days later I was able to get up for the first time, and a week later I was transferred to another hospital in a suburb of Athens. It was a former hotel, with big, high rooms with five beds on each side. There was practically nothing to do all day long but to sit on the beds playing cards, except that films were shown twice a week in the former hotel ballroom, and performances were occasionally given by concert parties sent by the organisation that provided entertainment for the troops.

She was part of an act that called itself the Transylvanian Quartet, consisting of three musicians and a singer. Her name, Thea Pichler, appeared in the programme in small

type. I don't remember much about the rest of the show, which consisted of the usual sketches and juggling and acrobatic acts. The chief attraction was a girls' band, consisting of three blondes and three brunettes, with three saxophones, which roused wild enthusiasm among the men, and some idiot had made her the next item on the programme—and there she was, poor thing, standing right in front of the footlights.

I had a new camera, and after her first songs, the applause for which was very meagre, I went up to the stage. There she was, looking rather thin, and there was something very touching about the way she kept putting her hand to her brow to push back her fair hair, which was combed back close to her head with a parting in the middle, though not a hair was out of place. She was nervous because of the restlessness in the hall, the clearing of throats and the buzz of conversation that betrayed the men's boredom. She did not know whether to go on singing or not, and some wag at the back of the hall called out *carry on*, and everyone laughed.

It was her bad luck that she came on immediately after the girls' band and that her repertoire did not include any of the hits of the moment, but only sentimental songs from Transylvania, and when she went on the applause was even more meagre and the laughter greater. I raised my camera and took a picture of her standing in front of the footlights. The flash startled her and she waited for the curtain to drop, but there was none, so she withdrew to the wings, where she turned and looked at me as if she were wondering whether I too were not just making fun of her.

There was another performance next day, and she had no better success. I had had the picture developed and enlarged, but it came back too late. I knew where the party were staying, and next morning I got to the hotel just in time; the bus that was taking them somewhere else for another performance, at which she would certainly not get more applause, was waiting to leave. She was one of the last, and

was just about to get in. She was dragging a heavy suitcase but, in contrast to the members of the girls' band, whose faces I could see behind the misted up bus windows, because it was early and it was a cool morning, nobody helped her.

When one was close to her she looked even thinner and more delicate. When I spoke to her, she stopped, turned hesitantly, and at first did not recognise me. I told her I had taken a photograph of her. She put down her suitcase and looked at it, as surprised as if it were the photograph of a stranger. I remember that her Transylvanian accent was discernible when she said:

'Is that me?'

'Don't you like it?'

She shook her head, and I thought what a pity it was that she didn't wear her hair loose, why didn't someone tell her? They put her on immediately after the girls' band, and on top of it she had that impossible hair-do.

'No-one has ever taken a photo of me like that before,' she said. 'I mean, it's very flattering. I've never seen a photo in which I look like that. Do I really look like that?'

'In reality you look even better. But you ought to wear your hair loose.' The driver sounded his horn, and she wanted to hand me back the picture, but I said: 'It's for you. I took it for you.'

A man appeared in the doorway and asked her impatiently to get in. The members of the girls' band, all the nice girls who were going to steal the show again that evening, were pressing their brows against the windows. So I said:

'Tell me, could we meet again?'

'I don't know. Do you really want to?'

'Yes, of course. Write to me, or telephone. Soon!'

She telephoned the same evening. The telephone was down the passage, in an alcove full of wildly luxuriating plants and tall rubber trees. It was late when the call came through, and my first thought was that it was Julia, but a strange voice said:

259

'I promised to ring you.'

'Yes, of course. Where are you?'

'At Larissa.'

'How did it go this evening?'

'Hopeless. I ought to give it up.'

'Nice of you to ring.'

'Are you sure it's really me in the photo?'

'Of course I'm sure.'

'I'm not.'

There was a pause, and that might well have been the end of all, but then she said: 'I wore my hair loose,' and I heard her laugh. 'But it made no difference,' she went on. 'I'm hopeless. You must have made a mistake.'

'Are you going on tomorrow?'

'Yes.'

'Don't you ever have a rest?'

She hesitated, and then said:

'Yes.'

'When?'

'In ten days' time.'

'Where?'

'At Schulerau.'

'Where's that?'

'Near Kronstadt. Where the songs come from. That's where I come from.'

'That's not so very far away. What would you say if I came over?'

'Would that be possible?'

I said something commonplace, like where there's a will there's a way, and after I was discharged from hospital I spent my three weeks' convalescence leave at Schulerau, and on the last day but one we got married.

I had written to Julia, telling her I was going to get married, and waited for a reply. I don't remember much about the three weeks there, except that every day I waited for a letter from her saying how absurd it was for me to marry

someone else, because she loved me. But no letter came.

Thea's father, was a simple, straightforward man who worked hard all his life, a Kronstadt confectioner who worked his way up to owning two hotels at Kronstadt and Schulerau. Olga Valmy had got married to him at the age of thirty-six, and how happy he had been to lay everything he had at the feet of this prima donna with a past, and how little it amounted to in her eyes. I can still see him in my mind's eye, small, thickset and a trifle bald already, busily arranging everything for our wedding in 1943, rushing excitedly about all day long, determined to give his daughter the best and grandest wedding possible in the middle of the war, while Olga Valmy found fault with everything, the food, the wine and the silver. I should never have left Thea with her afterward.

At Schulerau Thea and I stayed at the Butschetsch, one of the two hotels belonging to her father to which people came from Kronstadt on Sundays to eat and see the Carpathian deer and the bears in the enclosures belonging to the hotel; there were mountain bears which, as Thea said, were among the finest and biggest in the world. No letter had come, and so we got married. We drove in an open Tatra to the so-called Black Church at Kronstadt, and Thea looked happy and pretty. In her hair she had a lot of coloured ribbons that fluttered behind her in the breeze in the open car. Poor, happy Thea—even on that day I clung to my dream; I kept feeling in the left-hand pocket of my jacket to make sure, not that I had not forgotten the ring, but that Julia's telegram of congratulations was still there.

Thea came on a visit to my parents, and we spent one more leave together. After that we did not see each other for five years. When Gottfried Lehr arranged my transfer to Neuschwanstein I suggested she should go and live with my parents, but she did not want to leave her father alone; she had given up entertaining the troops, and was working in the hotel at Schulerau. When the German south-eastern front

collapsed at the end of 1944, she could have got away, but her father did not want to abandon his hotels, and he still hoped the worst would be avoided.

Then for nearly two years I had no news of her and did not know whether she was alive or dead, until a message from her came through the Red Cross. Her father was dead, and her mother was making a living by giving singing lessons. Nearly another three years passed before I was able to travel to Kronstadt, which by then was called Brasov, and bring them both out.

When we met again after five years in 1950 we were practically strangers to each other. We both wanted to make a new start, but too much had happened, both to her and to me. I never talked about Julia or her death, and she never talked about her father's death, or about the time when the Russians confiscated his two hotels and put them on the street. We tried to put the broken pieces together again, but failed.

She had begun to drink, which was something completely new to me; previously she had never touched alcohol—at our wedding she had got tipsy over a single glass of champagne. Her colleagues in the concert party used to join the officers in the evening after the show and used to drink a good deal, but she always kept out of it, because she thought it would be bad for her voice. But now she drank, and she started singing in American clubs.

It was her own idea. She said she wanted to do something and not be dependent on me—and she began practically overnight. The former organiser of entertainments for the German troops on the south-eastern front was now a well-known agent, and he got her the engagement. This too was a surprise for, if there was one thing she regarded with contempt, it was *good* singers who demeaned themselves by singing *cheap* songs. But now she sang in American clubs, the best things about which were invariably their names. The

six-man band with whom she sang was called the Alpine
Swingers, and instead of her old songs she sang *Don't fence
me in* and *I'm in the mood for love.*

There are snapshots of her taken at that time, showing a
slender blonde in a long dress, her arms at her sides, her
always serious face bent over the microphone, with five men
at their instruments in the background, looking hollow-
cheeked and with cropped hair (or so it looks to-day), waiting only for the interval, the free meal and the packet of
American cigarettes that was given to each. Thea was never
smiling in these snapshots, for she never forgot that she was
wasting her voice on all those GIs who whistled through
their fingers. She reached the high point of her career with
a three-week engagement at the Casa Carrioca at Garmisch
—which was then *the* club in the American zone—and two
discs that were made of her singing with the band. They
were shellac discs, which she later smashed, whether deliberately or not, when she was drunk. I realised that she
did all this as a kind of self-punishment, because as a serious
singer she had been a failure.

Then everything changed because of the child Julia. I had
not told her about Julia immediately. I went practically
every weekend to Lauingen to see the girl, or invented trips
as an excuse. Seeing that they had again cut off her fine,
long, dark hair, the cotton dresses they made her wear, the
fact that they did not call her Julia, which was far too
worldly a name, but Little Sister Severa, was horrible. She
was nearly six now, and saying goodbye to her, leaving her
standing at the end of the long avenue while she waved to
me until one of the sisters took her hand and led her away,
grew more and more difficult and more and more of an
ordeal.

So eventually I summoned up my courage and told Thea
about her. The reason why I put it off for so long—more than
six months—was that the first thing Thea told me after she
came back was that she wanted no children—not in these

times and in this world; she said it was unfair to bring a human being into the world without his or her having any choice in the matter. I was uncertain how she would react when I at last told her, and I did so half-heartedly and uncertainly, as at the time she was drinking more heavily than ever before. But her reaction was a complete surprise. She insisted on going to Lauingen at once, the very same day. I had told her very little about Julia's mother, and she did not ask many questions, either then or later, and I did not tell her who the girl's father was; all I told was that Julia must never find out that it was not I. To her I was her father, and so it must remain.

We drove back that evening with Julia in the car. Thea insisted on taking her away immediately; she told the nuns that, now the girl had both a father and a mother, she must not spend another day with them. I had been totally wrong about Thea. She gave up the Alpine Swingers immediately and stopped drinking overnight. With Julia's arrival everything changed.

Looking back at it now, I feel certain that the next ten years were the happiest in Thea's life and, incidentally, the happiest in our marriage. Everyone was always astonished at how like me Julia was as a child; she had the same complexion, a similar physique, the same way of walking and moving, and the same tendency to keep her mouth open when doing something on which she had to concentrate. This did not prevent Thea from thinking of Julia as her child. She was a daughter after her own heart, very shy and reserved with people, and very serious and thoughtful in everything she did. She was also always very punctual, and later, when she was older, she never wanted to go out alone in the evening, never wanted to eat ices when the weather was too cold, and never objected to the clothes that Thea chose for her or to the hair-do that Thea decided on. Also she rewarded Thea's efforts. It was never necessary to read Julia's school reports —Thea could see at a glance the double row of ones and

nothing but ones; and what a tragedy it was when a wretched two occasionally appeared among them to spoil the picture.

The first rift appeared when Julia took up tennis. Thea objected from the start; she said it distracted the child from more important things, robbed her of valuable time for her school work and it was bad for her figure. For a long time I could not understand Thea's exaggeratedly violent reaction; I failed to appreciate that it was the first sign of a deep jealousy of everything that brought me and Julia together.

Things nearly reached the breaking point when, in spite of all her many ones, Julia announced her determination to leave school after obtaining her school leaving certificate. It was her own decision, uninfluenced by me. Thea fought for her with appeals and tears. She insisted she must stay on at school and go to the university; only a university degree would assure her of independence. But at sixteen Julia was no longer a child. Her mind was made up, and she presented us with a *fait accompli;* she was going to Pforzheim to qualify as a goldsmith and play tennis. It was all settled; a big jewellery manufacturer, a survivor of the great age of tennis and a pioneer of the game in Germany, had seen her playing in a youth tournament and had offered to back her. She would have all the time she needed for practice and travelling, and she would learn a trade at the same time. Of course we could have put our foot down and simply forbidden it, but we never got to that point; Thea gave in, but not finally, for she went on trying to persuade Julia to change her mind, but her efforts grew weaker and weaker. In the end she surrendered completely, and reconciled herself to our often going off alone together, to my accompanying her to all the tournaments she played in. Poor Thea—again she had lost me to Julia.

When Julia went off, she began working again and, as I soon discovered, drinking again. She passed her driving test —it was six years ago now—at the age of forty-one, and became one of the Avon Ladies—*Avon rings at your door.* She

was often away for weeks at a time, staying at small hotels, and it was not difficult to imagine the rooms, the long evenings, the conversations with other travellers. Now and again she spent a few nights at home while minor repairs were done to her car—dents in the bodywork that grew more and more frequent. I found out what was at the back of this when she stayed at home for a longer period and a court reporter told me what had happened. She had had an accident driving home one evening, and the car had had to be written off. No-one else had been involved and no-one was hurt, but the blood test was 2.8 per 1000, and there was a long list of previous offences of the same kind; this time she had lost her license for eight years. After this she found the job at the Ilona Institute and commuted to Munich every day by train.

I was standing by the window when the taxi drove up. It was the same driver in the same black leather jacket, and she wore the same suit. She did not dismiss him immediately; they stood chatting on the pavement for a few minutes. I wondered what there was to say that had not already been said. I looked at the packed bag and the coat on the bed, and again I felt tempted to leave without talking to her. I knew in my bones that she would be better off after I had left her, not immediately, not next day, but certainly in the long run.

When I went out she was standing at the door opposite, looking for the latch-key in her handbag. She heard me, but did not turn, but went on hunting for the key, now nervously. I thought it would be better to postpone things till she had had her first drink, and said nothing. But then, with the key in her hand, she looked at me. She tried to smile, that slightly frightened, crooked smile of hers she used when she wanted to be left alone.

'Hallo,' I said, as to a stranger. 'What sort of a day have you had?'

266

'The same as usual.'

I was surprised that she did not open the door, but stayed there, still holding the key-ring, to which the old car key, out of sheer habit, was still attached.

'I should like to talk to you,' I said. 'Some time in the next few hours, when you have time.'

She came over towards me. She was wearing a tight skirt, and took short steps. I noticed for the first time that she was not wearing a wig. I held open the door for her. The first thing she noticed in the studio was the packed bag and the coat on the bed, and she seemed to realise immediately what this meant. She stopped in front of them, and, still with her back to me, said:

'Are you leaving?'

'Yes. I'm taking the next train.'

All she said was:

'Is that all you're taking with you?'

'Yes.'

'What about all the other things? Are you having them fetched?'

'No. I've got everything I need.'

I told her what I had done during the past three days, and showed her the folder.

'There are 27,000 marks in the current account,' I finished up, 'and 60,000 in securities deposited at the bank. The collection of clocks should be worth 20,000, you should get 10,000 for the photographic equipment, and I've sold the postcard publishing business for 40,000, payable in four annual installments. Also there's the surrender value of the life insurance.'

It seemed horrible to detail everything to her like this, but it had to be done.

'Don't you want a divorce?' she asked.

'I might.'

'If you want it, you can have it at any time. Desertion is a valid reason.'

She looked round the room.

'And what about all this? The books, the photographs?'

'I don't need them.'

For the first time she looked alarmed, as if my leaving her were less alarming than being left with all these things without knowing what to do with them. She was one of those people who cannot throw anything away.

'But what on earth am I to do with it?' she said.

'If that's worrying you, I can ring someone who'll take it all away.'

'Yes, please do that,' she actually replied. 'I wouldn't know what to do with it.'

It was absurd that she should be so worried at such a thing, but it was so, and it made everything easier. Then she suddenly said:

'So you're leaving me. Do you love her?'

She had no need to say whom.

'Yes,' I said. It seemed simpler to say yes than to enter into a long discussion. 'But I should have gone in any case. I should have done so a long time ago. If I had done it sooner, you might have had a chance. Perhaps you've still got one. At all events, it's the best thing for me to do, and I should have done it long ago.'

She turned and smiled. It was a rather painful smile, but not the crooked smile of before. I had not expected her to take everything so calmly, and that smile surprised me even more.

'I had my chance, hadn't I?' she said.

If I had been honest at that moment, I should have said no, you never had a chance, even when we got married I was in love with someone else, but I said nothing. I took out my latch-key and put it next to the folder. To our landlady nothing was worse than when latch-keys were lost and new ones had to be made. I almost made a remark about it. Otherwise I could think of nothing to say.

'Has it ever occurred to you that you might lose her if

you told her you were not her father and were in love with her?'

Of course it had occurred to me.

'Yes,' I said. 'I've often thought of it.'

'And what will happen if you lose her?'

'It won't happen. And even if it did, it wouldn't bring me back.'

Again I was surprised at her calm, and above all at her showing no sign of restlessness at not yet having had her drink. But perhaps when I had gone she would stop drinking.

'I know that. That's not what I'm talking about.' She shook her head, as over something she was very worried about indeed. 'What you want is impossible,' she said.

I looked at her in surprise.

'What is impossible?'

'It's hopeless. If only you'd understand. I hate saying this, because it's bound to sound as if I still wanted something for myself. You think you're in love with her, but it isn't true. You're no more in love with her than you're in love with me. It was hopeless for me, and it would be just as hopeless for her. That's something you must face up to at last. You've always been in love with one woman only, and you still are. It sounds abnormal, but I know it's true. And perhaps you're right, perhaps it's the only way of loving and knowing it will never change. . . . It's impossible to compete with that. It was impossible for me, and it will be just as impossible for Julia.'

I looked at her. It was a long time since I had looked at her properly. Even with all the years on her face and the powder and the paint, there was something there of the girl who had stood in front of the footlights waiting for the curtain to drop, with a forced smile on her face, while the audience grew more and more restless and there was more and more laughter. Once I had been capable of making her forget that evening and other things too, and then I had suddenly been able to do so no longer. That was our story,

and there was no more to say about it. One could make a person happy, and then one could do so no longer. I felt grief, not for her, not for myself, but just grief that such a thing could happen. But it had happened. It happened every day

XX

I spent the greater part of Friday at the hospital, and on
Saturday morning went to see Professor Blum, to be told the
results. I was put through the whole rigmarole—blood tests,
smears, ECG and EEG, my eyes were examined, my stomach
and lungs were X-rayed, in fact I was subjected to all the
items on the long list Blum had marked with a cross and,
as I was one of his privileged patients, he let me know the
most important results within twenty-four hours. I was rather
under weight, my blood pressure was a little too low, but
it had been for many years. Blum had always told me one
could reach a ripe old age in that condition, and he repeated
the assurance that morning. He thought me a trifle tense and
nervy, and he asked his old questions about whether I was
sleeping badly, or had headaches, or bad dreams, or sudden
memory gaps; and, as usual, he seemed rather disappointed
when the answer to them all was no.

He then asked me whether I would be willing to take the
new American test he had mentioned at the garden party.
I had practically forgotten all about it, but I was already
aware of his habit of subjecting patients whom he knew well
to tests, of course, as he always insisted, without permitting
any interference from his colleagues in the psychiatry department. He had been interested *in my case* ever since he
had operated on me in Athens. He handed me a thick packet
of questions worked out by a computer—five hundred ques-

271

tions for me to answer spontaneously with RIGHT or
WRONG. It was the latest and best thing of its kind, and
an IBM computer would then work out in a matter of seconds whether I was normal or *non compos mentis;* it would
say whether I was introverted, hysterical, hypochondriac,
paranoid, psychasthenic, psychopathological, manic-depres-
sive or schizophrenic. Those were the eight possibilities, not
stated so succinctly, of course, but in more solemn and cere-
monious medical terminology. I glanced at some of the questions—*I have the feeling that people talk behind my back;
I believe in angels; I wish I were dead,* and then took the
whole thing away in an envelope without the slightest intention of answering any of the five hundred questions.

I had arranged to fetch Julia at the Doerner Institute. It
was a Saturday, but she had wanted to finish her Holbein
that morning, after which we were going to look at a flat—
she had found one that seemed suitable, and the agent
wanted a decision that day.

I had not seen her after the tests at the hospital, which
always depressed me, and I spent the evening alone in a
hotel. I needed time; time to think what to say to her. I had
decided it would be best to take her away to some new place
so that, however she reacted, I should never have to go back
to it; for there were enough places in my life that were associated with painful memories, and I did not want to run the
risk of adding to them.

The institute is in one of two buildings that used to be
known as Führer buildings, hideous lumps of stone with two
flagpoles standing out like gallows over the two entrances.
The central files of the Nazi party had once been housed on
the ground floor and basement, and during the war, they had
been used to house art treasures, like Neuschwanstein Castle.
I had never thought of this before when I went to pick up
Julia there, but now it seemed impossible to find a place
that did not awaken memories.

Just when I was approaching a car drew up outside; it was the Mercedes, and Lehr and Winter got out. Winter opened the boot and took out a flat brown paper parcel, which he carried up the broad steps in front of Lehr, and the two of them disappeared between the pillars. I had not telephoned Lehr on Friday, so he knew I had accepted and was going to fly to Madrid. He certainly did not expect anything else; Fritz Lehr was always very sure of himself in whatever he did.

I waited. After a while Winter came out alone. He went back to his seat at the steering-wheel, picked up a newspaper, and began reading. I looked up at the windows on the second floor, the two windows on the extreme right behind which Julia worked. I felt sure he was there now, and for a moment I thought there was going to be a repetition, that Julia was about to emerge from the entrance with Fritz Lehr by her side, and that Winter would open the door for them and drive them away. . . . Obviously I needed a computer test, and it was obvious what it would say—a man who was continually remembering could only be schizophrenic.

I went on waiting. How long was he going to be? Only very exceptionally did the institute accept work from private individuals; it was kept busy with its own pictures, and the stores were full of pictures that were never shown because their turn for restoration never came. But an exception would of course be made for Fritz Lehr. He would get his own way, as he always did.

What could he and Julia be talking about? He had no right to be with her—but then I remembered he was her father. Her father? The idea seemed as absurd as the idea that he might become her lover. Her father. That gave him no rights whatever. Julia herself had said *the father won't worry you. He knows nothing about the child. It's my child only, and I don't want him ever to find out.* But wouldn't Julia find out now? Lehr always got what he wanted. Julia had not loved

him, and yet it had happened. I should have to tell her. But how could I tell her without breaking my promise? My promises to Julia counted more than anything else.

Perhaps I ought to answer the test questions. I have the feeling that people talk behind my back: WRONG. I believe in angels: WRONG. You have sometimes thought of suicide: RIGHT. You have wished you were dead: WRONG. When possible you always sit with your back to the wall: WRONG. You sometimes feel you want to run away: RIGHT. As a child you did not want to undress in front of other people: RIGHT. You reject your father: WRONG. I should never see the answer the computer came up with, but I was not interested. The accused is abroad, outside the jurisdiction of the court: RIGHT, I said to myself.

Winter had got out of the car, and Fritz Lehr came out alone, without the parcel. He was again wearing one of those blue suits, but since Tuesday, when he had looked tired and strained, he had changed; he walked out quickly and energetically, and he seemed to have lost weight during the short interval. A man like him was quite capable of such a thing if he set his mind to it, I said to myself. But it was time I stopped thinking about him. It was time for me to forget everything, the commemorative volume and people like Fritz Lehr. I waited for the car to drive away, crossed the street and walked up the steps.

The room in which Julia worked was big, almost a hall, with high windows. In the middle there was a big table at which several people could work at the same time. She sat on the left side, with a tall cupboard behind her, in which paints were kept in bottles in powder form. There were rows and rows of them in every conceivable shade; I counted eleven different shades of green alone. The one that came closest to the colour of her eyes was labelled Schweinfurt green. When she looked up from her painting and saw me

I forgot everything else; I really had been worrying for nothing.

'Sit down for a few minutes,' she said. 'I've nearly finished. We've plenty of time. We're meeting the agent at eleven.'

I went and stood behind her. She was wearing a green sleeveless pullover, and a long-sleeved jacket of the same colour was hanging over her chair. I looked at her hands; I had never before been so struck by the fact that she too had big white half-moons on her nails.

'What did Professor Blum say?'

'He was satisfied with me. Whenever he says that, he almost sounds as if he were disappointed.'

Her tennis racquets were on one of the window seats. The parcel Winter had taken from the car was on the table, unopened. 'I saw Lehr driving away,' I said. She went on concentrating on the painting in front of her, to which she was applying a transparent fluid with a fine brush.

'I can't make up my mind whether I like him or not,' she said. 'At the garden party he was very nice, I mean, much nicer than one imagines a man of that type to be. He came here today and wanted to have a picture restored. I told him we accepted no private work, and that he would have no better luck if he talked to the director. He laughed, and said I could safely leave that to him. I know the type. Lots of them come here and throw their weight about, and the worst of it is that they often get their way. I resent that more than anything else.'

'And what do you like about him?'

'I don't know. I've been thinking about it, and I can't make up my mind. Perhaps it's his direct, uncomplicated way of going about things. One can't imagine anything being complicated to him. He wastes no time beating about the bush. He doesn't create difficulties, he sweeps them out of the way. I don't know.' She got up, took the picture, put it on an easel and stood and looked at it. 'Hasn't it come out well?' She half

turned to me. 'Look at that. No more gowns, no more wreaths of roses and nuns' coifs, but simply the Schwarz family, husband and wife, the whole family, and lots and lots of children.' She started counting the figures in the picture, and I noticed the paint stains on her hand. 'Thirty-four of them all told. Just imagine a family of that size. I've been working on the picture for nearly two months now, and I feel I know every one of them.' She went over to a wash-basin to wash her hands. There was a slight smell of turpentine in the room.

'You like big families,' I said.

'Yes, I think I do.'

'I've talked to Thea.'

She remained bending over the basin.

'You didn't tell me anything about that yesterday.'

'I'm telling you now. I've left her for good. And now I know I should have done it long ago.' I realised she did not know what to say. She was quite right. What was there to say?

'I've been thinking we might go away together.'

I went over to her. I noticed a spot of paint on her brow, a brownish-red spot, rather like an Indian caste sign. I took a piece of cloth and some turpentine, and she kept very still while I wiped it away. A slight trace remained, but she did not bother about it. She looked at me, rather helpless and embarrassed.

'You've finished your picture, and the two of us could go off together somewhere. Do you realise we've never been away together except when there was a tournament on somewhere?'

'Where?'

'Wherever you like. What do you say to Tunis?'

'Tunis?' she said. Then she added: 'It sounds a good idea. I've always wanted to go to Africa. I think I'd like the colours, the light. Everyone who has ever been to Tunis writes about the colours and the light. It's a splendid idea.'

'I've got a job to do first.'

I had decided that, if she asked what it was, I could use the Hamburg job, which I had turned down, as an excuse. 'I've got to go to Madrid, and I could fly to Tunis direct. You could fly from here, and I'd meet you there.'

She smiled.

'This seems to be the day for invitations,' she said.

'What other invitations have you had?'

'Lehr is taking his boat to Genoa. It's late in the year, but not too late, he says. The weather's often at its best at the beginning of October. He invited me to go to Genoa and join him on a cruise. To Corsica and Sardinia.'

'And what did you say?'

'He's married, and he has a nice wife and two children.'

'Is that what you told him?'

'Oh, no, and if I really fancied him that certainly wouldn't stop me, at any rate I don't think it would. I like his father, for instance. I'm almost sorry I turned down his offer. Strange, isn't it?'

'What's strange?'

'That I should keep thinking about it, but I can't help it. We've been there only once. They're not at all my kind of people, they're strangers really, and yet I often think about the old gentleman and the evening we spent there, and the big table at which we all had dinner. I think it really may be connected with what you said—that I like big families of the kind they had in the old days, as on that picture, parents and children, grandpa and grandma, lots of aunts and domestic staff, a woman to do the washing, a cook, a coachman, and all in a big house under a single roof, with a garden, a park and a big cage full of singing birds. Old-fashioned, in fact. The sort of thing that has presumably totally ceased to exist. Or does it still exist?'

'No,' I said. 'It no longer exists.'

'What a pity.'

'Will you come to Tunis?'

'Of course I will.'

'You turned down Fritz Lehr?'

'Did you expect me to do anything else?'

She laughed, went over to the door and took her coat, which was hanging on it. It was one of those shiny red PVC coats, which made her look very young.

The two flats were behind the English Garden. The situation was ideal; the park was on one side and it was only a short way to the Isar on the other. They were in a big villa, the outside of which was unchanged, except for new windows that had been put in when it was converted. The flats were on the top floor, with big rooms, high ceilings and big windows, and everything was painted white. There would be two rooms for each of us, as well as two bathrooms and two kitchens, but one of them could easily be converted into a dark room. The two flats were not connected, but this could easily be remedied by breaking through a wall in the hall; it was not a supporting wall, and the owner was willing to give permission.

It was not cheap, but it was not unreasonably expensive; it was, in fact, exactly what we were looking for, and it was ready for immediate occupation. But, walking through the empty rooms with Julia, and at last standing in the window overlooking the park in one of the empty rooms, I felt that I was seeing all this for the first and last time. It was a fine day, the sky was grey in spite of the sun, but it was higher than usual, a high, radiant grey vault. You could see the park, and the watercourse at the end of it, the paths and the trees, which were beginning to turn red and yellow.

'The view's marvellous, isn't it?'

Her voice sounded loud in the empty room. I turned away from the window and looked at her in her shiny red coat, which looked redder than ever against all the white. I now know that I should have told her right then. I remember that the various ways in which she might have reacted passed through my mind. It was as if I really had gone up to her, put

my arms around her, and said: *I love you, Julia.* She laughed, and said: *But yes, of course you do, do you think I would come and live with you otherwise?* She responded to my embrace by embracing me, and then changed the subject to the agent who was waiting for a decision.

That was possibility No. 1. The next was that I went on: *No, you don't understand. I'm not your father, and I don't love you like a father. I know I should have told you long ago, but* . . . She tried to laugh and shook off my embrace and looked at me in horror. *But in that case it's impossible for us to live together, isn't it? Why did you have to tell me? Did you have to spoil everything now, at this moment, when we were so happy?* . . . I also thought of the third possibility: Julia melting in my arms, but happy. *I felt it the whole time. I felt I must be quite abnormal thinking such a thing when I was alone with you.*

But then I thought of what Thea had said, and what I had felt, and something in me decided to put it off till Tunis. What I really said was: 'Yes, the view's marvellous.'

'Well what do you think? We've got to make up our mind. Shall we take it? I think it's a piece of luck. If you had seen the other places. We're the first to have seen it. The painters only moved out yesterday. Don't you think we ought to take it? I do.'

'Yes, we must,' I said. She put her arms round me and dragged me away to show me something she thought I had missed.

XXI

A photograph would have preserved the moment for ever, the sight of the Munich station hall on a Sunday afternoon; even a stranger would have recognised it, and the clock would have been visible, and the crowded concourse, groups of dark-haired men in dark suits, white shirts, shiny polished shoes. They were standing or sitting on the luggage racks in front of the ticket windows, talking or reading their newspapers, the *Expres Español*, the *Corriere d'Italia*, or the *Cumhüriyet*.

The woman at the foreign booking office window was wearing a blonde wig which did not fit very well and left some dark hair showing. She was about Thea's age.

'One to Zürich, please.'

'Single or return?'

'Single.' I never knew exactly how close to the glass one ought to speak in order to be understood.

'You could save by taking a return.'

'No, just a single to Zürich.'

'First or second?'

'Second.'

She hesitated, looked at the clock, and said:

'Are you taking the next train? That's the Trans-Europa express, first class only.'

'All right, then, first.'

Julia, who was standing beside me, smiled. She had insisted on coming with me to the station.

I had spent the night at a hotel near the station, and she had arrived in the morning with plans of the two flats; she had made sketches of every room and of all the furniture she possessed, and she spent the whole morning trying out the various possibilities. She decided where my books and photographic files were to go, and she produced samples of paint and coloured cards to harmonise the colours of the carpets, curtains and lamp-shades. I was glad when the telephone rang at about three o'clock and I was told that I must either vacate the room or pay for another night.

I paid the bill, and we went across to the station.

Now, with Julia standing beside me and smiling, I almost regretted not having a camera with me. I could have asked anyone there to take us, I have never known anyone refuse such a request. I saw clearly that all of the photos that people put in wallets, behind the cellophane of driving licenses, in bags and purses, all the snapshots they carry about with them on their persons and near their heart, are all intended to hold on to moments in life, to preserve them—that was you at that time and at that place, and you were happy.

No, it was a good thing I had left my cameras behind. I needed no more cameras. I knew why I had left them behind.

I bought some newspapers and magazines. It was a sunny day, but I could feel my knee when we passed through the barrier, and knew that the weather was going to change. The train was waiting on the platform, six red carriages. I looked for a non-smoking compartment and a seat on the left-hand side, from where I should not be able to see the graves. I put my bag on the seat and opened the window.

'There's no need for you to wait,' I said.

'Will you telephone?'

'Yes,' I said, 'I'll phone you and tell you when I expect you in Tunis. There's plenty for you to do at the flat.' I had given her the cheques that Fritz Lehr gave me for the commemora-

tive volume. 'You'll hear from me any way.' I wanted to say no more, and I kept thinking about Tunis and the money and that twenty-six years was not really such a tremendous difference in age. *A man only gains with age. Age, which can ruin a woman's face, can't do anything to a man.* Julia had said that, Julia, who was so young and wise with her twenty-four years.

'What are you smiling at?' she said.

'I was thinking about something you said.'

'Something nice?'

'Something very nice.'

'I can tell you want me to go.'

'Yes. One never knows what to say.'

She went, and at the end of the platform she turned once more in her shiny red coat.

The compartment was empty. I sat on the side away from the window, next to the corridor and with my back to the engine. Then something moved; I was not sure whether it was our train or the one beside it.

The sky looked blue, but when we were outside the city we would discover that it was really grey. Another train appeared, and for some moments the two trains appeared to be motionless, but then the green carriages disappeared from view. I saw house-fronts, fenced in areas, big containers, and big piles of concrete; over them, in the middle of a crane running on tracks, were the words F. Lehr & Company. Someone had forgotten to switch off the current, and the neon lights were still burning; they were light blue, rather like the colour of the sky, but when it got dark they would look nearly white.

I picked up the newspapers, and looked for the exchange rates. The revaluation of the Deutschmark had continued and the dollar had fallen, it was about DM 3.80. That meant that $250,000 was not quite a million, at any rate not exactly.

The train moved smoothly; the cushions, the small white cushion at the back of my neck, had never felt so soft. I was

alone in the compartment, I had room, plenty of room, any amount of it. I wished I had not had to travel along this line again, through this area I knew so well.

I was now passing through it for the last time. The trip, according to the white leaflets left on the empty seats, took thirty minutes, of which ten had already passed. At Buchloe the morainic topography of the Lech, with its large gravel deposits, ended, and the names of the stations would not rouse too many memories.

I followed the numbers on the white kilometre stones along the track. 46.5. . . . 46.7. . . . 46.9.

It had been useless to pretend that choosing a seat on the other side of the compartment would be enough. I knew exactly when the triangular junction at Kaufering, would be coming up, Ewi's hut, the camp.

Don't think about it, I said to myself, you're in a harmonious ancient morainic topography between Ammersee and Lech. Those were my own words. *A landscape of peculiar charm that breathes harmony and peace.* See Our Landsberg Homeland; Calendar for 1969, published by Hans Pikola, publisher of postcards and calendars and printed by Pikola Brothers, Augsburg.

The morainic deposits meant gravel, every hill you looked at consisted of best quality pure building gravel. . . . Stop thinking about it. *Here Bavaria becomes a feast for the eyes.* Landsberg and the Lechwehr; Winkl in the isolated Bach; St. Alban-am See; the high altar of the monastery church at Diessen; sailing boats at Utting. If you have ever bought a postcard in this neighbourhood you would have been able to find my name on it in small print; I didn't leave out a single chapel, or putto, or John the Baptist, or gate, or notable façade, or curve of the Lech.

And, if you live there, I have certainly photographed your house from the air—genuine air photograph in colour, item N.15, plain copy 14 x 20, framed, DM 305, including value added tax, excluding carriage and packing. . . .

We Pikolas fertilised the landscape and were fertilised by it. We absorbed it into ourselves, illuminated it, reproduced it, dug it up. We have an old tradition in the matter. And, don't forget, it was my father to whom we owe the discovery of the plague burial ground at Kaufering dating from 1630, together with the felt-wheeled car in which bodies were noiselessly taken to their last resting place during the plague, 'so that the living should not be alarmed beyond due measure.' So remember that principle, and avoid alarming the living beyond due measure.

How could I forget? In spite of the speed of the train, I saw the gardens where the huts of Camp 1 had stood. The siding was still there, with a few trucks standing on it. The green-painted hut had been torn down. And then that too was over. The landscape changed, clouds covered the sky, and my knee hurt; we might yet have snow, because somewhere the train would reach 3,000 feet.

I picked up the newspapers and looked for the weather forecast. I could not find anything about the temperature in Tunis. But in one of the papers there was a table showing the temperatures in the various European capitals. In Madrid it was 56 degrees, and the sky was overcast.

Madrid, October 7 1969

I looked at the signature, the strange name in the black reception book, and wondered why I had taken all this trouble, come all this way, to kill a man who wrote his name like a child.

But there was no going back now. I went through a side door into a corridor that ran past the motel rooms. The man in the oily overall had finished refuelling the car and had gone back into his hut; through the window I saw him lighting a cigarette before his head disappeared. He could be summoned by a bell fixed on the wall outside that rang whenever a car passed over a cable placed across the entrance to the parking bay.

There was constant traffic in the Avenida de Burgos, most of it in the outward direction; the wooden boards of the corridor vibrated slightly whenever heavy lorries passed. There were gaps between the boards, so I could see the tops of the cars parked underneath.

The rooms I had to pass all seemed empty. I heard no voice, no radio, nothing, only the noise of the traffic and that of my own footsteps. I felt the pistol under my belt. The barrel with the silencer attached pressed against my left thigh. I remembered how real and genuine it had looked when I found it in the box in the steel strong-room at the bank; but now it seemed to me part of a strange game, a kind of race, as if it were the baton in a relay race. I was the

last runner, and whatever the game was called, whoever had made the rules, I had such an enormous lead that I could afford to take it easy, to take my time. I had all the time in the world, for I was bound to reach the tape first.

Room 16 was the last at the end of the corridor, and the only one from which any sound was coming. There were voices, speaking Spanish, two or three different voices. In my imagination he had always been alone, I had always faced him alone, he was a man who lived only for himself and was always alone. This changed nothing of what I had to do, and I hesitated for only a moment; it was simply that I was disappointed that something in the course of events that I had imagined had turned out to be wrong. So far everything had gone exactly to plan—the flight to Madrid, the hotel, the bank, the trip in the Metro and in the bus and the last part by taxi, and the walk along the Avenida de Burgos until the motel turned up on the left.

Now I was facing the door. I knocked. The voices went on talking, but another voice intervened, and said in Spanish: 'Come in. The door's open.' It was Spanish, with a pretty strong accent. This was the second surprise. After twenty-one years in a country in which one was taking refuge, one ought to have mastered the language. This would seem to be especially important to a man who wanted to be inconspicuous; but the way he spoke Spanish immediately betrayed that he was German, or at any rate a foreigner. Perhaps the reason might be that in the past twenty-one years he had not had much opportunity to talk to people in his hiding places. But I did not propose to worry my head too much about a man who was going to die in a few moments.

I opened the door, walked in, and shut the door behind me. I had to go through a small ante-room, and then entered the room itself. It was in half darkness, and the brightest spot was the television set standing in the corner. It was switched on, and the voices I had heard came from the loud-speaker. The man was alone

He was sitting on the unmade bed against the wall to my

288

left, facing the television set, but I still avoided looking straight at him. I remained standing in the doorway, with the bag in my left hand, to make him think I had brought the money. It was a small, square room, too small for the television set, there was not enough space between the viewer and the screen. The set was on a small table, and apart from that there was only a double bed, two bedside cabinets, a chair, and a photograph of a bullring. The window in the background was half covered by dirty yellow curtains; through it one could see out on to a yard with piles of oil barrels; beyond this there was some waste land, and the mist-covered Guadarrama range in the distance; again it looked as if the peaks were covered with snow.

On the only chair there was a pile of newspapers and magazines, and others were scattered about the floor; I noticed they were German newspapers, there was not a Spanish one among them; he must have fetched them or, more probably, had had them brought to him; the whole room and the man on the bed created the impression that he had not left it for weeks.

I looked at him as he sat there, leaning against the back of the bed with his knees drawn up on the crumpled blanket and wearing shoes. He wore beige khaki trousers and a shirt of the same colour. I stood there without moving, and he too remained motionless, looking at me, saying nothing, as if he had exhausted his strength with the first and only words he had spoken. He had a small black box in his hand; his finger-nails were dirty, the nails were broken, and the veins on the back of his hands were swollen. He switched off the television sound, but let the pictures run on, and from time to time he glanced at them. I said nothing, and I had the feeling that he was safe from me so long as he did not speak, so long as he did not move his lips, as if it were impossible to shoot a man who said nothing.

In my imagination I had done it. Outside, during my last steps along the corridor, it had all been very simple. In my imagination I had never stood there as long as I had done

289

now. Instead I had opened the door, drawn the pistol, fired, and left again. But my imagination no longer existed.

It was hot in the room, hot and stuffy, much hotter than outside. When he raised his arm and put the little black box on the night table beside him, I noticed that the shirt under his arms was dark with sweat. The shirt was open over his chest, and you could see grey hairs, which were also gleaming with sweat. He looked much older than I had expected, somehow I still had before my eyes the photograph his wife had shown me. His face was yellow and he looked unhealthy, there were big bags under his eyes. It was not a face, but only a skull over which thin yellow skin had been stretched. I looked at the dead man, who still had said nothing. He half turned away from me, slowly turned his head to the left towards the window; he turned it only a fraction of an inch at a time, as if it were tremendously difficult, and his face, which was no longer capable of expressing any feeling, even fear, grew contorted with pain; he went on turning it until he was almost looking over his left shoulder, out of the window, where you could see the mountains in the distance. I suddenly realised he was seeing nothing, that his eyes were shut, that he was showing me the back of his neck, as if giving me the opportunity to draw the pistol and aim and fire at leisure. I felt sure of it, he was waiting for it, he had been waiting for it all these weeks, he had been sitting on the bed and waiting, waiting for the steps outside, for the knock at the door, for the man to enter. He had been waiting in this room for three weeks, and perhaps he had spent months and years waiting in other rooms exactly similar to this, except that there had been no television set or German newspapers. I knew that this was so, and that I was not making a mistake; and when at last he turned his head just as slowly and looked at me, really looked at me for the first time, my certainty was confirmed. For the first time a sign of life appeared in his face. No, it was not fear, but disappointment, deep disappointment.

'Have you brought the money?' he said.

I did not answer. I lifted the bag, which was light and empty and had been intended to deceive him. I no longer looked at him. A suitcase half protruded from under the bed. Remnants of a meal were on the night table. Through the half open doorway I could see a shower. Another khaki shirt and underwear were hanging on a line.

I summoned up all my hate which had been so fresh and vital; it was like having to gather and fit together a large number of scattered fragments. There were fragments, but they did not fit together. I thought of Julia and how she had died; I thought of the jeep with its waving serial disappearing behind the slight eminence, and of the man that followed it—and how he had stood at the edge of the gravel pit. But there was also something else, Julia saying 'I despise them'; and that last moment when she took my hands and pressed them to her lips.

Hate still remained—and the will and determination to revive it, but it had nothing to do with the man in front of me. Also there was something else.

I thought of the money in the safe, the many bundles of new bank notes, twenty-five bundles in all; I thought of them so intensely because it seemed to be my last chance, because I thought it would help me to pull myself together and kill him. The strange thing was that it did not help at all, just the opposite, because I realized now what I had really hoped for in coming here: I had wanted to kill Boettcher in order to be close to Julia again. That had been a pure feeling, but the money, and what it meant, stood in my way. It interfered, it contaminated, and at last, it undermined. The whole of my hate collapsed and broke. In offering the money to me Fritz Lehr had made a mistake; he did not make many mistakes, but this was one of them.

'Tell me just one thing,' the man said. 'Do you know my wife and children?'

His voice was old, dry, dead. I did not answer. Whatever

he wanted to talk about, whatever he still clung to, it was no affair of mine. I would have had only one question to ask him, one single question, but I needed only to look at him to know that he would not answer, perhaps could not after so many years. He would not even understand. He would not remember the name, and I did not want to speak it in front of him.

I raised my right hand to take the safe key from my pocket. He watched the movement, and for a moment there was once more something like a glimmer of hope in his dead eyes; as if he still hoped I might draw the pistol and kill him. His hand moved. A newspaper was on the bed beside him, and when he moved it I saw the pistol that had been hidden underneath it; it was a heavy calibre pistol with a long barrel. It was only to be expected that such a man would be armed, but it was as pointless as the cyanide capsules he had once carried about on his person; he was not a man to commit suicide.

He said nothing, but hoped the sight of the weapon might induce me to do something; but he could not coerce me by such means into doing something that no longer made sense. I shook my head, and threw him the safe key. I gave him the name of the bank, and told him I would fill in the form authorising him to use it. The last I saw of him was that he once more picked up the little black box and turned up the sound on the television. I heard the voices behind me as I went out.

The Fénix at 2, Paseo de la Castellana, is a big luxury hotel. My room there had been booked by Fritz Lehr. It was the kind of room he liked, an oversize room with thick, soft, wall-to-wall carpeting and, of course, a bar and a television set. I switched it on, and turned up the sound pretty loud.

On the way back I had bought one of those lined envelopes, and stamps. I addressed the envelope to Julia, by air mail, and stuck on so many stamps that it was bound to

reach her. All I would have to do would be to put in these two notebooks and close the envelope with the staples.

Fénix is merely the Spanish for phoenix. I do not assume that Fritz Lehr chose it for any symbolic reason, but merely because of its convenience. It was said, if I remember correctly, that when the phoenix felt death approaching, it chose a shelter of sweet-smelling wood, burnt itself to death in the flames and rose rejuvenated from the ashes. But that is not my hope.

The only thing I think of is Julia. She will understand my fear. The old questions remain: Why did she choose death when she could have chosen life? And what should I have done at the time?

I love her, and her only. What I will do did not happen now, did not happen in this room in Madrid; the bullet that stopped my heart struck me twenty-five years ago, on the night when she took my hand and pressed it to her lips and I did nothing.

No hotel likes finding a dead body in a room. But I assume it's easier for a five-star hotel like the Fénix to deal with such a situation; they are used to fulfilling their guests' wishes, even the most eccentric, and they'll know what to do.

Now I shall close the envelope. I shall put the 'Do not disturb' notice outside the door, and then I shall shave. True, I shaved this morning, but I don't want anyone to find out that my beard is turning grey. . . .